One

'Mr Tibbs!' Amelia Beaufort called, looking anxiously towards the road that wound past her front garden. She hadn't seen her beautiful Persian cat since the previous evening, and in view of what Mrs Henderson had just been saying on the telephone, that was worrying. Several cats had gone missing from the village recently and some of them had been found mutilated. 'Mr Tibbs, come to Mummy, there's a good boy,' Amelia coaxed.

Mr Tibbs was five years old and had a beautiful nature. It distressed Amelia to think that he might have been taken by whoever was killing other people's cats.

'Mrs Beaufort, there's a telephone call for you, ma'am.'

Amelia sighed, making her way along the little moss-grown path to the house. She still wasn't truly used to being summoned to answer the telephone, though she had to admit it was a useful instrument. She took the telephone from her house-keeper, holding the trumpet to her right ear, her left hand curled round the long black stem.

'Hello, Amelia Beaufort speaking?'

'Gran darling!' the girl's voice bubbled with life and vivacity. 'How are you? I was thinking about you this morning and I decided to give you a ring.'

'Sarah my love,' Amelia said, all trace of apprehension gone as she heard her granddaughter's voice. 'It is lovely of you to think of me. I dare say you are busy?'

'I have been, but I'm resting now, as we say. At least I shall be from the day after tomorrow. But you haven't said how you are? You sound a little out of breath. You aren't ill?'

'No, quite well, thank you. I've been searching for that wretched cat. But what do you mean by resting? You're not ill yourself, are you?'

Sarah's laughter was warm and delightful. 'It means I'm out of a job, Gran, that's all.'

'Oh, I see.' Amelia smiled, glancing at her own reflection in the wall mirror. She was a small lady, her grey hair curled under in a roll at the back of her head. The neat collar of embroidered silk she wore to complement her dress owed nothing to the dynamic thrust of the twenties and everything to lingering memories of the more elegant age of her youth. 'Well, if that is the case, why don't you come and stay with me?'

'I can't impose on you, Gran. It might be a long visit.'

'The longer the better. You know I always love to see you, my dearest.'

'Well, perhaps I shall,' Sarah said. 'I'll let you know in a few days, Gran.'

'I shan't take no for an answer – unless you have a better offer?'

'Nothing could be better. Oh, there's someone at the door. I'll ring you again soon . . .'

Amelia replaced the telephone stand on the hall table. She was about to go back out to the garden when Mr Tibbs came from the sitting room, mewing plaintively as he wound his way round her ankles, transferring smears of his silky hair on to her skirt.

'Where have you been, you terrible animal?' She bent down to pick him up. 'I suppose you've been chasing all the ladies in the district, and there was me thinking someone had chopped off your head.'

As she walked towards the kitchen, still carrying her pet, Amelia wondered if she ought to let Miss Bates know what was happening to the local cats. Miss Bates lived at the bottom of the hill, but she didn't have a telephone. It was too far to walk these days, Amelia decided, especially when it was cold. She would ask Andrews to call in on Miss Bates when he took her to the market later in the week.

'Buy some lucky heather, lady?' Morna Scaffry offered her basket to the woman she had just met on her way up the hill. 'Tell your fortune for a shilling.'

The woman shook her head. She was wearing a dark brown fur coat with the collar turned up against the cool wind and

MISCARRIAGE OF JUSTICE

MISCARRIAGE OF JUSTICE

Linda Sole

This first world edition published in Great Britain 2007 by
SEVERN HOUSE PUBLISHERS LTD of
9–15 High Street, Sutton, Surrey SM1 1DF.
This first world edition published in the USA 2007 by
SEVERN HOUSE PUBLISHERS INC of
595 Madison Avenue, New York, N.Y. 10022.

British Library Cataloguing in Publication Data

Sole, Linda
    Miscarriage of justice
    1.   Murder - Investigation - England - Fiction
    2.   Great Britain - Social life and customs - 1918-1945 - Fiction
    3.   Detective and mystery stories
    I.   Title
    813.9'14 [F]

    ISBN-13: 978-0-7278-6492-5

All Severn House titles are printed on aci

Typeset by Palimpsest Book Product
Grangemouth, Stirlingshire, Scotland
Printed and bound in Great Britain b
MPG Books Ltd., Bodmin, Cornwall

an expensive silk scarf. The heavy sunglasses she wore made it impossible to see her eyes, or much of her face other than her glossy red lips. She seemed to be loitering, uncertain of her bearings. It was the combination of fur coat and dark glasses that had made Morna take notice of her. Who did she think she was, prancing about in a coat like that – a bleedin' star out of one of them there silent films?

'Go on, lady,' Morna wheedled, pressing her opportunity. Strangers were fair game and deserved what they got, especially them what could afford a fur coat like that. It was them sort that was behind the move to destroy the ancient woods at Thorny. 'It will bring you luck – only sixpence a bunch.'

'Please go away and leave me alone.' It was obvious that the woman thought Morna a dirty gypsy and wanted nothing to do with her. She wasn't local and wouldn't know that Morna's caravan was as clean as a new pin or that she was well liked in the village.

'You look as if you need some luck,' Morna went on, knowing that persistence usually paid off. She sensed that the stranger would do anything to get rid of her, because she was obviously nervous. Her face looked unnaturally pale. 'Been ill 'ave yer, love?'

'Damn you, I told you to leave me alone!' The woman pushed her hand into the pocket of her coat and came out with a sixpence, which she thrust at Morna. 'Take it and go!'

'Here's your heather, love.' Morna grabbed the money before it was withdrawn. She pocketed the coin, smiling inwardly as the woman shoved the heather into her coat pocket. There was one born every minute, but Morna thought that today might be her lucky day, her chance to earn some real money. If her plan worked, she wouldn't be standing on street corners waiting for someone to buy her heather this winter.

She wondered whether to call at some of the cottages first. Janet Bates always bought something from her and sometimes she asked her to go in for a cup of tea, probably because she liked to hear the village news. Wandering about the village the way she did, Morna saw most of what was going on. Just as she and her brother Jethro knew all about the goings-on in the wood.

She noticed a spade and a pair of men's heavy work boots by the back door of the flintstone cottage. Perversely, the back door was really at the side and in full view of the village street, whereas the front door faced the lane to the woods because the cottage was set at an angle. Morna decided against stopping. Why bother with sixpences when she might soon have a fortune within her grasp?

She cursed softly as she heard the backfiring of a car, turning to see the scruffy-looking vehicle that drew up at the side of the road beside her. She looked at its driver impatiently.

'What do you want?'

'To talk to you. Get in, Morna.'

'Why should I?'

She tossed her head, her long black hair flying in confusion about her face. Her eyes were defiant, her face proud and patrician. There was something regal about her, something very sensual in the line of her body, her ankle-length red skirt giving her a wayward appearance.

'I'm asking, but if you're stubborn I'll come and get you.'

It was on the tip of her tongue to refuse, but the look on his face warned her to do as he said. Her bid for a nice little nest egg might have to wait until another day. Getting into the car, she noticed that the woman in the fur coat was still hesitating outside the front gate of Janet Bates's cottage. Only a stranger would go to the front door – the locals used the back door – but it looked as if the woman might have changed her mind. She was walking away . . .

'Ah, I thought so,' Janet Bates murmured her satisfaction as she witnessed an interesting occurrence near the entrance to that part of the woods that backed on to her garden. From her vantage spot she could see most things that went on. She continued watching; she had been right all the time. Jethro Scaffry had been taking game from Thorny Woods again, despite his last warning. 'Sir James will have a word to say if he catches you, my lad.'

Both bedrooms of Janet's period cottage looked out towards Thorny Woods, but the spare room also oversaw the road that wound up the hill to the Manor. Besides, it was more private and her telescope wasn't as likely to be noticed as it might have been at the front.

The big house at the top of the hill was actually named Thornhill Manor, but the locals called it the Manor and laughed about his lordship. Sir James Beecham sometimes carried on as if he were a feudal lord, imagining that he had the right to order the lives of those who lived at Beecham Thorny. The villagers resented his interference, especially the plans to tear up part of the ancient woodland to build expensive houses. If the plans went through, it would bring more strangers into the area, and the local people were not keen on the idea.

Something else was happening near the woods. Janet bent her head to the telescope and watched as a man and a woman got out of a car and entered the woods. 'I wonder what your uncle would think if he could see you now!' she murmured, and chuckled. 'Ought I to tell him – or shall we just keep our little secret?' She decided against, because part of the fun would go out of her secrets if she shared them – at least before she was ready.

Janet Bates spent several enjoyable hours each week gazing out of her windows, because she loved poking her nose into other people's business. It had been a lifelong hobby, and what she had just seen was very interesting, very interesting indeed.

Tucking a wisp of grey hair behind her ear, she made a note in her exercise book, writing down the exact time and date. At the far end of the room was a large old-fashioned sofa, and behind this was a boarded-up fireplace in which she stored her notebooks. There were sixty in all, thirty of them containing the things she had noted from time to time, the others the beginnings of the novel she was writing.

If she had been inclined, she might have blackmailed quite a few people over the years. She knew so many secrets, and not all of them were about her neighbours. But Janet had never considered using her secrets in such a way. After all, she had no need of money. She was very comfortably off and had been for the past several years. Not that it had changed the way she lived in her little cottage. She didn't have much in the way of modern conveniences. There was an outside toilet and only cold water inside. It didn't matter. She was content as she was, though when she finished writing her novel she would be famous, and some people would be sorry . . .

She tucked her current notebook behind a cushion on the sofa for safety. She was smiling as she went downstairs. It would be such fun to see all that in print. She knew how scandalous her book was, and the amusing part of it was that everything she had written was absolutely true. Oh, she'd changed the names, of course, but dates, places and events were all exactly as she had recorded them.

The book would cause an uproar, but that was the reason she had decided to write it. It was her way of reaping revenge on people with whom she had a score to settle. Yes, she would keep all her secrets until she was ready to make the maximum impact. Quite a few people were going to get a nasty shock one day.

Janet was well aware of what people said about her. They thought she was just a batty old spinster who had never done anything but live quietly with her cats, but they were wrong. She had assumed the role when she came to this small community, but her mild manner was a façade. A lot of anger and resentment was simmering beneath the surface. She had held it in check for all these years, but the book was almost finished and she was savouring the prospect of its publication. She had already sent three chapters to a publisher who had expressed a wish to see the rest, and if he didn't take it she would publish it herself.

One of her cats came to her as she went down to the kitchen. It was a large ginger tom that she'd had neutered to keep him from straying. He rubbed himself against her legs. The skirt she wore was as shapeless as the rest of her and nearly as old, and she didn't care that it looked as if she had slept in it for a month.

'Here you are then, Tiger,' she said, bending down to pour the cat a drink of milk. 'Where has Pansy gone, then? Did she go out earlier or is she hiding somewhere?'

She glanced at the paper on her kitchen table. She hadn't had time to read it properly, because she liked to go through the local news line by line. She had noticed the advert for the film at a cinema in Norwich, because it was Valentino and she liked his films. She had read in the paper that they would soon be showing talking films at cinemas, but for her nothing could replace the silent movies.

Hearing a noise in her parlour, Janet went to investigate. Her female cat hadn't been in the cottage all morning and she was a bit concerned about her. Perhaps she'd got herself shut in the front parlour.

'Pansy . . . puss, puss . . .'

However, when she went into the hall, Janet saw that the door to her parlour was open. She frowned when she saw her gardener. He was looking through the photograph album she usually kept in the bottom drawer of her Georgian secretaire, along with some other personal treasures.

Ronnie looked up and grinned at her. His normally vacant eyes were bright with excitement as he jabbed at a picture with his grubby forefinger.

'I seen her at the pictures,' he said, and giggled. 'She's pretty, she is. I like her . . .'

'How dare you pry into my things!' Janet was furious. She had employed him because she felt sorry for him, but now she wished she hadn't. 'You had no right to come in here – and you certainly have no right to look at that!'

She snatched the book away from him, feeling as if he had sullied it merely by touching it. She could see a smear on the photograph. Why did it have to be that one? She took out her handkerchief and wiped the mark away. It came off easily, but the mental smear was still there. He should never have touched her photographs – and especially not that one.

She went over to the secretaire and opened the cash box that she kept just inside. She took a ten-shilling note and two half-crowns out and shut the box, replacing it and closing the drawer. Then she went over to where Ronnie was standing, watching her expectantly. She usually invited him into the kitchen for a cup of tea and a slice of her seed cake – but she wouldn't today, because she was angry.

'There's your money,' she told him. 'Don't come next week. I don't want you here again.'

Money meant very little to Ronnie, because he gave his wages to his widowed mother, who fed and clothed him but allowed him nothing else. What Ronnie liked was Janet Bates's cake and he looked at her in bewilderment, not understanding that he had offended her.

'Seed cake today?' he asked hopefully. The fact that he had just been dismissed had not sunk into his head. If you wanted Ronnie to understand something you had to tell him several times, very slowly.

'No. There's no cake today,' Janet said. 'Go away, Ronnie. I don't want to see you again.' She took hold of his arm, propelling him from the room into the kitchen and out of the back door, pushing him towards the lane that led to the village. He stood there staring at her and she made a shooing motion with her hand. 'Go away, lad! I told you, I don't want you to come again!'

'Cake?' Ronnie repeated, standing his ground. 'I ain't had me cake, missus.'

'Go away!'

'Miss Bates told you to go away.' A man riding by on his bike put a foot to the ground as he saw that the gangling lad was staring at the old lady oddly. He was a big lad and strong, but he had the mind of a child. 'Off with you now, Ronnie! If you cause trouble for Miss Bates your mother will take her stick to you.'

Ronnie stared at him. His mother's temper and her readiness to take it out on him with the stick she kept in the corner of her kitchen was the one thing that really got through to him. He shuffled off down the road, looking over his shoulder resentfully and muttering to himself.

'It's just as well you've got rid of him,' Harold Jackson said. 'He's a mite short of a shilling, Miss Bates. He works hard if you keep him at it, but he can turn nasty if he gets upset. Folk say as he should have been shut away years ago, but his mother won't hear of it. She rules him with a rod of iron and most of the time he's no trouble – but you're well rid of him.'

'I suppose so.' Janet was regretting her impulsive dismissal of Ronnie now. He worked well for her and she had just paid him for three weeks' labour. Usually, she gave his mother two weeks' money in one go, but today she had paid him an extra week to make up for sacking him. 'He isn't a bad lad, Mr Jackson.'

'Not intentionally,' Jackson agreed. He worked up at the Manor as head groom and had employed Ronnie on a couple of occasions. 'You have to keep after him mind – but as long as he doesn't drink beer he's fine. It's when he's had a drink or two that he gets into trouble. That's why his mother always collects his money for him.'

'I just gave him fifteen shillings,' Janet said. 'I completely forgot that his mother said he shouldn't have it. She didn't tell me why.'

'Let's hope he goes home and gives his mother the money. Otherwise he'll be down the pub this evening causing trouble again.'

'Oh dear! I was so upset at finding him in my parlour going through my things that I forgot.'

'Well, it isn't your fault he's the way he is,' Jackson said, and mounted his bike again. 'I shouldn't worry about it. His mother will sort him out, don't you worry.'

Janet nodded. She had always given the money to Ronnie's mother before but she hadn't realized that he couldn't be trusted with it. Not that it was her problem. If Mrs Miller couldn't control her son properly, she should have had him locked up long ago.

It was only as Jackson rode off that Janet Bates realized Ronnie had left his boots and his beloved spade by the back door as he always did when he came into the house. He was seldom parted from that spade of his, which had a very sharp edge. She had worried the poor lad so much that he'd run off and forgotten them, but no doubt he would return and fetch them later.

She went back into the house and through to the parlour. Tiger was sitting on the kitchen windowsill now, but there was still no sign of Pansy. It was all a bit worrying. Her cats meant everything to her these days.

Perhaps she ought never to have invited Ronnie in for tea and cake, but at the start she had liked him, felt sorry for him. She would never have sent him off like that if she hadn't been so upset over him touching that picture. It was so special, a precious link to the happy days of her past.

It was her fault for leaving the album on the table. It wasn't often left lying around. She had taken it out that morning because she was thinking about the past, remembering. She looked at the picture Ronnie had pointed out. He wasn't so simple that he hadn't recognized a famous face, even if it was one from the past. She supposed he must have been into Norwich and seen one of the silent films they showed at the flea pit every Saturday morning. It didn't cost much to go in, just a few pence for the kids, but if Ronnie's mother never allowed him to have money, she wasn't sure how he managed to pay.

She remembered something she'd read somewhere about

children sneaking in without paying. Poor lad! She felt a surge of pity for him, half wishing she hadn't lost her temper with him. He wasn't daft, as people liked to think, just slow, but he did have a good memory; it was just that he couldn't always put his thoughts into words. He knew how to look after a garden, even if you did have to watch that he didn't pull up flowers thinking they were weeds, but once you told him he didn't make the same mistake again.

Carrying the album carefully, Janet placed it in the bottom drawer of the secretaire where it belonged, and then went through to the kitchen to put the kettle on. She could do with a cup even though she hadn't made one for Ronnie. She had just taken the cake tin out of the pantry when she heard the ringing at her front door.

Janet frowned as she went to answer it. She didn't often have visitors, which meant it was probably the vicar's wife. She must be on her usual rounds, begging things for the church fête or for help at the bazaar. Janet sometimes made cakes or she gave a hand with the stalls, but she wasn't sure she wanted to this time.

The bell rang again, insistently. She glared at the door, annoyed by whoever was there. There was no need to be so impatient! She wrestled with the key and lock, which was tight because it was seldom used. Most people came to the back door. She felt annoyed, and then the key turned and she opened the door. A shock ran through her as she saw who it was, and she felt a flutter of nerves in her stomach. She hadn't been expecting this and wasn't sure what to do.

'You had better come in,' she said, and stood back, allowing her visitor to enter. 'When I wrote, I didn't expect you to call . . .' She looked back at her visitor, eyes opening wide in horror as she saw the cut-throat razor, its blade exposed. 'What are you doing?' Her heart started thumping and she was suddenly frightened.

'I don't take kindly to blackmail . . .'

'But it wasn't . . . I wouldn't . . .' Janet protested. Her eyes fixed on the razor as an arm lifted and she realized that she was going to die. 'No, please don't. You don't understand . . .' She was frightened but disbelieving, too stunned to move or attempt to fight. 'Please, you must . . .'

Her words were lost as the blade slashed across her throat

and the blood spurted everywhere. She collapsed, the darkness folding around her, her last thought of the photograph album that Ronnie had besmirched with his dirty hands.

The murderer stood looking at her for a moment as the blood seeped on to the kitchen floor, then turned and walked away. One of the cats had come into the room, watching with green eyes as the murderer left by the front door, closing it with a bang.

The cat meowed plaintively, its back hunched, as if it realized that it was now a prisoner, shut in with its dead mistress.

Two

Sarah saw her grandmother's car waiting for her outside the station and was pleased, because she wouldn't have fancied the long walk to Amelia Beaufort's house. The road passed by Thorny Woods and there were no streetlights, which meant that it could be a little bit lonely at night. Besides, it had turned cold and she wore only a thin silk dress under her coat. She'd worn it to the end of show party the production manager had given, and hadn't bothered to change before leaving for the station.

'Miss Beaufort.' The chauffeur came towards her and smiled. 'Did you have a good journey down?'

'Yes, thank you, Andrews,' she said and smiled back. She liked Andrews, because he was reliable. He had been with her grandmother for nearly seven years. After his demob from the army at the end of the war, he had just turned up one day looking for a job. Amelia Beaufort had liked him so much that she had gone out and bought a car so that he could drive her around in it. 'The train was a little late and I was afraid you might have given up and gone home.'

'I would never do that, miss. Your grandmother would have my guts for garters.'

Sarah laughed. Andrews didn't mince his words and she liked him all the more for it. You knew where you were with him. He didn't take liberties, but he wasn't a servant in the old-fashioned sense of the word, and Amelia thought of him as one of her family.

'Yes, I expect she would,' Sarah said. She shivered a little in the cold wind. The porter was carrying her bags, and Andrews stowed them safely in the boot of the Rolls Royce, having already opened the door for her. However, she did not immediately get into the car, preferring to watch as her luggage was packed in, filling the available space. The bags and cases contained all she currently had in the world. 'How is Gran?'

'Happy that you are coming to stay, miss.' He glanced at her. 'Jump in or you'll get cold. Mrs Beaufort is very well. I dare say she will live to be a hundred.'

'Yes, I expect so. I hope so.'

Sarah slid into the back seat of the car. She liked the smell of the leather and the comfort the car offered. Her grand-mother could afford the best and she had certainly bought the best on offer, recently replacing her rather clumsy old Phaeton with this very smart Silver Ghost town car.

Sarah looked out of the window as they left the station behind and approached the village. The main street comprised a few cottages facing the green and a duck pond; the church, church hall, post office and general shop; also the baker's, a pub, a butcher's and the vicarage, this last a large Victorian house a little in need of repair. Most of these buildings were of the same faded rose brick and had a cosy look, as if they belonged on the lid of a chocolate box. There were several more houses scattered about the area and the village shared its doctor with another a few miles away. The library van called once every two weeks, and a market visited once a week, and for everything else they needed, the villagers caught the train into Norwich from Thorny Station.

At the top of the hill was Thornhill Manor, which had presided over the scene for centuries, and, a little down the road that branched to the right, was her grandmother's house. It had once been the dower house for Thornhill, but had been sold off some forty years earlier and bought by Gran's husband. He had intended that they would move on in time, but a fever had cut short his life and Mrs Beaufort had refused to move. Her son – who was much richer than his father had ever been – had tried to get her to move into his mansion in Hampshire, but she had steadfastly avoided being made his prisoner. She loved this part of Norfolk, and particularly the house she had been brought to as a bride.

'He doesn't mean to be patronizing,' she had told Sarah once with a wicked smile, 'but I would rather starve than live under Edward's roof. I love him dearly, but quite frankly, he is impossible to live with.'

'I expect that was why Mummy ran off and left him,' Sarah

said and looked affectionately at her grandmother. 'He isn't on speaking terms with me at the moment, because I've been on the stage and he warned me against it. He thinks I am a fallen woman now.'

'That's exactly what I mean. Ridiculous!' Amelia snorted. 'Edward is a snob and thinks too much of himself.'

Sarah smiled at the memory. They were passing Miss Bates's cottage at the bottom of the hill and she noticed there were no lights on, which was unusual. Miss Bates usually sat up late in the evenings, beavering away at her writing. No one was sure what she was writing, though Sarah thought it might be a novel. Janet had mentioned something about a publisher the last time she was down.

Sarah's last visit had been in the spring. She'd been between jobs at the time. But then she'd been offered a summer season at Bournemouth in a theatre that catered for the holidaymakers, who flocked there. She was of course just one of the chorus girls, but on a couple of occasions when the star had been taken sick, Sarah had been given a chance to sing some of her songs. None of the cast was truly famous, though some of them had played with Marie Lloyd and Harry Lauder in music halls and were justly proud of it. Sarah's father certainly hadn't thought much of it.

'You have let me down, Sarah,' he'd said when she was first offered a job singing on stage. 'You might have done anything but you choose to stand on the stage of a tuppeny variety show and sing rubbish.'

'It isn't rubbish, Daddy,' Sarah had told him. 'I sing popular songs – some of them are by Oscar Hammerstein. And I sing them very nicely.'

'If it was a proper concert . . .' Edward Beaufort looked angry. 'You have no need to work, Sarah.'

'I want to sing,' Sarah had smiled to soften her words. 'And I'm sorry you don't approve, Daddy darling, but I'm going to take the job at Bournemouth.'

'Then you can expect nothing more from me while you continue to make a fool of yourself and me.'

Sarah had hardly believed that her father would cut off her allowance but he had. She knew that he was trying to force her to go home to him, but she was determined not to do so. Amelia had offered her a bolthole whenever she needed it, and she was taking advantage of the offer until another job came along.

The car slid smoothly to a halt in front of the house, rousing Sarah from her reveries. It was a beautiful Queen Anne-style cottage with a sloping thatched roof and small windows; the gardens were neatly kept with rose beds, herbaceous borders and an immaculate lawn.

Lights were burning in the front parlour and the door opened as soon as Sarah got out. Amelia always seemed to know things a few seconds before they happened, and Sarah had often told her she was a witch. It was their private joke, but there was no doubting that Amelia had the knack of forecasting things a little in advance.

'Sarah, my darling!' she cried, opening her arms wide. 'That wretched train was late again. I was afraid it might be.'

'Something to do with leaves on the line,' Sarah told her as they embraced affectionately. After Sarah's mother had run off with her rich American, the two had grown very close. 'We had to go dreadfully slowly for a while.'

'Well, you're here now. Come in and get warm, my love. You look frozen.'

Sarah took her coat off. Her arms were bare and she shivered, feeling the goosebumps as she went into the parlour, going to stand in front of the fire to warm her hands. Her pale apricot silk dress was low-waisted, very fashionable with its short skirt and squared neckline, but also highly impractical for a late autumn afternoon. She looked what she was: a pretty, much loved and indulged young woman of the twenties.

It was a welcoming room, the soft furnishings deep and shabby but comfortable, the gleam of old polish on tables, chairs, and a handsome bookcase, which took up the length of one wall, was filled with a mixture of books, silver items and china figures. The whole room smelled of rose petals, which had been dried and lay in porcelain bowls dotted about the place, amongst a collection of much-loved clutter, including stones given to Amelia by Sarah from childhood visits to the beaches on the Norfolk coast. There was also a wind-up gramophone and a pile of records, some by Paul Robeson and other stars from the stage shows in London and on Broadway, of which Amelia was a great fan, and lots of family photographs in frames.

'How are you, darling Gran?' Sarah asked. 'Your last letter, which I received just before I left the hotel, said you were bothered about something?'

'Was I?' Amelia wrinkled her brow. 'I was bothered about Mr Tibbs when you rang, because cats have been going missing in the village they tell me, but I don't think it was that . . .'

'No, it was something to do with the wood,' Sarah prompted.

'Oh, yes,' Amelia smiled as she remembered. 'They want to cut a large chunk of it down to build expensive houses. Those woods are ancient, Sarah. People have been protesting. Some believe there is a sacred pagan shrine somewhere in there – and there are certainly badgers and lots of wildlife. Sir William was very angry about it. He has offered to buy the land at a sensible price, but Beecham won't hear of it.'

'I suppose it is worth more for houses,' Sarah said, 'but surely there are other places they could build without cutting down ancient woodland?'

'Agricultural land is more useful. People haven't forgotten that we went short of food during the war, and the wood is adjacent to where they want to widen the road. It's right on the other side of Thorny Woods and doesn't really affect our village. It's Sir William's land it will scar. They will need to take a part of his land too.'

'Can't he just say no?'

'He has been saying no for the past two years, but it looks as if the council is behind this scheme and they might make a compulsory purchase order.'

'That's not fair. I shouldn't have thought they could do things like that.'

'It's because of the road. The traffic has been increasing since the war ended, Sarah. People are coming this way more often, especially in summer. A lot of our Norfolk roads were made for the horse and cart. I must admit I find a car very useful. I can't imagine how we used to live without one.'

'I suppose you had a carriage – or perhaps a bicycle like Miss Bates?' Sarah said with a teasing smile.

'Oh, don't!' Amelia sat down on the sofa, her tiny frame almost disappearing into the piles of soft cushions. 'Of course you don't know, my dear. Poor Janet was murdered. It happened

just a few days ago. I didn't write to you about it because it
was so shocking.'

'*Murdered?*' Sarah shivered as a chill trickled down her
spine. 'That's horrible. I noticed her light wasn't on as we
passed the cottage but I had no idea why. How was she killed?'

'Someone cut her throat with a gentleman's razor and there
was a lot of blood. It was at least three days before she was
found, apparently.' Amelia shook her head. Her skin looked
pale and she appeared more fragile than usual. 'Most unpleasant. Mrs Hayes found her when she called about the
fête. Janet always used to help out with the cakes. Vera said
she had called previously and got no answer so she went round
the back and when she saw the cat lying on the path . . .'
Amelia shuddered. 'It was a nasty thing to do. Janet loved
her cats.'

'The murderer had killed the cat too?'

'Chopped its head off. Quite appalling! The other cat was
still inside, trapped with Janet, apparently, and it was hungry
. . .' Amelia broke off, for there was no need to go into that
kind of detail. 'It has all been rather unpleasant. Nothing like
that has ever happened in Beecham Thorny before.'

Sarah sat down in the large, comfortable wing chair by the
fire, her greenish-brown eyes clouded with distress. She could
see the murder had upset her grandmother, and the mutilation
of the cat was macabre.

'Who could have wanted to kill Janet Bates? She lived in
that cottage alone and caused no trouble for anyone.'

'Well . . .' Amelia looked thoughtful. 'She was a bit nosy.
I've seen her at her window, watching people, and she had
a telescope at her back bedroom window. I saw it when
she took me into her garden to show me her prize marrows
one year . . .' She was silent for a moment. 'I don't think
she gossiped about what she saw, but she probably could
have done if she'd wished. I suspect she rather liked keeping
her secrets to herself.'

'Surely no one would kill her for being nosy? I should think
she was just lonely and watched people for something to do.'

'She was invited to join in all the village activities, and I
had her to tea several times. I quite liked her, though some
people didn't. She won the flower-arranging contest last year,
and the prize for the best jam – and she might have won the

contest for the biggest marrow if someone hadn't crept into her garden one night and vandalized it.'

'Oh, Gran! They didn't? Whatever for?'

'You don't understand, my darling. Competition for these things is very fierce around here – and Janet was one of the worst. I wouldn't put it past her to vandalize someone else's produce if she got the chance. It was rumoured that she might have attacked Major Hurst's sunflowers last year, though it was never proved, of course.'

Sarah pulled a wry face. It seemed rather petty. She couldn't believe that people actually did things like that because of a village show.

'Major Hurst wouldn't murder her for that – would he?'

'I'm sure he wouldn't,' Amelia agreed. 'But someone hated her enough to do it. Some of the locals think it might have been Ronnie Miller. Apparently she turned him off the day she was murdered. Harold Jackson saw him that afternoon and he says the lad was resentful because she hadn't given him his usual tea and cake.'

'Ronnie Miller?' Sarah searched her memory and came up with the image of a gangling youth who had seemed a bit backward the few times she'd spoken to him. 'He looked after her garden, did the digging and the heavy work, didn't he?'

'Yes, for a couple of years now. She told me she felt sorry for him. I can't think it was him, Sarah. I know he is a nuisance when he's had a couple of drinks, but his mother doesn't let him have much money. No, no, I don't think it was Ronnie.'

'What do the police say?'

'Not much from what I hear. Our local man called in a detective from Norwich. He and his colleagues arrived in a small convoy, walked all over the garden, sealed the cottage and spent the best part of a day there, but no one has seen them since. I don't think there were many clues – except that it seems she must have let her killer in, so probably knew him, and of course the razor, which was dropped on the floor.'

'Wouldn't that have the killer's fingerprints? I don't know much about it, but I read somewhere about the police catching criminals that way. Detective work is becoming quite scientific now, I believe.'

'If the killer didn't wear gloves.'

'Yes, of course. If he planned it, he probably would. How

horrible.' Sarah shuddered at the idea of someone planning a murder in cold blood. 'Well, I suppose the police will work it out in the end.'

'And it's better if we don't talk about it. I'm glad that Andrews and Millie sleep in. I should be nervous without them at the moment.'

'Yes, it is very unpleasant. Miss Bates's cottage isn't far from you.' The dower house was a bit isolated, its nearest neighbour Thornhill Manor. It was something that had never bothered Amelia in the past, but was clearly a disadvantage now.

'Let's try to forget about it, dearest,' Amelia said. 'Tell me about your show. You sang on stage alone when that woman was sick, didn't you?'

'Angela Anthony,' Sarah supplied. 'She was off a couple of times. Everyone said that she was drunk, but the manager told us she was ill. I was a bit nervous to start with, but once I started to sing I was fine.'

Sarah chattered on about the wonderful time she'd had in Bournemouth and the new friends she'd made, but the murder lingered at the back of her mind. A violent killing like that was such a horrid thing to have happened. Miss Bates had been a quiet, inoffensive lady. What possible reason could anyone have had for killing her?

Sir William Meadows replaced the receiver of his telephone and frowned. He was not at all happy about what he'd just been asked to do and he needed time to think it over.

'Something wrong?' his wife asked as he returned to the dining table. 'You look extremely cross, my dear.'

'I'm not exactly angry.' He glanced down the long and beautifully set table at his son. Larch was a source of irritation to him. He had a brilliant mind and Sir William had hoped that he would take up the law when he was demobbed after the war. Instead, he spent his time painting pictures. People said he was good, but it seemed a waste of effort to his father. Larch hadn't sold a painting yet. He didn't actually need to, because his maternal grandfather had left him an obscene amount of money. Not that he bothered about that either, leaving it to the lawyers to administer.

'I've been asked to sign an order for Ronnie Miller to be put away in an asylum.'

'You won't do it, William!' His wife looked at him in alarm. 'You simply can't – that poor lad! And his mother too! He is all she has.'

'I might have to, Edith.' Sir William glanced at his son, who was toying with his food. 'What's wrong with that?'

'Nothing.' Larch focused his eyes. He was a mildly attractive young man, with deep blue eyes and a gentle smile, but his father thought his hair too long for decency. 'Just not hungry. I had a bacon sandwich earlier.'

'You should eat properly, darling,' Lady Meadows said, smiling at him lovingly. 'You're too thin.'

'You knew Ronnie Miller when you were at school, didn't you?'

Larch met his father's anxious gaze. 'Yes, sir. He wasn't there often and he's some years younger than me, but I stop and speak to him when I see him about, slip him a shilling sometimes. He's slow and he can be surly if he's upset, but I can't see him killing Miss Bates. A cut-throat razor wouldn't be his weapon. He might use a spade if she made him lose his temper. But it is possible that he killed the cat. I know he has never liked them. Yet I've never known him to be violent before.'

'There's always a first time.' Sir William was thoughtful. 'It seems the police think he's their most likely suspect. They couldn't get anything out of him when they questioned him, and there was no sign of blood on his boots or clothes. But they feel it would be best to put him away.'

'Case closed, just like that? They haven't even tried to find the real killer! They let our local plod do the leg work, questioning the villagers – and you can guess how much information he picked up, can't you?'

'Constable Arnold is a nice young man,' his mother reproved.

'Exactly!'

'Not enough clues, Larch,' his father said, though in this instance he agreed with his son. 'Apparently, they think she knew her killer. She didn't put up a struggle and it appears that nothing was taken.'

'Someone must surely have seen something?'

'Harold Jackson says she'd turned the lad off earlier that day – could that be reason enough for him to kill her?' Sir

William frowned. The whole business was very messy and worrying, because something didn't quite fit to his way of thinking.

'Perhaps, though I can't see him going back there with a razor. If he'd struck her in anger with his spade, yes – but the razor is too cold-blooded, too calculated.'

'As it happens, I agree with you,' Sir William said. 'I shall hold off on this section order for the moment. They could get someone else to sign it, but probably won't – it might not look too good if the local JP objected.' Sir William toyed with the stem of his wine glass for a moment. 'I might ring someone I know. Ben Marshall – an old friend. He was with Scotland Yard for years but he retired last year – ill health, they said, but I think it was more a matter of politics.'

'Will he want to be bothered?' Lady Meadows asked. An attractive, patient lady, she was much like her son to look at with dark hair and blue eyes that could still sparkle with youthful laughter. 'He probably has better things to do with his time.'

'If I know Ben, he is slowly climbing the wall and wishing his days away. He'll come down, if only for a few days' holiday. If he thinks the local plod has got it right, he can always go sea fishing off the pier at Lowestoft.'

'A bit cold for that at this time of year,' Larch said, and received an accusing glare from his father.

'Isn't it time you had your hair cut?'

'Is it?' Larch was surprised. The length of his hair never bothered him. 'I'll have it cut soon, Father.'

'Time you did,' Sir William barked. 'You might think about getting yourself a proper job, Larch.'

His son gave him a lazy, affectionate smile. 'Other people don't seem to share your good opinion of me, sir. Can't think of anyone who would employ me.' He pushed his chair back and went to kiss his mother on the cheek. 'Don't worry if I'm late back, Ma.'

'Going out?' his father asked.

'I thought I would drive over and visit Amelia Beaufort,' Larch said. 'Sarah is staying with her. I have to return a book she loaned me.'

'Yes, darling, enjoy yourself.' Lady Meadows smiled at her husband after Larch had gone. 'I have hopes. Sarah is the only girl he has ever bothered with.'

'Perhaps because she is as feckless as he is,' Sir William replied, and then conceded as his wife gave him a hard look. 'Well, all right, she's a nice girl, pretty too.'

'Sarah is lovely! All that wonderful hair – such a pretty shade of reddish-brown – and soft eyes, loving eyes. She would be a wonderful daughter-in-law.'

'Perhaps she can get him to find a proper job.'

'Larch has talent, my dear. You may not see it but other people admire his work.'

'Perhaps you're right. I think I'll go and ring Ben Marshall now.'

Larch was thoughtful as he drove past Janet Bates's cottage. He hadn't had a great deal to do with her himself, but she'd always waved when they'd passed in the village, him in his car, her on that bicycle of hers.

He thought he caught sight of a flicker of light in the upper window at the back of the cottage. It was only a flash in his driving mirror and gone so soon that he couldn't be sure. Could someone be up there having a look around? He considered turning back, but decided against it. The police were supposed to have sealed the cottage – and he was probably mistaken.

Miss Bates had owned her cottage. He thought she had a brother, because she'd mentioned him once, saying that he was going to meet her in Norwich for lunch. He might have turned up to see what he had inherited.

As he crested the hill and paused to turn right, allowing the oncoming car to pass first, Larch caught a glimpse of the woman driving. She was wearing a fur coat, dark glasses – at this hour of the evening! – and a headscarf pulled tight over her head. He wondered if she could see where she was going – she had certainly cut the corner off as she rounded the bend from Thornhill Manor. She must have come from there, because the road didn't lead anywhere else.

He hadn't seen the car locally before as far as he could recall, which meant she was probably a stranger. However, as she had come from Thornhill Manor he didn't make much of that, because Sir James was a businessman and had his finger in a few pies. Larch's father certainly didn't approve of some of what went on at the Manor, though he usually kept his opinions to himself. It was this quarrel over the wood that really angered Sir William.

'The man is a cheat and a stubborn fool,' Sir William had complained recently. 'There are plenty of alternatives to that woodland if he cared to open his eyes. I can't understand why he's set on destroying something that beautiful.'

Larch thought it was sacrilege. He had attended the various meetings to protest against the idea of both a new road and the housing estate. It was complete madness to contemplate such a project, and unlike the parish council to agree to the application. The only explanation was that Sir James was hand in hand with at least one of the councillors, and that money had changed hands.

That was illegal, and if it could be proved would cause trouble for both the councillors and Sir James. Larch had already talked to a few people about trying to find out what had gone on in dark corners. One of the local hotheads had suggested breaking into the council offices in search of proof that some collusion had gone on, but the proof would hardly be found there. It was far more likely to be the new car in the drive of one of the councillor's houses, or the mink coat his wife was wearing.

As he drew up outside the lovely old cottage where Amelia Beaufort lived, Larch saw that the lights were burning in the front parlour and his thoughts turned to the beautiful Sarah Beaufort.

His ring was answered swiftly by the chauffeur, who grinned when he saw him. 'Good evening, sir. I answered the door because it's dark out and Millie is a little nervous because of what happened to Miss Bates.'

'Very wise, Andrews,' Larch replied. 'I am very glad to see that you are here to look after the ladies.'

'Yes, sir. I shall be keeping a watch out until the police clear this matter up, don't you worry.'

'If they ever do – the police, I mean,' Larch said. 'The best idea they've had so far is to shut Ronnie Miller away in an asylum – and for my money they are on completely the wrong track.'

'Just so, sir. It was the wrong choice of weapon for that lad. He might have bashed her with whatever came to hand, but a razor . . .' Andrews shook his head. 'Not quite Ronnie's style. He's not a bad lad, just a bit slow if you ask me. I've let him help me out a couple of times, and I give him a few pence now and then . . . not much of a life for the poor devil with that mother of his.'

'Exactly my thoughts on the matter.' Andrews was a sensible man. No one knew much about him, because he didn't talk about himself, though he had a small scar on his cheek and a bit of a stiff shoulder as souvenirs from the war – but they all had their own souvenirs of that time. And Larch had his own ideas concerning Andrews. 'Is it convenient to see Miss Beaufort and Sarah?'

'Yes, I am sure it is,' Andrews said. 'Come in, sir. Shall I tell Millie you would like some tea – or would you rather have something stronger?'

'Not unless Miss Beaufort asks – I'm hoping Sarah will come out for a drink somewhere.'

'Ah, just so, sir. I should go through to the parlour. The ladies will be pleased to see you.'

Sarah jumped to her feet as soon as Larch entered the room, her face lighting up with a smile of welcome. 'Larch! I told Gran that I thought I heard you speaking to Andrews. How lovely of you to come over this evening! I was thinking about walking down to see you tomorrow.'

'I came to bring your book back,' Larch said, and then laughed. 'Well, that was my excuse, but I really wanted to see you, Sarah. I hear you've been doing marvellous things since the spring.'

'Did a little bird tell you that?' Sarah blushed and directed an accusing glance at her grandmother. 'It wasn't all that marvellous really, although I did get to sing a few songs solo on a couple of nights. I sang "Look For The Silver Lining" by Jerome Kern and an Irving Berlin song. The rest of the time I was just one of the chorus.'

'I wish I had been there on those nights,' Larch told her. He didn't add that he had visited the show once when she was in the chorus, but had lost his nerve and gone away after-wards instead of waiting at the stage door to take her out to supper. 'I thought you might like to go for a drink – if that's all right with you, Amelia?'

'Yes, I think I can trust you to take care of her.' Amelia's eyes twinkled. 'As long as you promise not to drink too much and bring her back safely.'

'Yes, of course,' he replied. 'Talking of driving safely, I passed a woman driving rather fast as I came here. She had been to the Manor and shot round the bend, but I had paused just in case so there was no bother.'

'A woman driver?' Amelia looked interested. 'She must be a stranger, then, because I don't think anyone drives around here – ladies, I mean. Sarah does, of course, but she was here with me.'

'She must have been a stranger,' Larch agreed. 'She was wearing a fur coat and sunglasses, and I wondered if she could see where she was going at this hour.'

'It does sound a little odd. It's rather American, don't you think?'

'Yes, perhaps,' Larch agreed and chuckled. 'Like one of the female stars from a motion picture.'

'Who could it have been?' Sarah wondered aloud. 'It makes you think . . . after what happened to Miss Bates . . .'

'She was killed by a man,' Larch said. 'It must have taken some force to slash her throat like that . . .' He saw that Amelia had gone white and apologized quickly. 'I'm so sorry. It's just that I heard Father discussing it with someone. I thought it must have been a man.'

'Some women are very strong,' Sarah said. 'But don't let's talk about it.' She got up and went over to kiss her grandmother's cheek. 'We shan't be late, dearest, but don't sit up for me.'

'No, I shan't sit up,' Amelia assured her. 'Have a good time, you two. Take care of her, Larch.'

'With my life,' he said and winked. 'We shall go to the Chestnuts, Amelia. It is all very proper there. My mother likes it so I'm sure you must approve.'

'Oh, are we going there?' Sarah questioned as they went out into the hall. 'I thought we might just pop into the King's Head.'

'I thought you would prefer the Chestnuts.' Larch arched his brows. 'Make it more of a treat?'

'I'm not really dressed for it,' Sarah replied. 'In Bournemouth, the girls just popped into the pub for a drink after rehearsals. Some of the men went with us, of course, but I'm quite accustomed to public houses, Larch. I'm a modern girl.'

'Yes, of course you are. The local it is then . . .' He saw the look on her face and assumed there was something more going on in her head. 'Any particular reason for that?'

'Well . . .' She put a finger to her lips and lowered her voice. 'Tell you in the car . . .'

Larch nodded. He rather thought Sarah had a bee in her bonnet, and he had noticed that Amelia had been upset at his speaking of the way Miss Bates had died. He waited in silence until they were in the car and then looked at her expectantly.

'I thought we might hear what everyone is saying about it – the murder, I mean.'

'I can tell you that the police want to put Ronnie away.'

'Oh, poor boy! Of course, I suppose he is a man, but he always seems like a boy.'

'Yes, he does – and he doesn't cause much trouble, unless he has a few drinks too many.'

'I don't think he killed her – do you?'

'No, not that way. He is a creature of impulse. He might have lashed out in a temper but he wouldn't have sneaked back with a razor – and he was seen to leave earlier that afternoon.'

'Then that means the killer is still walking around laughing at the police and thinking he has got away with it – if it was a man, and you seem to think a woman couldn't have killed her.' Sarah raised her brows at him.

'I think it was more likely to have been a man,' Larch said, 'but I am willing to be proved wrong.'

Her eyes sparkled as she looked at him. 'Do you think we could have a go at finding the killer ourselves?'

'You're not serious?' Larch had been thinking along those lines himself, but hadn't included her in his plans. Yet two minds were better than one and it would give him an excuse to see her more often. 'How do we start? The police didn't seem to find many clues – apart from the razor, of course, which was a very cheap thing available in most chemist shops. If they are stumped, what chance do we have of discovering anything?'

'I don't know. I thought we might sort of . . . well, you know, nose about, keep our eyes and ears open. I should like to have a look around the cottage.' There was a teasing light in her eyes, challenging him.

Larch was silent for a moment, then, 'You might not be the only one to have that idea. I thought I saw a light in one of the bedroom windows as I drove past on my way here.'

'A light? I thought the police had sealed it?'

'Yes, they did – but if the intruder knew where she kept her spare key . . .' he broke off, seeming rather pleased with himself.

'Do *you* know?'

'Yes, I do as a matter of fact,' Larch said. 'I saw her struggling near the bus stop in Norwich a few weeks ago. She had several heavy parcels so I put them in the back of the car and drove her home. She couldn't find her key immediately and said she kept an extra key hidden under one of the flowerpots.'

'What an original hiding place,' Sarah said, her lips twitching with unholy amusement. 'Almost anyone could have got in there.'

'Yes, but it was a key to the back door,' Larch said. 'The police think that the killer came in the front way, because the bolts were undone and she usually kept them locked. The door hadn't been locked again, so the murderer must have left the same way.'

'Most people used the back door,' Sarah said, turning it over in her mind as she tried to picture the scene. 'So it had to be a stranger, didn't it? A local person would have gone to the back door. Of course the front door faces the wood and wouldn't be so open to the public gaze. If the murderer went there intending to kill her it might have seemed the best bet.'

'Good point! Yes, that makes sense,' Larch agreed. 'It seems likely that she knew her killer, though that is not definite. We have to keep an open mind.'

'Which means if we have a drink at the local and ask a few questions . . .' Sarah murmured, a gleam of mischief in her eyes,

'We might hear about any strangers who have visited this past week or so.' He laughed softly. 'You really are interested in this, aren't you?'

'I should like the killer to be caught,' Sarah said and her expression was suddenly angry. 'This business has upset my grandmother and Millie. They are both feeling nervous, and it isn't nice, Larch. I shall feel easier myself when he is caught.'

'Or she,' Larch said and nodded as her brows went up. 'Well, we already know of one stranger in the village, don't we? The mystery woman in the fur coat . . .'

Three

Amelia was in the kitchen talking to her housekeeper when Sarah came downstairs the next morning. She hovered in the doorway watching them. She had always liked this part of the house, with its smells of baking and herbs, and the old-fashioned range and oak dresser. Wandering over to the table, she picked up a piece of crumbly, just-baked shortbread to nibble at, and then her grandmother waved her towards the breakfast room with a mock frown.

'Biscuits at this hour? Your breakfast is ready, Sarah. I'll join you in a minute . . .' She turned her head towards the front hall, seeming to listen. 'That will be the post, pick it up for me, my dear.'

Sarah went through to the hall. She looked at the doormat, which was empty of letters, but even as she was thinking that her grandmother was wrong this time, there was a swishing noise and a small pile of envelopes came through the letter box.

She took the letters into the breakfast room, placing them beside Amelia's plate before pouring coffee for herself and tea for her grandmother. She examined the contents of the silver chafing dish, helping herself to some scrambled eggs and bacon. Amelia came in and picked up her letters, looking through them.

'Drat that boy!' she said with a trace of annoyance. 'That's the second time this month he's brought me one of Sir James's letters. It is such a nuisance – for poor Sir James as well as me. As well it came here, though, because some people might open it before passing it on.'

'Surely not? Do people actually do that, Gran?'

'Oh yes, I am sure of it.' Amelia frowned. 'A letter came for me a few weeks back. It was in the afternoon, and we never have an afternoon post, and I am certain it had been steamed open and glued down again.'

'Was it important?'

'It was a letter from my doctor asking me to make an appointment for a routine check-up,' Amelia said and seemed annoyed. 'But it might have been important.'

'Do you know who brought it?'

'Yes, I do. I saw her cycling away afterwards.' Amelia hesitated, and then, 'It was Miss Bates, Sarah. I am quite sure that she would open any letters that were delivered to her by mistake. I told you I saw a telescope at her bedroom window, didn't I? I believe she spent quite a lot of time at her bedroom windows watching what people did and with whom they spoke . . .'

'Do you think that might have something to do with her death?'

'Well, I have wondered,' Amelia admitted, a trifle reluctantly. 'If she somehow got hold of something she wasn't supposed to see . . .'

'You mean a letter addressed to Sir James? Do you think he had something to do with this?'

'Oh, no! God forbid that I should give you that idea!' Amelia looked horrified. 'No, of course not. Quite out of the question.'

Sarah saw her grandmother's worried expression and knew that she was still disturbed that something of the sort should have happened in sleepy old Beecham Thorny, and clearly wasn't ready to consider that one of her neighbours may have been the perpetrator.

'I'll walk over to the Manor with this for you,' Sarah offered. 'I'm going down to the village so it will only take a moment or two longer.'

'That is so kind of you, dearest,' Amelia said. 'I had to take the last one myself, and he seemed to think it was my fault that it had been delivered here.'

'I thought you were friendly with him? Isn't he a member of your monthly bridge club?'

'Yes, he is,' Amelia said, 'and I saw him again the following night. He was as nice as pie then and apologized to me. Told me I had caught him at a bad moment . . .'

'Well, I'll take this one and pop it through his door,' Sarah said. She finished her coffee. 'You don't mind if I dash, do you? I'm meeting Larch in half an hour.'

'Again? Didn't you have enough chance to talk last night?'

'We had a lovely time, but we have a little project on for this morning.' Sarah shook her head as her grandmother looked at her inquisitively. 'Nothing much. I should think I shall be home for lunch but don't wait for me if I'm late.'

'Do whatever you like, Sarah. You know we only have something light at midday. Enjoy yourself, my darling. I have plenty to do myself. There are lots of leaves in the garden and Andrews is going to help me make a bonfire.'

Sarah correctly interpreted this as Andrews doing the work while her grandmother directed him and generally got in his way, but knew that he was perfectly happy with that arrangement.

She had arranged to meet Larch at Janet Bates's cottage that morning. Against his better judgement, she had persuaded him that they ought to have a quick look around, see if they could find any clues the police might not have noticed. Because apart from the razor, which had been left lying on the floor, the police didn't seem to have found anything of interest. Or if they had they weren't saying.

'It's hardly likely there are any obvious clues,' Larch had said. 'The police aren't complete idiots, Sarah, even if I do think they've made a bit of a mess of this so far.'

'But they might not have seen it with our eyes,' Sarah pointed out. 'I visited Janet a few times at her cottage. She showed me some programmes she had of shows at the music halls before the war. I think she knew some of the stars – Vesta Tilly, Marie Lloyd and others. She even had some signed photographs of early film stars. Mary Pickford amongst others.'

'How did she get those?'

Sarah shook her head. 'I think she was going to tell me once and then she spotted Ronnie doing something he shouldn't in the garden and rushed out after him. When she came back she had changed her mind. She only showed me the programmes and the signed photographs because I told her I was going to be in a variety show at the seaside.'

'I suppose she is a bit of a mystery, isn't she? She came here ten or twelve years ago and we've got used to her, living alone with her cats, helping at the church fête – but what do we know of her past life?'

'Very little. Janet didn't talk about herself much – but having been to her cottage, I might notice if something was missing. The police wouldn't know, but I might.'

'I'm not sure we ought to meddle in this,' Larch said, rubbing the bridge of his nose as he sometimes did when he was disturbed. He didn't much like the idea of snooping around the cottage. 'If we did stumble on a clue – well, it could be dangerous.'

'Not if we're together,' Sarah said. 'I mean, if I went alone . . .'

'You wouldn't!' Larch stared at her hard. 'Yes, you would, wouldn't you? All right, we'll have a quick look in the morning – that way I shan't be worrying about what you are up to all day long.'

Sarah's thoughts were interrupted by the sound of loud voices as she approached the Manor. She halted, listening to what was obviously Sir James venting his anger.

'Get off my land! If I ever catch you hanging around again I'll have my gamekeeper after you! Next time he'll break your legs. You've been warned before and this time I've had enough . . .'

Sarah saw the two men as she rounded the bend in the long drive, but it seemed as if the incident was over, and one was leaving. The man coming towards her looked as if he were a gypsy, dressed in dirty brown corduroys and a tweed jacket that might have been good once but now had patches on the elbows. He had a greasy-looking cap pulled down over his long hair, but she could see that he was scowling as he brushed past her. She thought he was Morna Scaffry's brother Jethro, but she wasn't certain, because she knew Morna better than her brother.

Sarah walked on, her heart thumping as she saw Sir James standing there just outside his magnificent old house, which was an early Georgian mansion built of faded rose brick. It had funny little twisted chimneys and a lot of later additions that had caused it to spread out on both wings. He had a shotgun over his shoulder. It had been broken so that the barrel was at an angle and was obviously not ready for use. He was wearing a tweed jacket and brown cord trousers with long leather boots that buckled at the side. His hair was short and wiry, beginning to turn grey at the temples, and his grey eyes narrowed as she approached. So much for her hopes of leaving the letter and getting away without seeing him!

'Sir James,' she said and smiled brightly. 'You may remember me – Sarah Beaufort? Unfortunately the post boy brought us one of your letters this morning.'

'What?' His expression darkened. 'Damn and blast the boy! Can't he get it right? That's the third time lately . . .'

'I am very sorry,' Sarah apologized, although it wasn't her fault and she had delivered it straight away. 'Anyway, it was only a few minutes ago. And you will notice that we did not attempt to open it.' She wasn't sure why she had said that, except that a little demon had prompted her.

The colour left his cheeks. For a moment his hands clenched at his sides and she thought he might strike her, and then he checked himself and shook his head.

'Of course not. I didn't imagine so for one moment, Sarah. Mrs Beaufort is far too honourable to do such a thing.' He forced a smile. 'Come down for a little visit, have you?'

'Yes, for a longish one I should think,' Sarah said, and handed him his letter. 'I'll be on my way then, sir.'

'I shall ask my wife to invite you both to dinner one evening,' he said. 'Please forgive me if I was brusque – that damned gypsy was caught red-handed in my woods again. He had been poaching. He has been warned once and my keeper told him that this time it was a police matter. He came to ask me to reconsider . . .'

'It must be very annoying,' Sarah said, turning away. Poaching was what the gypsies did, she thought as she walked off, leaving him still standing there, like selling lucky heather and telling fortunes. Most landowners put up with it unless it got too bad, though it wasn't so long ago that it had been a very serious offence that might be punished by hanging or transportation.

Sir James had been very angry, but was it just over a poaching offence? Sarah hadn't missed his slip of the tongue over the post boy's mistake. Two of his letters had been delivered to her grandmother but he had mentioned three, so perhaps one of them might have gone to Miss Bates. Her cottage, the dower house and the Manor were the last houses on the post boy's round, so if delivered wrongly, the letter would probably have gone to one or the other . . .

She saw that Larch was waiting for her at the bottom of the hill and ran the last bit. Some rooks were startled out of their perches and flew up, their wings making a loud noise as they circled overhead. Sarah arrived a little out of breath, her cheeks pink from the fresh air, long hair flying in the breeze.

'Something wrong?' Larch asked. 'You haven't changed your mind about this?'

'No, of course not. I was a bit late because I delivered a letter to the Manor. The boy put it in with ours. It seems he has done it a couple of times before, but only one of them went to Gran.' She gave him a meaningful look.

Larch was silent, his brows arching. 'So? There's more, isn't there?'

'Gran had a letter go astray as well. It was delivered to her in the afternoon and it had been steamed open and stuck back down . . . Miss Bates brought it on her bicycle.'

'Ah . . . yes, I see where you're going with this. You think she might have opened Sir James's letter as well.'

'Yes, it seems likely, doesn't it?'

'Yes, very likely, I should say. It depends what was in the letter, of course. If it was something she could blackmail him over—'

'It might have been a reason for murder,' Sarah concluded. 'If Sir James were the killer he would be able to reach the cottage on foot, perhaps through the woods – and that might account for no one seeing anything.'

Sir James might well be capable of murder. Sarah had heard him threatening Jethro Scaffry and he had looked so angry. He was a heavily built man and, she imagined, could easily kill with one slash of a razor.

'We should keep him in mind as a suspect. We don't have any others as yet.'

Their questions at the pub the night before had verified nothing except a lack of information, though there was plenty of speculation, but it seemed most locals favoured Ronnie Miller as the culprit.

'It is possible, of course. I don't like the man much, Sarah, but he does have influence locally. However, murder is a serious charge and we would have to be pretty certain before we said anything. Father knows from bitter experience how difficult it is to deal with that man, but that doesn't make him a murderer.'

'No, of course it doesn't,' Sarah agreed, 'but it is something to keep in mind, isn't it? Of course, even if blackmail was the reason Miss Bates was murdered, it might have been someone else entirely behind it. The letter going astray isn't proof of anything.'

'Well, as long as you remember that,' Larch said and grinned. 'Come on, let's go to the cottage now. No one is about and we're breaking and entering, you know.'

'Not exactly, not if the key is there,' Sarah argued the point. 'We're simply making use of inside knowledge.'

Larch pulled a face at her. His father would have a fit if he knew what they were up to, but he wasn't going to let Sarah do this on her own. If they got caught he would think of some excuse.

They went through the front gate and around to the back door. Larch turned up the flowerpot just a few yards away and discovered the key still there. He unlocked the door and turned to beckon Sarah just as she bent to pick something up.

'What have you found?'

'A sprig of lucky heather,' Sarah said. 'I know where it came from because I bought some from Morna Scaffry in the spring, and the stem was bound with ribbon just like this. She told me it would bring me luck and I got the job in Bournemouth the next week.'

'Coincidence,' Larch said. 'You don't believe in that rubbish, do you?'

'I'm not sure,' Sarah said, 'but that isn't the point. What was it doing there, lying in that flowerbed? It hasn't been there long because it would have fallen to bits.'

'Was Morna in the habit of calling on Miss Bates?' Larch said as they went inside and closed the door of the cottage. They were in the kitchen now and there was an unpleasant smell, perhaps because the floor was still bloodstained. The tiles hadn't been cleaned and Sarah felt a little sick as she saw paw prints all around where the body must have lain.

'Her cat was shut in with her for a couple of days. Do you think . . .?'

Larch took her arm and steered her into the hall. 'I don't

think about things like that and nor should you. Did you ever
go upstairs when you visited?'

'No, just in the kitchen and the parlour.'

'Right. I'll go upstairs and have a look around while you
do the parlour. If anything frightens you, call me.'

'Yes, all right,' Sarah said.

She took a deep breath and went through to the parlour. A
large, comfortable room, it had quite a few valuable antiques,
and the carpet was good quality, of Persian design. In here it
smelled of lavender and was much fresher than the kitchen.
She checked the things she remembered, because there were
some small silver pieces that might be valuable, also some
rather nice porcelain. It was all in place, though she thought
one framed photograph might be missing. It had stood on the
little table near the window when Sarah was here last, but she
couldn't be sure it hadn't been moved somewhere else. She
thought it had held a photograph of a woman, but she wasn't
sure of that either. The programmes and some photograph
albums were kept in the bottom drawer of the secretaire. She
went over and pulled it open, lifting them out.

'What are you doing?' Larch asked, coming in at that
moment. 'I'm not sure that you ought to be looking in drawers,
Sarah.'

'It was where she kept the programmes and these albums . . .'
Sarah laid one down and it fell open as if it had often been
used. 'Oh, look, she showed me a signed photograph of this
woman – but there are a lot more here, and she is with her.
She must have known her well.' She turned the pages and
found even more. 'She must have lived or worked with her
for some time, because these were taken over a period of some
years, I should think. The hairstyles have changed in this one.'

'Do you know who the woman is?'

'I'm not sure,' Sarah said. 'The face is vaguely familiar. I
think she might be something to do with acting but I'm not
sure.' She pulled a face. 'I believe there was a silver photograph frame on the table by the window. It might have been
of this woman but I can't be certain.'

'Nothing else missing?'

'No, I don't think so. I'm not much of a sleuth, am I?'

'I think you've done pretty well,' Larch said. 'Put the photos
back – oh, look, take one of that woman, and then put the

album back. It might be a good idea to find out who she is if we can.'

'Yes, all right. I'll have this one of her with Miss Bates. It must have been taken a long time ago. Miss Bates looks a lot younger . . .' She slipped the picture into her coat pocket and then returned the albums to the drawer. 'Did you find anything upstairs?'

'I wasn't looking for anything in particular. But there's no sign of a disturbance so it probably wasn't a robbery,' he said. 'The telescope is there as Amelia said and there was a pencil lying on the table near it – but nothing to write on. If there was a pad or something I suppose the police took it.'

'Well, they would if it was interesting,' Sarah said. 'Blow them! It might have told us something if we'd found it.'

'If she was making notes about what she saw it could have provided a clue,' Larch said. 'If the police did find it they have kept pretty quiet. Father doesn't know anything about it, and he made it his business to find out what he could.'

'Well, as the local Justice of the Peace he had the right, but I don't suppose the police gossip about these things,' Sarah said. 'I think we had better go before someone sees us, don't you?'

'Let's hope they don't,' he replied, and grinned at her. 'But I've thought of an excuse. We'll say we heard a cat in distress and came in to rescue it.'

'Where is it then?' She was amused, because it was just like him to think of it.

'Oh, it dashed off as soon as we opened the door. After all, no one knows how many of the things she had, do they?'

'She had several at one time,' Sarah said, 'although I think a couple of them disappeared mysteriously last summer.'

'Ronnie probably got rid of them,' Larch said. 'He didn't like cats. He told me they were nasty creatures once – and he may have been responsible for the dead cat they found on the path.'

Sarah shivered. 'That was rather horrible. If he did that, he might have . . .' the words stuck in her throat.

'No, I don't think so. I doubt if he even thought of killing her, Sarah. Cats, yes, I wouldn't put that past him – but not a woman who gave him work and fed him tea and cake.'

'But she turned him off, didn't she?'

'Yes – but did Ronnie take that in? I very much doubt it. I should say he turned up for work as usual the next day.'

'Do you think he saw anything? If he came back later that day for some reason . . . or the next day, because they aren't exactly sure when she died, are they?'

'They think it was two or three days before she was found. Forensic isn't always a hundred per cent, but they are finding out more all the time,' Larch said, and looked thoughtful. 'The police didn't get anything from Ronnie, but he often talks to me . . .'

'Be careful, Larch,' Sarah said. 'He might be dangerous.'

'I'm in no danger. I often speak to him in the village, give him a shilling or two. I've never seen him attack a human being even when he's had a few drinks. He can be surly, but that's because of the way people treat him, as if he were a complete idiot. You don't think I'm going to ask him if he murdered her, do you? I think I can manage to be more subtle than that.'

'Yes, of course you can,' Sarah said, a look in her eyes that spelled mischief. 'Morna usually sells her heather on market days, and that's tomorrow. I think I might see if she visited Miss Bates recently – and don't look at me like that, either! Morna wouldn't have killed her but she might have seen something. If I buy some of her heather she might tell me what . . .'

Morna Scaffry had made up her mind. She was going to do it this morning, right now. She had been ready to say something a week or so ago but *he* had turned up, and what happened after that had made her nervous.

She glanced at Miss Bates's cottage as she walked past, and a chill went down her spine. It was nasty thinking of her lying there with her throat cut for a couple of days. Folk were saying the cat had nibbled at her flesh, and that gave Morna goosebumps all over. The idea of that poor woman being eaten by her own cat was enough to turn her stomach.

She was being sick a lot of the time anyway now, and the reason for that was the reason she was intending to pay a visit to the Manor. She'd cared about *him*, and *he* was her only lover, but he had got angry over the baby, accusing her of betraying him. And then he had raped her.

He was going to pay for what he'd done to her in the woods that day if it was the last thing she did! The easy way would have been to tell Jethro. She knew her brother would thrash the man who had raped her so brutally, but he was unpredictable, and might turn his fists on her first. Jethro was already suspicious, because he'd seen her crying and noticed the scratches on her arms. Thankfully, she'd managed to get rid of her torn clothes, though he had asked where her favourite red skirt was.

She would never wear that again! She had burned it when she got back to the caravan that day, and it had been her favourite – another reason that he should pay for what he'd done.

'You must be mad!' His words echoed in her ears even now. That was when she'd told him that she would let his uncle know that she was expecting his child.

'He'll laugh in your face,' he said. 'Anyway, by the time I've finished with you, you won't dare to tell tales to anyone . . .'

His brutal attack on her had hurt her physically, but it hadn't broken her spirit, and now she was determined to speak to his uncle. If he wouldn't pay up, then she'd get the money elsewhere – and if the uncle was as scornful as his nephew she would go to the papers, because she knew something that would cause a lot of trouble for both of them.

Morna glanced at the cottage again, feeling shivery as she thought of what had happened to Miss Bates. She remembered seeing a woman in a fur coat before she got into *his* car. She had sold her a piece of lucky heather and the woman had looked annoyed.

Perhaps she ought to have told someone about that, Morna thought a little guiltily. But who could she have confided in? Jethro was in a foul mood because he had been warned to expect a visit from the police for poaching, and Morna hated the police as much as he did. Besides, Ronnie Miller's boots had still been outside the cottage, and she wouldn't want to get him into trouble. She liked Ronnie, who sometimes did little jobs for her, and she didn't trust the police anyway.

Until they'd settled in Thorny Woods the police had always been moving them on. She wasn't sure why they had been allowed to settle this time, but she hadn't asked questions. Sometimes it was best just to accept your luck. The local

Bobby wasn't too bad; he sometimes winked at Morna when she was selling her heather in the market.

She had her basket with her now, though if she got what she was after from his uncle, she wouldn't have to bother with that much longer. She might be able to afford something she'd always wanted: a nice little flower shop in Norwich with rooms over the top. She would settle down then, because it was a lot warmer serving behind the counter than standing on icy pavements all winter. And she would be away from Jethro and the threat of his fists.

Four

'I'm sorry you've had a wasted journey, sir,' Mrs Miller said as she stood at the back door of her cottage. 'Ronnie isn't here. The police frightened him out of his skin and he ran off after they brought him home. To tell the truth, I'm worried about him.'

'I'm sure he will come back when he's hungry,' Larch said. 'It must have upset him a great deal to make him bolt like that.'

'Oh, it did, sir. The police told him they were going to take him away, and I think he thought they were coming back for him so he ran off when my back was turned.'

'They simply don't know him,' Larch said. 'If they did it would be clear to them that he isn't really violent.'

'He's just a great daft boy,' Mrs Miller said. 'Mind, he doesn't like cats. I've seen him kick them. They don't like him either and they scratch him if they get the chance.'

'Well, I'll be off then,' Larch said. 'Let me know if Ronnie turns up, won't you? I'm on his side. I want to make sure there isn't a miscarriage of justice.'

'It's good of you to take an interest,' Mrs Miller said. 'Don't you worry, sir. I'll let you know when he comes home.'

Larch went out to his car. As he drove home, he saw Morna Scaffry walking in the direction of the village. He caught sight of her face and thought that she looked rather pleased with herself.

Sarah saw Morna almost as soon as she reached the market-place that morning. She was talking to someone, a man. Another glance told Sarah that it was Jethro Scaffry and it looked as if they were having an argument of some kind. It was obviously quite unpleasant because Jethro took hold of his sister's shoulders and shook her.

Sarah hesitated, wondering whether she ought to interfere, but even as she started to walk in their direction, Morna broke away from him and ran off across the marketplace, getting on to a bus that was going to Norwich.

'Oh, damn!' Sarah muttered as the bus drew away. She had walked all this way for nothing, it seemed. It was too cold to stand around thinking about what she might have done so she went into the little shop that also served as the post office and bought a quarter of a pound of Tom Thumb Drops and a couple of sticky buns. She was the only customer in the shop.

'You're usually so busy, Mrs Roberts,' she said. 'Where have all your customers gone?'

'It's always like this on market days,' the woman said, looking annoyed. 'They think they're getting a bargain, but it's more likely rubbish, that's what I say. And what would they do if I weren't here the rest of the week, answer me that? If I go the post office goes, and there will be some long faces then.'

Sarah realized that she had touched on a sore spot. 'Oh, I do hope you won't close the shop,' she said. 'I know Gran relies on you for so many things, and your stuff is much nicer than what they're selling on the market.'

'Well, you're a sensible girl,' the woman said, somewhat mollified. 'Is there anything else I can do for you?'

'Well, yes, now I think of it,' Sarah said. 'I would like a packet of those big envelopes and an exercise book.'

'Are you taking up writing like Miss Bates?' Mrs Roberts said. 'She was always popping in for her pencils and her exercise books . . . poor woman. I still can't believe it happened. Things like that don't happen in a place like this.'

'No, it seems all wrong doesn't it?' Sarah said. 'We've been wondering who it might have been. I can't imagine that anyone local would have done it, can you?'

'It doesn't bear thinking about,' Mrs Roberts said, and shuddered. 'Mind you, we don't get many strangers here. It's the sort of thing you'd notice . . . there was her, of course . . .'

Sarah sensed that Mrs Roberts was in two minds about saying anything. 'Have you seen any strangers in the village recently?' she prompted.

'There was one . . .' Mrs Roberts frowned. 'I don't mind telling you, Sarah, though I wouldn't say anything to the police.

Besides, she wasn't the sort to do a nasty trick like that. Quite the lady, she was, wearing a fur coat and dark glasses, an expensive silk headscarf too. You can always tell quality. She took off her gloves to pay me for the cigarettes, and I saw the diamond rings on her fingers. Must have cost a fortune.'

'Did she say why she was here?'

'Just passing through on her way to the coast, I think. She asked me for a map but I hadn't got one to sell her.'

'Was she driving a car?'

'Oh yes, a large black one. Don't ask me the make because I wouldn't know – but she drove off down that way.' She pointed in the opposite direction to Thorny Woods. 'Besides, it wouldn't have been her. Women like that don't go round murdering people, do they?'

'No, I shouldn't think so,' Sarah said. 'You didn't mention it to the police, then?'

'They didn't come and ask,' she said, looking indignant. 'Never even came in for some snacks. Went to the pub instead, I expect.'

'I suppose they wanted beer and sandwiches,' Sarah said, giving her a sympathetic smile. 'You don't have an off-licence, do you, Mrs Roberts?'

'I don't hold with strong drink. Miss Bates agreed with me there, said drinking led people into trouble, seemed quite cross about it too. We'd had that little bit of bother with young lads at the time.'

'I didn't know about that. Was it recently?'

'In the summer. Miss Bates said they were in the woods at night, making a lot of noise and leaving litter. She said that she'd had experience of drink ruining people's lives, but she didn't say who – just went a funny colour and left suddenly.'

'She didn't come from around here, did she?'

'Oh no, I'm sure she didn't. I imagine she'd done a bit of travelling. She might have been in service – as a personal maid or a companion.'

'What makes you say that?'

'I was in service as a personal maid before I married Mr Roberts – God bless his soul. Good man, he was. Never had a moment's bother with him, and he left me this shop.' She looked pleased with herself and patted her hair, which was styled in tight little curls and a mousy shade of brown.

'But you sort of know when you meet others who have done the same kind of work – little things, just a feeling.' She handed Sarah her change. 'Anything else?'

'Oh no, thank you.' She nodded and left.

Sarah felt that her trip into the village had been more than worthwhile, even though she hadn't managed to speak to Morna Scaffry. She had learned quite a bit, though she wasn't any nearer to discovering who had killed Miss Bates. This sleuthing business was harder than she had supposed.

It was as she approached Miss Bates's cottage that Sarah saw Ronnie Miller leaning against the low garden wall. His thin face looked disconsolate and he was staring fixedly at the road to the village, as if waiting for something.

Sarah hesitated and then stopped. 'Miss Bates isn't there, Ronnie.' He turned his vacant gaze on her. 'She isn't there anymore.'

'Gone shopping,' he offered. 'Might bring some cake when she comes back. Ronnie likes cake.' His vacant eyes brightened for a moment and he looked like an overgrown schoolboy, touching Sarah's heart. He obviously had no idea what had happened to Miss Bates. She held out her paper bags with the buns inside. He took it, his eyes gleaming when he saw what was inside. 'You're nice,' he said, taking a bun and cramming it into his mouth, spitting crumbs as he went on, 'Ronnie likes you. You're pretty.'

Sarah smiled at him. 'I should go home, Ronnie. Miss Bates won't be back today. She has gone away.'

She walked on up the hill, feeling desperately sorry for the poor lad, because he was nice enough to look at and to talk to if you were pleasant to him.

Her thoughts returning to the murder, Sarah decided that she would make a note in her exercise book of all she'd discovered. It was strange that they hadn't seen any books lying about in Miss Bates's cottage. Sarah thought she might go back there alone sometime and have a more thorough look round . . .

'Telephone for you, Sarah,' Millie said, coming into the parlour that afternoon. Sarah had her nose in a copy of *Vogue* magazine, but she got up at once because she guessed it was Larch.

'Thank you, Millie.' She dropped her magazine on the coffee

table and walked into the hall, picking up the receiver Millie had left lying on the beautiful Regency half moon table.

'Just connecting you,' chirped the operator.

'Larch? Is that you? I was hoping you might ring me.'

'Did you see Morna Scaffry?'

'No, but I had an interesting chat to Mrs Roberts in the post office.'

'She's quite a gossip, isn't she? At least you've done something positive. I've had a wasted morning. Ronnie has run off. Mrs Miller is very upset. She says he has never done such a thing before.'

'Do you think the police frightened him?'

'Yes, I would imagine that's what happened.'

'I saw him standing outside Miss Bates's cottage as I came home. He was waiting for her to come back, seemed to think she had gone shopping.'

'Probably doesn't understand what happened. I'm glad you saw him, because his mother was very worried about him, but doesn't want to contact the police. She's frightened they may lock him away if she admits that she has lost control of him.'

'That would be very unfair. He hasn't been any trouble before this, has he?'

'Not really. A few scuffles at the pub when he's had a couple of drinks, but they could lock up half the population for that if they wanted.'

'We're not getting on very fast, are we?'

'Well, that might change soon. We could have professional help by the day after tomorrow, Sarah.'

'What do you mean?'

'My father rang a friend of his. Ben Marshall was an inspector at Scotland Yard until he retired. He has agreed to come and stay with us, see what he can find out about this business.'

'Oh . . .' Sarah was oddly disappointed. 'I suppose that's a good idea.'

'Of course it is. As you said yourself, we're not getting on very fast. It doesn't mean we can't be a part of the investigation, Sarah. Mr Marshall will only be here unofficially, and he'll need someone who knows the locality.'

'It won't be quite the same, though.' She swallowed her disappointment. 'When can we meet again? I have a little news and I've been making notes of everything we know – though it isn't all that much really.'

'I'm afraid I can't make it this evening,' Larch apologized. 'Mother has friends coming to dinner. I can't get out of it I'm afraid. Perhaps tomorrow afternoon? We might go out for tea somewhere. There's a meeting in the village hall in the evening – to do with the wood . . .'

'Shall you go?'

'Yes, I think so. They are talking about forming an action group. Father is keeping clear of it, but I intend to help.'

'Could I come with you?'

'Yes, of course. We'll have some tea, talk things over and then go to the meeting – how's that?'

'Lovely. I'll see you tomorrow then.'

Sarah replaced the receiver and went back to the parlour. She was feeling restless, frustrated because they had made so little progress, and disappointed that Larch's father had brought in a retired inspector of police. He was bound to turn his nose up at their efforts, and would probably solve the mystery just like that.

She sat on the sofa and picked up her magazine but then threw it down again.

'Are you bored, Sarah?' Her grandmother looked at her anxiously as she got up and went over to the window. 'You must miss all your friends and being in the show. There's nothing much for you to do here.'

'No, I'm not bored. Sorry, Gran. I had something on my mind, that's all. Shall we have a game of chess?'

'You're not going out with Larch?'

'Not this evening. I'll set the board out, shall I?'

Ronnie put his head down. The rain was driving into his face and it was cold. He was hungry and he wanted to go home but his mother had shouted at him after the police came. He wasn't sure what he was supposed to have done. He thought it might be to do with Miss Bates, though he couldn't understand what had happened to her. He knew that she'd been cross with him that last day but he didn't know what he'd done to upset her. She must have been cross though, because she hadn't given him his cake.

When he'd gone back to fetch his boots later, he had glanced through the kitchen window and seen her lying there on the floor. She had looked very strange and he'd been too frightened to go in, though he knew where she kept her key. He'd grabbed his boots and run home, but he hadn't dared to tell his mother what he'd seen, and he hadn't gone to work the next day.

When the police came they had taken him to the police station in a car. They shut him in a room with only a tiny window high up. A different policeman had stood under the window and looked at him. He didn't say anything and it was a long time before anyone else came near, and then two of them came in and said they knew he'd done something very bad. They sat down at the table and asked him if he'd killed Miss Bates in a temper, but he didn't know what they meant and wouldn't answer them. He had just kept shaking his head over and over, and then he'd started crying. After a few minutes the men left and then a woman had come into the room. She had taken him away to give him a cup of tea and a biscuit. He'd liked her and if she'd asked him questions he might have answered her, but then they had put him in a car and driven him home.

His mother said that they might come back and that he should tell them the truth, but he didn't know what the truth was. Miss Bates had looked strange lying there, her eyes open and staring as if she'd had a fright, and there was blood all over the floor. But he didn't know what had happened to make her like that. He'd jerked away from the window in fright and that's when he'd stepped on the cat. Something had happened to the cat. Ronnie wasn't sure what. Things got muddled in his head sometimes and he couldn't remember what he'd done or where he had been.

After he'd seen Miss Bates on the floor, he'd grabbed his boots and run so fast that he was halfway home before he realized that he hadn't put his boots on. His feet hurt, and when he got to bed that night, he saw that they were bleeding just like Miss Bates and the cat.

Ronnie had black periods when he lost track of time. The police thought he'd done something bad, and perhaps he had. It made him feel frightened to think about it, because it reminded him of something he'd seen in the churchyard a couple of years earlier. He'd come across some people doing strange things and he'd watched them, laughing because he thought it was funny to see them dressed up that way. One of them had got very cross and he had been warned not to tell what he'd seen, because people who told tales got punished. He hadn't told about that, and he wouldn't tell anything now.

He was so cold and his stomach was empty, rumbling. He was just wondering where he could go to find some shelter when he saw the lights of a caravan ahead of him. He smiled as he remembered that that was where the gypsy girl lived. He even knew her name, because he'd thought it was pretty – like her.

He'd seen her in the village lots of times, in the woods too. She always smiled at him, asked him how he was, and once she'd invited him into her caravan and she'd given him something to eat. It wasn't as good as Miss Bates's cakes, but it was good and he was so hungry. He felt better as he walked towards the caravan. Morna Scaffry was kind and pretty too. She had such soft skin that looked as if it would be nice to touch. Ronnie thought that he would like to touch her, but even if she wouldn't let him, she would give him something to eat. Perhaps she would let him stay until it stopped raining.

He walked faster, eager now to reach the warmth and comfort of the caravan. He was looking at the lights, not taking notice of anything around him, and so he didn't see the figure lurking in the trees a little to his right. It was a strange figure, dressed in a long black gown. If Ronnie had seen it, he might have been frightened because the face wasn't human.

Sarah spent the morning helping Andrews in the garden. It wasn't really his job but Amelia couldn't manage it herself, and her obliging chauffeur had taken it over as part of his duties.

'I don't mind a bit of digging now and then,' Andrews had told Sarah that morning. 'It helps me to keep fit, but I'm not much of a plants man, miss. Your grandmother asked me to dig up some clumps of Christmas roses and move them – but I'm not exactly sure where they are . . .'

'I suppose you've been looking for rose bushes that flower at Christmas?' Sarah smiled as he nodded. 'They aren't really roses at all. Gran means those plants under glass at the bottom of the garden. I think they have become too crowded in that frame, and she wants them moved into the larger one near the back of the house.'

'Ah, I see, no trouble,' Andrews said and chuckled. 'That explains why I couldn't find them.'

'I've found some bulbs that need planting,' Sarah said. 'If you could dig the holes for me, I could put them in the earth.'

'Feeling restless, miss?'

'Yes, but not because I'm out of a job. I hate the idea of that murderer getting away with it. Larch and I have been trying to find out what happened, but we haven't got anywhere yet.'

'It was a nasty business,' Andrews said, 'but the murderer has probably gone far away by now.'

'What makes you think that?'

'I can't think it was anyone local, miss.'

'It's discovering the reason for her murder that's the problem,' Sarah said. 'If we knew that we should be halfway there.'

'I expect that's what the police think too,' Andrews said with a smile. 'Now, where do you want those bulbs, miss? I think we'll do those first, and then you can show me the Christmas roses.'

They had finished planting the bulbs, and Andrews was about to start on the Christmas roses when Sarah saw Mrs Hayes cycling up the drive towards them. She went to greet her with a smile, but as the vicar's wife parked her bicycle against the wall and turned to her, Sarah went cold all over. Something had to be very wrong to make Mrs Hayes look like that.

'What has happened?'

'It's awful, just awful,' Mrs Hayes said. 'I heard about it half an hour ago, and I decided to call and tell your grandmother myself rather than telephone.'

'Please come in,' Sarah said. 'I've been gardening with Andrews, but I was about to stop for coffee – or tea if you prefer?'

'Either, my dear,' Mrs Hayes said. 'Though you may need something stronger, both of you. It is such a shock. One body was bad enough, but two . . .'

'*Two?* You mean someone else has been killed?'

'Yes, my dear. I am afraid there has been another murder.'

Sarah led the way into the parlour, feeling the coldness spread through her. Amelia was sitting by the fire, reading the paper. She got up at once and came to greet her visitor.

'Vera, how lovely to see you. I've sorted a few things out for the fête – mostly books and some clothes.'

'Thank you, Amelia. I knew you would have them ready, but I didn't come just for that . . .' She looked serious. 'I think you should sit down – you too, Sarah. This is most unpleasant!'

'What has happened?' Amelia's hands trembled slightly and she clasped them together, sitting with her back very straight. 'Don't tell me there's been another murder?'

'Yes, that is it exactly,' Vera Hayes said. 'Her body was discovered this morning. Apparently, some men from Norwich Council found her. They had gone into the woods to have a look around – I suppose they were considering the site for these new houses – and she was lying there, stark naked and strangled.'

'Oh, my goodness!' Amelia gasped. 'How awful! I can't imagine what's going on here, Vera. First Miss Bates and then this . . .'

'Who was it?' Sarah felt the shivers down her spine. One murder was terrible enough, but two was frightening – especially a murder of this kind. 'Do they think . . . was it rape?'

'Sarah!' Her grandmother looked shocked. 'Please, my dear, you shouldn't ask such questions.'

'I don't know the answer,' Vera admitted. 'I was told the news when the police called on us this morning. They wanted to know if there was any connection between her and Miss Bates, but of course I couldn't tell them.'

'But who was murdered?' Sarah asked.

'Didn't I say?' Vera sat down, clearly feeling a bit faint. 'I thought I'd said – but it was that gypsy girl, Morna Scaffry. She used to come round selling sprigs of lucky heather . . . all nonsense of course . . .'

'*Morna* – it was Morna who was murdered?' Sarah felt sick as she realized that she might have been on the right track all the time. That sprig of heather hadn't been lying in Miss Bates's garden for no reason. Someone had dropped it there – but was it Morna herself or someone else?

'I saw her in the market yesterday but she caught the bus into Norwich. Do they know how long she has been dead?'

'I have no idea. The police just said she'd been found, told us to warn as many of the parishioners as possible to stay away from the woods, and then left.'

'Well, I suppose that's all we need to know.' Amelia shuddered. 'It makes one feel so unsafe. I mean . . . what is behind all this? Are the murders connected?'

'That's what the police want to know,' Vera Hayes said. 'It doesn't seem likely, and yet we've never had anything like this before in Beecham Thorny. I think it may have something to do with all this trouble over the wood.'

'What makes you think that?' Sarah asked.

'I have no particular reason, but tempers are raised over this, Sarah. I know that the bit they want to use isn't as old as some of the rest, and it certainly isn't the best part – but some people think the wood is special. Henry gets very cross about it, but he believes there is a pagan shrine in there. And with that girl being found naked . . . well, pagan rites, you know.'

'Vera!' Amelia was horrified. 'You can't think there is anything like that going on in our woods?'

'Well, I know Henry has suspected it for a while,' Vera said, and frowned. 'Naturally, we don't talk about it – the bishop would have something to say if it got out, and Henry can't stop it. But the diocese will think he should.'

'I haven't heard any of this before.' Amelia frowned.

'It started about five years ago,' Vera said. 'Henry discovered some grisly remains in the churchyard on four or five occasions – the mutilated bodies of cats and rabbits. He scrubbed the gravestones, and spent a few nights in the graveyard trying to catch whoever was doing it. It stopped as suddenly as it started, and someone told him that whoever these people were, they had transferred their attention to the woods. Apparently there is some kind of a flat stone in there with strange markings on it, and people think it's a relic from pagan times.'

'Who told you about the change?' Sarah asked, because all this was very interesting.

'I shouldn't say – but I know it won't go any further,' Vera said, looking guilty. 'Henry told me that it was Sir James Beecham. He was very angry about it, said that his keeper had found dead cats and other animals that had obviously been sacrificed. Apparently, they cut the hearts out of the poor things. He demanded that Henry do something about it, and they had a blessing in the woods to try and put off these pagans or witches, whatever they are – but I don't think it worked.'

'Does Henry know who these people are?' Amelia asked, looking sceptical and a bit green.

'Some of them come from outside the village,' Vera said. 'Strange types – arty, Bohemian. Weird, I call them! I mean, to practise that kind of thing, well, I ask you! They aren't all local, though Henry does suspect that one or two are . . .'

'What do they do – apart from kill cats, of course?' Sarah asked, feeling amused even though she knew she oughtn't to. 'Do they dress up in white togas and flowers or dance naked by the light of the moon?'

'It isn't funny, Sarah. The bishop would take a very dim view of it if it came out, I can tell you – but what can Henry do? He did ask Sir James if they should inform the police, but Sir James was against it. In fact he seemed to change his mind altogether and said it was probably just some idiot who didn't like cats.'

'Ronnie Miller hates cats,' Sarah said, and then wished she hadn't as the others looked at her. 'Oh, I shouldn't have said that. I'm sure poor Ronnie wasn't behind all that stuff in the churchyard.'

Millie brought in tea and biscuits and the conversation lapsed for a moment, and then Amelia looked at her visitor. 'I'm going to ask Andrews to put your bicycle in the boot of the car and take you home, Vera. It was very good of you to come out here to warn us, but I shouldn't feel right if I let you go home alone.'

'Don't you worry about me,' Vera said stoutly. 'I don't intend this wretch, whoever he is, to make me a prisoner in my own home – and nor should you, Amelia. I don't know what Morna Scaffry had been up to that landed her in trouble, and I can't imagine why poor Miss Bates was killed, but I'm not going to let it stop me doing my duty.'

'I'll send Andrews to the vicarage with the things I looked out then,' Amelia said. 'You can't possibly carry them all on your bicycle.'

'Yes, you do that,' Vera said. 'I must get off now, Amelia. I wanted to tell you myself, but I've got lots to do.'

Sarah went to the door with her. Vera Hayes looked at her in concern.

'Amelia seems very upset about all this, my dear.'

'Yes, she is,' Sarah replied. 'I'm glad I'm here with her, though of course she has Andrews.'

'Thank goodness for that,' Vera said. 'I should be very worried about her living out here if it weren't for him. I think anyone who wanted to harm Amelia would need to do it over his dead body! Amelia is lucky to have him.'

'Yes, she is,' Sarah agreed. 'Thank you so much for coming.'

'Well, I didn't want to tell Amelia this over the telephone.'

Sarah watched the vicar's wife peddle away on her bicycle, then returned to the parlour where her grandmother was pouring another cup of tea. She noticed that Amelia's hand was trembling and felt anxious, because this had been an awful shock for her.

'I wish Vera had let me send her home with Andrews, Sarah.'

'I think she's right, Gran. We can't let this take over our lives – but we can be careful. I shan't go walking in the woods alone until the murderer is safely locked away.'

'No, I'm sure you won't, my dearest, but it is worrying.' Amelia set her cup down. 'Do you think the same person killed both Miss Bates and that poor girl?'

'I'm not sure,' Sarah frowned. 'Morna was strangled, and according to Mrs Hayes, she was naked. I don't think that sounds as if it was the same person, but it might have been.'

'It is all very worrying,' Amelia said. 'Do you think you should go and stay with your father until all this is over?'

'I most certainly do not,' Sarah replied. 'I have no intention of leaving you while this is going on, and I wouldn't go to Daddy if I did.'

'Don't think I want you to go, dearest, I was merely thinking of your safety. I know you won't want to be cooped up in the house all the time.'

'Larch is coming to take me to tea this afternoon, and we're going to a council meeting this evening. If I want to go out when Larch is busy I shall either borrow your car or ask Andrews to drive me, Gran. Please don't worry about me. Besides, Sir William has asked a friend of his to come and stay. Mr Marshall used to be an inspector at New Scotland Yard, so I expect he will clear this mystery up in a few days.'

'I wish he would.' Amelia looked so upset that Sarah was glad Larch's father had asked his friend to help them. She had realized that her earlier disappointment was foolish; this wasn't a game they were playing, and it had suddenly become that much more serious with Morna's death.

It wasn't that she was more important than Miss Bates, but Sarah had thought it might just be a private quarrel between the murdered woman and someone in her past. Now it seemed that wasn't the case.

'I've been writing everything down,' Sarah told her grand-mother. 'I shall add what Vera told us and give it to Mr Marshall when he arrives.'

'Do you think you ought to do that? Vera told us in confidence.'

'And I shall make sure that Mr Marshall understands that,' Sarah said, 'but I think it is important he has all the information possible. He is a stranger here, Gran. It will be like someone who can't swim jumping in at the deep end of the pool. I want to throw him a lifeline.'

'Well, yes, perhaps you should. I think Vera was making too much of that angle anyway. If there are any pagan rites going on it's just a bunch of rather silly people behaving in a reprehensible way – don't you think so?'

'Yes, I do,' Sarah said. 'I think Morna may have been killed because she saw something at Miss Bates's cottage. Larch and I found a piece of her lucky heather in the garden when we had a little snoop around . . .'

'I hope you didn't go inside!' Amelia stared at her hard. 'You did, didn't you? Oh, Sarah, you really shouldn't have, my dear.'

'We didn't do any harm,' Sarah replied. 'The police had finished searching – and I discovered something. I think a photograph frame was missing, and I believe the picture was of this woman.' She had placed the photograph in an enve-lope but now she took it out and showed it to her grandmother. 'I think she may have been an actress.'

Amelia looked at the picture and smiled. 'She was a bit before your time, Sarah. I remember seeing her in two of the earliest motion pictures I ever watched, long before the war. Her name was Shirley Anne Asbury, and I think she was all set to be a big star, but then something happened. There was some sort of scandal and she disappeared. I'm not sure whether she's still alive, but she will be much older than she was when this photograph was taken. I should think she must be almost fifty now . . .'

'You don't remember what happened to make her drop out of sight? It must have been something awful if she was all set to become a big star in the cinema.'

'It eludes me at the moment . . .' Amelia shook her head. 'I think someone died. A young man if my memory serves me right, and there was some talk of foul play, but it was a long time ago and I may have it wrong. I don't know where Miss Asbury came into it. I don't think she was accused of the murder, but she was mixed up in it somehow.'

'Well, Janet Bates knew her well. Mrs Roberts at the post office thinks that Miss Bates may have been in service as a maid or a companion when she was younger.'

'Are you thinking that she knew the truth about some old scandal?'

'Well, blackmail could be a reason for murder, couldn't it?'

'Yes – but why now? If she had kept the secret all these years, why would she suddenly decide to blackmail an old friend?'

'Do you think she could have been short of money?'

'Oh, I shouldn't think so. She had sufficient for her needs, which weren't very demanding. I remember calling at the cottage to collect for a charity one day. She gave me ten pounds. I don't think she would have done that if she was short of money.'

'No, probably not,' Sarah agreed. 'Besides, my theory may be completely wrong. We don't know that Morna saw anything the day Miss Bates died. She may have been killed for another reason entirely.'

Amelia shuddered. 'Well, I hope this friend of Sir William's can clear the mystery up, Sarah. I don't think I shall feel safe again until the murderer has been caught.'

Five

Sarah spent the time between lunch and Larch arriving in writing up her notebook. She made a list of all that they had discovered, adding in all the gossip and hearsay under a separate heading, and her own theory that Miss Bates might have tried to blackmail someone she had known in the past.

When Larch arrived they spent some minutes discussing the terrible news about Morna Scaffry's death. Then Sarah showed him what she'd done, giving him the book and envelopes to pass on to Mr Marshall.

'I know it's all very amateur,' she said, 'but it may be of some use to him, and I think anything we can do to help him catch this murderer must be worthwhile.'

Larch glanced through the book. 'You have been busy, Sarah. I think this is all rather splendid. You've discovered much more than I have, though Ronnie's mother sent me a note this morning to tell me he had come home earlier. She says he's in a bit of a state and asked if I would go over in the morning and talk to him, so perhaps I shall learn something then.'

'I wonder where he was all night. It rained for hours and it was cold out. He must have had a very uncomfortable night, poor man.'

'Yes, that's the curious thing. Mrs Miller said he was dry when he came home, and he must have had something to eat because he didn't want his breakfast.'

'So he found somewhere to stay then. It's a pity he wasn't at home. Especially as Morna Scaffry has been found dead.'

'Of course, I know what you mean.' Larch looked concerned. 'If Ronnie had been at home he would have been in the clear. The police may think he had something to do with this – as of course he could have done. I still can't believe it, but maybe I'm just refusing to see the truth.'

Sarah didn't believe that Ronnie was behind the murders

either, though she knew quite a few people suspected it. 'Do you think Morna was killed because she saw something near Miss Bates's cottage that day?'

'Yes, perhaps, but it was a very different kind of murder, wasn't it?'

'Yes, very different.' Sarah looked out of the window as they passed the woods in the car. She had known Thorny Woods most of her life and played in them often as a child. She had never thought of them as a sinister place, but today they looked dark and uninviting. The rooks were circling overhead, as if in warning. 'I'm not sure I shall ever feel the same about those woods. Do you think Mrs Hayes is right about what is happening there, Larch?'

'It all sounds rather fanciful and lurid to me,' he said. 'If there is anything out of the ordinary, it's probably a Bohemian crowd having fun – just as an excuse to dress up in weird costumes and drink too much. There may be some immoral behaviour going on, Sarah, because these covens or whatever they call them are often an excuse for this kind of thing.' He saw she was shocked and apologized. 'I ought not to have said that – forgive me?'

'I am shocked, but not because you mentioned immorality. You don't think that they are really calling up the devil then? I think the vicar believes it's some kind of devil worship.'

'John Hayes is a good man, but I've never had a great opinion of his intelligence – and don't let that go any further.'

Sarah giggled, her feeling of foreboding evaporating as they passed the village. She saw several villagers gossiping outside the post office, and was glad that not everyone had been driven to stay behind locked doors by the terrible news.

She thought that the villagers were probably talking about the murder, but of course it might just have been the council meeting.

'Do you think they really intend to cut down part of the woods to build houses?'

'It's just that wedge-shaped bit on the far side, where it adjoins one of Father's fields. They want to take a road across his land to avoid traffic having to pass through Thorny village. I suppose it would be better for the children and protective of some of our old buildings. The guildhall in Thorny is fourteenth century and there are some Queen Anne cottages near the Green. But building those houses is another matter. People need houses and I've no quarrel with that, but they will bring in an influx of newcomers, because they will be too expensive for local people, and that's what is upsetting everyone. I wouldn't mind if they put them somewhere else.'

'They could build nearer Thorny village, couldn't they? I should have thought that would be more sensible. There's a bit of land next to the forge that's only used for pasture at the moment. Why don't they use that instead?'

'Presumably because it belongs to us rather than Sir James. That bit of the wood is useless to him as it is, too scrubby to be of use as timber – but if the council grant planning it could be worth a few thousand.'

The subject lapsed. Sarah didn't feel strongly about it herself, but obviously some people were very upset. She wondered if the trouble over the woods could be connected to the murders, but it didn't seem likely.

'What are you planning to do next in your career?' Larch changed the subject. 'Shall you look for another show?'

'One of the girls at Bournemouth suggested I try pantomime or perhaps nightclub work.'

'You wouldn't think of that?' Larch shot a surprised look at her.

'No, I don't think so, but I shall have to find something. I can't sponge off Gran for ever.'

'No, of course not.'

Larch had driven into the gravel drive leading to the Chestnuts Hotel. It had once been a beautiful old mansion but was now a popular venue in the district. They served lunches and dinners most days of the week, also afternoon teas. Every few weeks there was a splendid dinner dance, which was always packed out.

When Larch and Sarah walked in that afternoon only two tables were occupied, both of them by ladies. Larch smothered a groan as one of the ladies waved at him enthusiastically.

'Don't say anything, just smile,' he murmured in a low voice as they were led to a table. 'If she corners us we shall never get rid of her.'

Sarah laughed as she saw his expression. He looked like a long-suffering martyr condemned to the stake. They had asked for a quiet table in the corner by the window, which was sheltered partly by a large aspidistra plant, but no sooner had they been seated than the woman left her companions and came bouncing over to them. She was tall and thin-faced with long red hair, wearing a floral afternoon dress, pink cloche hat and heavy beads that flapped against her flat chest.

'Larch, darling!' she cried. 'How lovely to see you here! Do introduce me to your charming companion.'

'Madeline,' Larch said, 'this is Sarah Beaufort, a friend of mine. She is visiting her grandmother.'

'Amelia, of course. How nice to meet you, Sarah. Amelia and I play bridge sometimes. She often speaks of you.'

Sarah stood up and shook hands. Madeline turned her attention to Larch. Her smile was rapacious and Sarah felt an immediate dislike for her. The woman was a maneater!

'When are you coming to look at my paintings?' she asked with a coy smile. 'You did promise, you know.'

'Yes, I remember,' Larch said, remembering the rash moment. 'Forgive me, I have been very busy. Perhaps next week.'

'Well, see you keep your promise this time. Otherwise I shall be very cross with you.' She glanced over her shoulder and saw that her friends were preparing to leave. 'I must go. Don't forget this time, Larch.'

'I shall try,' he said, and pulled a face at Sarah as Madeline walked away. 'She scares the hell out of me. I suppose I shall have to go, but heaven knows if I'll ever be seen again!'

Sarah laughed. 'Poor Larch. Do you want me to come and protect you?'

'Yes please!' He grinned at her. 'What shall we have – the full tea or just cakes?'

'If we're going to that meeting perhaps we'd better have something more substantial. I wouldn't mind the crumpets.'

'Me too,' he said. 'With lashings of their strawberry preserve.'

'Yes, why not?' Sarah said and glanced out of the window, which was opened just a crack. Two men were standing outside in the gardens, clearly having an argument. 'Who's that with Sir James?'

Larch turned his head to look. 'That's his nephew, Simon. Goodness, they are having a go at each other, aren't they?'

Sarah pushed the window a little wider. The men were standing a few feet away, but she heard what Sir James was saying because he was shouting.

'You are an utter disgrace, sir. A disgrace, do you hear me?'

'For goodness' sake, it was only a bit of fun,' Simon replied. 'You're not exactly whiter than white yourself, Uncle.'

'And what is that supposed to mean?'

'You know what I'm talking about. A lot of people might be interested to know what I know . . .'

'Is that a threat?'

'No, of course not. Just a reminder.'

Larch reached over to pull the window shut. Sarah arched her brows at him. 'That was just getting interesting.'

'But private,' he said. 'You know what they say about eaves-droppers.'

'Yes, but we might have learned something.'

'You don't seriously think that Sir James had anything to do with either of the murders, do you?'

'He might have done. If it was a case of blackmail. I think he is quite capable of murder, Larch. I saw him threaten Jethro Scaffry once and I don't much like him. There's no saying what he might have done if Miss Bates discovered something he didn't want known.'

'Even if that were true, he would hardly be having an argument with his nephew about it in a public place, would he?'

'No, I don't suppose so. But it was still very interesting, didn't you think so? I mean, what does Simon Beecham have on his uncle that could be used as blackmail? If he knows, perhaps Miss Bates did too.'

'Sarah!'

She pulled a face at him, but as the waitress had arrived to take their order, she turned to look out of the window again. Sir James was getting into his smart black saloon car, but his nephew had a rather elderly black Phaeton, which rattled as he shot off down the drive.

'What does Simon Beecham do for a living?' she asked nonchalantly as the waitress left them.

'He runs a nursery just the other side of Thorny Wood,' Larch said. 'They supply trees and shrubs to hotels and parks, stately homes, things like that. I believe they also do cut flowers . . .'

'Oh . . .' Sarah realized why he drove a rusty old car, which must be handy for transporting that kind of thing.

'Why did you ask?' Sarah shook her head and Larch gave her a stern look. 'This is all getting a bit dangerous, Sarah. When we started it was just Miss Bates, but after what happened to Morna Scaffry . . .'

'You are as bad as Gran. I'm not going to do anything stupid. Anyway, I expect Mr Marshall will have the mystery under control in a day or so.'

'Perhaps,' Larch said. 'I have to go and visit Mrs Miller tomorrow morning, and then I need to see someone in Norwich. You won't do anything foolish while I'm away, will you?'

Sarah smiled at him sweetly. 'Now whatever makes you think I might?'

Ben Marshall realized that he must have taken the wrong turning. He wasn't supposed to come this far. Beecham Thorny was only just ahead of him. He had taken the wrong road back at the junction. Possibly because he hadn't been listening properly when Sir William gave him the instructions. His mind had been elsewhere, namely with the Siamese cats he was planning to enter into a prestige show very shortly.

His wife, Cathy, was looking after the cats. He had given her full instructions before he left, which he knew she would carry out to the letter, even though she wasn't a fan of his cats. She preferred her own tabby, an old tomcat that prowled constantly around the cattery cages, eyeing the sleek inmates with a lecherous obstinacy that he had been fighting with an equal determination for weeks. He didn't want that tabby getting in with his best female now that she was due to come into season.

He just hoped it didn't happen while he was away, but this case shouldn't take up too much of his time. He had agreed to come and help out following a telephone call to his Norwich colleagues, some of whom he knew from past cases. They seemed to think it was probably a young lad called Ronnie Miller, though they hadn't been able to provide any positive evidence as yet, and Sir William had refused them a section order until they came up with something concrete.

That was just as it should be in Ben's opinion. Otherwise it would be a clear case of miscarriage of justice. He wouldn't want to see anyone shut away for life without good cause.

He backed his car into a gateway and headed back towards the crossroads. He was just coming up to that rather nice hotel he'd passed earlier. Some people were standing outside talking – three women dressed in fancy afternoon frocks and hats. Glancing at them, he had an odd feeling that he knew the one in the fur coat, and checked in his driving mirror to get another look. Unfortunately, she had turned her back his way and he couldn't see her face.

Now where had he seen her? Ben puzzled over it as he approached the crossroads and took the right turning this time. He thought it might have been when he was working on a case, but he couldn't bring it to mind for the moment. Not that it mattered. It would come to him in the end.

Any plans Sarah might have had for taking another look inside Miss Bates's cottage were scuppered that morning by the arrival of her father. She happened to be looking out of the window as his car arrived, and groaned. She was probably in for another lecture. However, differences aside, she was actually very fond of him and smiled as she went downstairs to see Amelia greeting him in the hall. He had brought a huge basket of hothouse flowers and some expensive Belgian chocolates for his mother.

'You are always so extravagant, Edward,' Amelia scolded. 'But thank you all the same. Have you come to stay or is this a fleeting visit?'

'I shall take you both out to lunch,' he said. 'We could go to the Chestnuts.'

'Why not stay and have a light lunch with us? We have cold beef or chicken, and Millie will do some nice roast potatoes especially for you.'

'I wanted to take you both out as my special treat.'

'Mending fences, Edward?'

'Yes, I suppose you could call it that . . .' He saw Sarah on the stairs and frowned. 'Have you come to your senses at last, young lady?'

'If you're wondering whether I've given up all hope of a singing career, the answer is no, Daddy. I'm staying with Gran because I'm between jobs at the moment.'

'I thought as much. You've thrown your reputation away for nothing. Goodness knows what you imagined would come of it!'

'That's enough of that, Edward!' Amelia gave him a hard stare. 'Behave yourself please. I shall not allow you to be unkind to Sarah in my house.'

'It's all right, Gran, I'm not upset. Daddy thinks he's right and perhaps I shan't get far in my career, but at least I shall have tried.'

'I thought perhaps you might have decided to do something sensible.'

'Singing is all I've ever wanted to do,' Sarah told him with such a lovely smile that he was left with nothing to say. 'Now, if you really want to take us out, I think that will be very nice. Where shall we go, Gran? The Chestnuts or a hotel in Norwich?'

'The Chestnuts would be best,' Amelia said. 'Ask Millie to make some coffee while I go up and change, Sarah.'

'Yes, of course. If you go into the parlour, Daddy, I'll arrange coffee . . .' She was about to walk away when he caught her wrist. 'Yes?'

'Are you all right for money, Sarah?'

'Yes, I'm fine. Please don't worry.'

'I know I said I wouldn't give you anything, but I've been anxious in case you were short.'

'I'm fine, really,' she said. It wasn't quite true but she was determined to prove that she could be independent.

'I'll start your allowance again next month, shall I?' He looked uncertain, his usual confident manner surprisingly absent. He was a tall, strong man, still attractive despite his receding hair, and sometimes arrogant.

'I would rather you didn't. I'm managing very well.'

'But you wouldn't come to me if you weren't, would you?'

'Not unless I was desperate,' she said. 'I want to prove I can do this, Daddy. If I fail . . . well, then I shall have to eat humble pie, shan't I?'

'No, I don't think I would want you to do that,' he told her. He smiled wryly as she arched her brows. 'I suppose I'm proud of my girl for standing on her own two feet – and I feel bad about stopping your allowance.'

'I think it has done me good,' Sarah said, tossing her long

hair, her eyes bright with laughter. 'You did rather spoil me, and now I'm learning what life is all about.'

'And enjoying it?'

'Yes, I am.'

'Then I can't ask you to come home, but remember that I care about you, Sarah. I know I said a lot of harsh things, but I have regretted them – and I do miss you.'

'Then I shall come and stay with you at Christmas if I can,' she said. 'It isn't a promise, but I'll try.'

'All right,' he said. 'At least that's something . . .'

'Ah, there you are, Larch,' his father said as he came into the front parlour that morning. 'I should like you to meet Ben. He arrived while you were out yesterday and he is very intrigued by what you and Sarah have been doing. I gave him that book of yours to look at earlier this morning.'

'Sir,' Larch shook hands with his father's guest. Ben Marshall was grey-haired, clean-shaven, tall and lean. His eyes were a slate grey and intelligent, full of questions. 'I am very pleased to meet you. We've been doing a bit of sleuthing, but we haven't got very far, I'm afraid.'

'I'm not so sure about that,' Ben said. He picked up the exercise book. 'I understand it was Miss Beaufort who wrote the information in this book?'

'Sarah has discovered most of what we know,' Larch admitted. 'I went to see Ronnie Miller again this morning, but the police were there before me and he's done a bunk again. His mother said he was very upset about something, but he wouldn't talk to her, just kept mumbling something about her being hurt. And before you ask, Mrs Miller has no idea who he meant – except that the police seem to think he strangled Morna Scaffry.'

'I see . . .' Ben's eyes narrowed in thought. 'And what do you think, Larch? I see from Miss Beaufort's notes that neither of you believed he had anything to do with the first murder.'

'I can't think he is the killer this time either. If I had managed to see him this morning . . .' Larch sighed. 'I can't tell you any more than Sarah has already.'

'Well, I think your friend has given me quite a bit to go on,' Ben said. 'I find her style of case notes most interesting. I am especially taken with the stuff about the devil worship . . .'

'Really?' Sir William looked at him in surprise. 'I should have thought that was all nonsense.'

'As anyone would in the normal way of things,' Ben said. 'But I recall a case I had about five years ago. It was in a small village in Devon – and near some ancient woods. These people seem to like woods; they think it puts them in touch with the spirits they are trying to conjure up. There were a couple of murders there, and I got called in because I happened to be on holiday there. We arrested one chap for the murders, but I was never convinced that he was acting alone. He pleaded guilty but wouldn't tell us anything else.'

'You think he was covering up for someone else?' Larch asked, fascinated.

'I'm pretty sure there was a lot more beneath the surface than we ever touched,' Ben said. 'They were pretty grisly murders, too – mutilated bodies, and that sort of thing. You haven't got that here so I'm inclined to discount that side of it, but even so it is interesting that something appears to be going on here. I shall keep an open mind.'

'Do you have any ideas yet?' Larch asked. 'Or is that expecting too much?'

'Ideas? Yes, I have several,' Ben said, 'but I imagine Miss Beaufort got there first on most of them. It sounds very much like blackmail, and that gentleman . . .' He frowned as he searched his memory. 'Sir James Beecham, I believe – well, he may be involved somewhere . . .'

'Or you may have been influenced by some silly scribbling from a young girl who has no idea of police work,' Sir William said, and then, looking at his son, 'Not that she isn't a perfectly nice girl, of course.'

'I should like to meet her,' Ben said. 'Could you introduce us, Larch?'

'Not this afternoon I'm afraid,' Larch said. 'I have to meet someone in Norwich, but perhaps this evening. I'll ring her when I get home.'

'Then I'll have a walk around the village on my own and see what I can find,' Ben said easily. 'What happened at the council meeting you went to last night?'

'Oh, the council told us that more new homes were needed,' Larch said with a shrug. 'They said the land earmarked was a good place because it would enlarge Thorny village without crowding it and would be on the right side of the new road.'

'And what was the reaction to that?'

'A lot of protests,' Larch said. 'The councillors got shouted down several times and afterwards the local hotheads were coming up with some rather wild schemes for stopping it.'

'I hope you're not thinking of getting involved in any of that, Larch.' His father frowned at him.

'I shall protest,' Larch told him, 'but peacefully.'

'Do you think the protesters have anything to do with these murders?' Ben asked. 'Could there be something going on – bribery and corruption in high places?'

'I thought that,' Larch said, 'even before the murders happened. I mean, if Miss Bates got hold of a letter intended for Sir James that gave the game away . . .' He pulled a face. 'Very amateurish stuff I'm afraid, sir.'

'Fresh minds are often good in these cases,' Ben replied. 'It is one theory and a plausible one, but my nose is telling me something different.' He laughed as Larch looked bewildered. 'It's a way I have of describing hunches. My hunch is that there is a lot more to this than meets the eye.'

It was on the way back from lunch that they saw the police cars parked at the entrance to the woods just beyond Miss Bates's cottage. A scuffle seemed to be going on, and several policemen were trying to capture someone. Sarah craned forward in her seat in the back of the car and saw that it was Ronnie Miller.

'Oh, poor Ronnie! The police are arresting him!'

'Is that the idiot that used to do Miss Bates's garden?' her father said over his shoulder. 'I should say it is a good thing.'

'Not if he didn't do anything.'

'Obviously the police think he did,' her father said. 'And they should know, Sarah. Personally, I think it would be sensible to put him away.'

Sarah decided it was best not to say anything more. Her father had gone out of his way to be pleasant during lunch, and she didn't want to quarrel with him over this. She was sure in her own mind that Ronnie hadn't killed either Miss Bates or Morna Scaffry, though she was no nearer to finding out who the real culprit was – but she might be if she could get into Miss Bates's cottage again. She decided that she would do it first thing the next morning.

Naturally, she didn't mention this to either her father or her grandmother. She smiled and kissed her father goodbye when he said he ought to be getting back.

'I have an appointment in London tomorrow, so I'll be staying at the flat for a few days,' he said. 'You can telephone me there if you need me.'

'Yes, Daddy, but I'm sure we shan't need anything.'

'Well, if the police have caught this killer I shan't have to worry about you two,' he said. 'I can't tell you how relieved I am that this sorry business is all over.'

'Yes, Daddy, I am sure you are.' She gave him one of her lovely smiles, which reassured him until he thought about it later.

Six

Sarah waited until her father's car was out of sight, and then turned as the telephone rang. Millie answered it and she heard her name mentioned.

'It's Mr Larch, miss.'

'Thank you, Millie.' She held the receiver to her ear. 'Larch, thank goodness you've rung. Have you heard about Ronnie?'

'No, what's happened to him? I knew he'd done a bunk again.'

'The police have arrested him. We saw them as we came back from lunch. Daddy took Gran and me to the Chestnuts. Ronnie was fighting and it took several of them to subdue him.'

'I should think he was terrified,' Larch said. 'I missed him again this morning, but I have a hunch that he knows something about Morna's death.'

'You don't think he killed her?'

'No, I don't believe so – but he may know something about it. He was muttering about her being hurt. His mother didn't know who he meant and he was too upset or scared to tell her, and then, when he saw the police cars arrive he ran out of the back door and disappeared. Would you believe, they sent three cars to the Millers' cottage?'

'Anyone would think he was a dangerous maniac!'

'Apparently, that is exactly what they do think. Ben has been talking to someone he knows in the force in Norwich, and it seems they are convinced that Ronnie is the killer. They found his spade outside Morna's caravan.'

'But that doesn't prove anything.'

'It proves that he was there. You remember that it rained the other night and Mrs Miller said Ronnie was dry when he got home – and he wasn't hungry? He could have been with Morna.'

'That doesn't mean he killed her.'

'No, and as a matter of fact, Ben doesn't think so either – from what he has to go on, that is. He says he is keeping an open mind, and wants to meet you, Sarah. He was very interested in your notes.'

'Oh . . .' She felt pleased. 'Did he actually say that?'

'Yes, and he means it. He has gone out for a snoop about himself so he doesn't know that the police have arrested Ronnie, but I'll tell him when he gets in. Perhaps we could come over this evening?'

'Yes, that would be good – about seven?'

'Sounds about right. I'll see you then.'

Sarah was glad that the retired Scotland Yard detective seemed interested in what she'd managed to find out, even though she knew it wasn't much really. Perhaps if she went to have a good look round the cottage by herself she might find some real evidence to give him that evening.

She popped her head round the door of her grandmother's sitting room. 'I've got something to do, dearest. I shan't be long.'

'If you're going out, be careful, Sarah,' Amelia said. 'I'm not sure all this is over, even though your father was.'

'I shan't go near the woods,' Sarah said. 'Don't worry, Gran. I'll be fine, and I'll take the car if you don't mind.'

'Andrews will drive you if you like.'

'Yes, of course,' Sarah replied, though she had no intention of asking him. He wouldn't approve of her entering the cottage any more than Larch had.

She took the spare set of keys from its hook behind the back door, and went out. She loved driving her grandmother's car. It was the one thing she had missed when she'd left home, because she'd left her car behind. It had been a twenty-first birthday present from her father, but it was an expensive roadster and she had decided against taking it to Bournemouth with her.

It took her only a few minutes to drive to Janet Bates's cottage. She parked the car off the road not far from where all the fighting had been going on a little earlier and walked to the cottage. She shivered in the wind, because she was wearing only a light jacket and it was colder now. She walked up the front path, turning to her left to go round to the back door. She was just about to look for the key when the door opened and a man came out.

'Hello,' he said. 'Can I help you?'

'Oh . . .' Sarah hesitated and then remembered Larch's clever notion. 'I was just wondering if the cat was all right. I think it bolted when the police came . . .'

'Did it? Poor thing,' the man said. He was in his mid-thirties perhaps, a small, thin person with light brown hair and greenish eyes. 'I'm Keith Bates – Janet's brother. The police have told me I can hold the funeral for my sister now.'

'You must let us know when and where,' Sarah said. 'I'm sure my grandmother will wish to attend.'

'No, Janet didn't want that. It's to be a cremation and a private ceremony in Norwich.'

'Do the police agree to that?' She looked at him doubtfully.

'Yes, I imagine so. They seem to think they have it all tied up.'

'Do they?' Sarah said. 'I doubt if Ronnie Miller killed her, Mr Bates. He isn't usually a violent person.'

'No? Well, I wouldn't know. I've never been here before. Janet never wanted me to visit her. I sometimes wondered why, but then I didn't know much about her. We were parted when we were children, you know. She was a lot older than me, anyway. She went off when our parents divorced . . .' He pulled a face. 'I don't know why I'm telling you this. I suppose it feels a bit creepy here alone. You wouldn't like to come in for a cup of tea, would you?'

Sarah hesitated for a moment. She didn't know he was who he claimed to be, but on the other hand he seemed harmless enough.

'Yes, of course,' she said. 'I used to visit Janet sometimes. She showed me some pictures she had of people connected with the theatre, and I think she may have been writing something.'

'Janet was a personal dresser for more than one actress,' Keith Bates told her. 'But perhaps she didn't say? She was a bit secretive about her life. She told me a few things, but not much.' He ran his fingers through his hair as if under some stress. 'That's one of the reasons I've come here. I want to discover who she really was. It was a shock when the police told me she was dead. She found me about three years ago.

She'd had a private detective looking for me for years, and we started to meet sometimes – but I still don't know much about her. I know about the book, though. I've found a letter from a publisher. He's very interested in seeing the manuscript – wherever it is.'

'You haven't found it yet, then?'

'No. I only arrived an hour or so ago. Just before all that noise and trouble in the wood.'

'The police were arresting Ronnie Miller.'

'Oh . . .' he frowned. 'Poor devil. He probably doesn't know what he did or why.'

'No, perhaps not,' Sarah said. She watched as he filled the kettle and set two cups on the tray. It had a much fresher smell in here now and she saw that the floor had been washed. 'Has someone been in to clean up for you?'

'Yes, the police arranged it,' he said. 'A local woman, I think.'

'You wouldn't have wanted to come as it was.'

'No . . .' A little shudder went through him. 'I keep wondering why anyone should want to kill her. Unless . . .' he broke off and shook his head. 'No, I'm sure she wouldn't have . . .'

'Wouldn't have what?' Sarah asked. 'Do you know something that you ought to tell the police, Mr Bates?'

'No, not really,' he said and picked the kettle up as it began to whistle. He was frowning as he made the tea and poured it. Sarah was certain there was something on his mind, but whatever it was he wasn't going to share it with her. 'Besides, if that chap killed her, the man who has the mind of a child – well, it wouldn't have anything to do with it.'

'With what?' Sarah asked. 'You do know something, don't you?'

'No,' he said. 'No, I don't. I think you had better leave, Miss Beaufort. I don't know why you came, but I should like you to go now.'

'Are you staying here?' Sarah asked.

'No, I only came for a look round. I shall have it cleared and put it on the market as soon as the lawyers give me the go ahead.'

'So Janet left the cottage to you then?'

'Yes, of course. Why shouldn't she?' He glared at her. 'If

you're thinking I killed her for the money you're wrong. Janet would have given me anything I wanted. I had no need to kill her. Besides, we were both lonely. Neither of us had anyone else . . . anymore.'

'Did you once?'

'I asked you to leave,' he said. 'And don't come poking your nose in here again. You thought the key would still be where it was, didn't you? Well, I'm taking it with me so you won't be able to get in next time.'

Sarah hesitated, but he looked really annoyed so she decided to leave. At least she knew that Janet hadn't left her exercise books lying around, which meant they were probably hidden. Why would she hide them – unless she kept notes about other people's secrets? If she had, then she could have been using them as blackmail . . .

'It doesn't necessarily follow that she was trying to blackmail someone,' Larch said that evening, when Sarah told them about her meeting with Keith Bates, and how talkative he'd been until she asked the wrong questions. 'He might not have meant anything like that.'

'Then again he might have slipped up and said something he didn't mean to,' Ben said. 'Something made him throw Miss Beaufort out so it must seem important to him.'

'Oh, please, do call me Sarah,' she begged. They were sitting in her grandmother's parlour that evening, Amelia having gone to her bedroom to leave them to talk in private. 'He was so friendly, telling me all that stuff about his sister and how they had been parted when he was very young and their parents divorced. All of a sudden he became touchy and practically threw me out.'

'What made you go in in the first place?' Larch asked. 'It was a bit of a risk with a murderer running around loose.'

'Yes, I did hesitate, but he seemed very pleasant. Not at all the kind to kill anyone – sort of sad really. I don't think he has anyone else and it had overwhelmed him being alone in the cottage.'

'But he could have been the murderer,' Ben Marshall said, looking grave. 'You have given us some more interesting information, Sarah – but it might have been dangerous. I would like you to promise not to do anything like that again, please.'

'Are you going to let us continue to help?' Sarah said, and when he inclined his head she smiled, 'Then I shall promise not to take any more risks. The thing is that I know there were several exercise books, but Janet's brother hadn't found them, so that probably means she hid them.'

'That is what you were hoping to find, of course. They would be useful, but I don't think we have the right to go looking, not until we've exhausted all other avenues of investigation anyway.'

'But they might tell us who killed her.'

'Yes, they might,' he agreed, 'but perhaps we shall discover that for ourselves. Let's give it a few days, and if we aren't getting anywhere I'll see if I can get the police to search the cottage with me as an observer.'

'Would they do that?'

'If I ask nicely,' Ben said, and smiled at her. 'I have some friends on the force, Sarah, and a little influence. In fact Inspector Harrison has told me he will be grateful if I can help in any way.'

'I thought they were convinced that they had their killer?' Larch said, arching his brows.

'Well, they are half convinced, but they don't have any real evidence against Ronnie. He was at both crime scenes but at the moment they can't prove he killed either victim.'

'Why should he?' Sarah asked. 'Miss Bates dismissed him for some reason and that may have upset him, but where did he get the razor? Surely he didn't go home and fetch it? His spade was there. He could have used that instantly if he'd been planning to kill her.'

'Yes, that was my argument. I spent some time on the phone with Harrison this afternoon, and he says they are going to question Ronnie again with a psychiatrist present in the morning. Depending on what she thinks, they will either have him sectioned or bring him home again.'

'But they can't put him away if he isn't guilty of anything!' Sarah cried. 'Surely they can't?'

'They can if they consider him a danger to himself or the public. I know it seems unfair, but the laws are there to protect all of us. But it hasn't come to that yet. I'll do what I can – and the best way to get Ronnie home is to solve these crimes.'

'That's what we all want. I liked Morna. She was a gypsy

and most people don't have a good word to say about them, but she was different. I should like to see her murderer pay for what he did to her – and to poor Miss Bates, of course. But I think—' she broke off and blushed. 'No, perhaps I shouldn't say . . .'

'Go on,' Ben encouraged. 'That's the way crimes get solved. We need to talk it over again and again, and that way we may see things we've missed.'

'I think there are two murderers.'

'Ah yes, I can see why,' Ben said. 'They were very different – though both violent crimes. There certainly isn't a pattern.'

'That's not what the police are saying: they think that Ronnie committed both murders,' Larch said. 'But if they're not sure . . .'

'I think the next thing is for me to have a talk with Miss Bates's brother,' Ben said. 'It's possible that he might have found something after you left – and I should like to hear what he has to say for himself.'

'Yes, that's a good idea. I'm sure he knows something that might help us,' Sarah said.

'I am also going to talk to Ronnie if the police will allow it – and one of us has to speak to Jethro Scaffry. He's a suspect for his sister's murder. I've heard he has a nasty temper and they might have fallen out over something.'

'Yes, I saw them together in the village,' Sarah said. 'He did seem to be very angry with her . . .'

'Yes, perhaps,' Ben agreed. 'So you see, he must be interviewed, too. I doubt if he would speak to me because I was a policeman, but perhaps to you, Larch?'

'Yes, I'll have a go, if I can find him,' Larch agreed. 'Morna's caravan is usually in the woods but I think Jethro comes and goes. The police would have scared him off when they were all over the woods. He probably thought they were looking for him, because of the poaching.'

'Been poaching in Thorny Woods, has he?'

'Yes, that's what I've heard,' Larch said. 'I was speaking to Harold Jackson – he's the head groom up at the Manor – and he told me that Sir James had threatened to have the police on Jethro this time. He warned him off his land with a shotgun.'

'Then perhaps I'd better have a word with Sir James too,' Ben said. 'If I talk to him about the poaching, I might learn something of interest.'

'Then you think he might know something about all this?' Sarah said. 'I know Gran says he couldn't possibly be mixed up in this, but I'm not so sure. I think he has a nasty temper too. And I did hear Sir James threatening Jethro. We also saw him having words with his nephew when we had tea at the Chestnuts. He might have something to hide – and he might be capable of murder if he was angry.'

'Yes, I saw that you had noted both incidents. Your notes were excellent,' Ben said. 'I think you might have another chat to the postmistress, Sarah. He might have called there to buy his milk.'

'Yes, perhaps.' Sarah felt as if she were being given the safest task, but she supposed that Ben Marshall was the best person to speak to Keith Bates and to Sir James, and she knew that neither of the men would have allowed her to go in search of Jethro Scaffry. 'But you will tell me everything you find out, won't you?'

'Yes, of course,' Ben said. 'We are a team, Sarah. I shall value your opinion, and we'll all meet again tomorrow evening – but not here. We can't turn Mrs Beaufort out of her own parlour again . . .'

Sarah took her grandmother's old bicycle from the shed the next morning. Andrews used it occasionally himself, so the tyres were pumped up and the brakes worked. She was thoughtful as she cycled past Janet Bates's cottage, remembering her conversation with Janet's brother and wishing she'd been more careful. If she had phrased her questions differently, he might have been inclined to tell her more.

Oh well, Ben Marshall was going to check out his home address and talk to him again. She wondered what the villagers thought about this second murder. Did everyone still blame Ronnie Miller?

Sarah wished that she had thought of talking to Morna sooner. If she had done the killer might have been caught and the gypsy girl might still be alive. And yet the more she went over things in her mind, the more she believed that the murders were committed by two different people. She knew that Larch was sceptical of her theory, and Ben Marshall was keeping an open mind, but she had a feeling deep down inside.

Sarah shivered, feeling a tingle at the nape of her neck. It was as though the village had been abandoned, the main street deserted. Although she could see a black car parked down at the far end, and a couple of dogs were nosing about on the Green. The wind caught her hair, blowing it across her face. She brushed it back, somehow uneasy.

As she left her bicycle outside the general shop and went in she heard something, a sound from the back room. The shop itself was empty, which was unusual. Mrs Roberts was normally behind the counter most of the day, and she came through almost at once if she happened to be in the back. The back rooms consisted of a small sitting room where Mrs Roberts made herself a hot drink and sat for a while when she had her break, and a store room. Her living quarters were upstairs.

Sarah had a look through a rack of magazines, deciding to buy one and ask Mrs Roberts for some boiled sweets from one of the two rows of jars on the shelf. Her grandmother wanted some thick-cut marmalade and a packet of biscuits, so that gave Sarah plenty of excuse for a good gossip.

She waited for a few minutes, placing her purchases on the counter, but there was no sign of Mrs Roberts so she called out. She was beginning to feel uneasy. It just wasn't like the shopkeeper not to come through when her bell rang.

Sarah hesitated. She had promised Ben Marshall that she wouldn't take any risks, but supposing Mrs Roberts had had a fall? The woman wasn't exactly young and Sarah had heard something when she came in, she was sure of it.

She took a deep breath and then lifted the hinged flap in the counter. The door that led into the back rooms was slightly open, so she pushed it back and called out again.

'Mrs Roberts – it's Sarah. Are you there? Are you all right?'

She heard something but it was muffled, odd. Certain that something was wrong, Sarah walked through the door and into the room beyond. Almost at once she saw the slumped figure of Mrs Roberts lying on the floor and ran to her.

'Mrs Roberts . . .!' she cried. 'Mrs Roberts, are you hurt?'

She knelt down on the floor beside the woman, who was lying face downward. As she did so, she saw that there was blood in her hair. It looked as if she had been struck from behind.

'Mrs Roberts . . .' Hearing a faint moaning sound coming

from the woman, Sarah realized that she wasn't dead, only hurt. She turned her over on to her back, and saw that her eyelids were fluttering. 'I'll get help . . .'

Mrs Roberts reached out, her fingers closing over Sarah's wrist. Her eyes were open now, fearful and yet determined as she said, 'I know who killed her. Morna was . . .' A sigh issued from her lips and her eyes closed, her hand falling away from Sarah's wrist.

Sarah gave a little cry of alarm. She jumped to her feet, intending to telephone for the doctor, but as she did so, a figure rushed from the storeroom at the back and pushed her so hard that she fell to her knees on the floor. The intruder dashed on through the shop before Sarah could recover enough to realize what she had seen or catch her breath. A few moments later, she pulled herself up and went through to the shop. It was empty, the bell still clanging as she ran to the window to look out.

The intruder had gone – but that wasn't possible. He or she hadn't had time to run the length of the street.

There was no time to waste puzzling over what had happened. Mrs Roberts was alive but badly hurt. Sarah returned to the counter and reached for the telephone, dialling the emergency number.

'I'm phoning from the post office stores in Beecham Thorny,' she said. 'I have just discovered a woman who has been attacked and badly hurt. I need an ambulance and the police . . .'

Sarah was sitting in the corridor of the hospital in Norwich when Larch arrived. He came hurrying towards her, his expression one of extreme anxiety.

'Are you all right, Sarah? Father told me that you had phoned and asked if I would collect you. How is Mrs Roberts?'

'I don't know,' Sarah replied, a catch in her voice. 'She was still alive when we came in but she had been hit with something hard and was unconscious. She did manage to tell me something before she passed out again.'

'Tell me later,' he said. 'Shall I take you home or do you want to wait for some news?'

'I think this is the doctor who attended her when she was brought in coming now,' Sarah said as she saw him walking towards them. She started forward. 'How is she, Doctor?'

'We have placed Mrs Roberts under observation in case we have to operate,' he said. 'It may be some days before we know how that blow to the head has affected her.'

'Will she live?' Larch asked.

'Yes, I think there is a good chance that she will survive,' Doctor Peters replied. 'But there may be some damage to her brain. We cannot say for certain as yet.'

'What does that mean exactly?'

'Perhaps a loss of memory, perhaps worse. We shan't know until it happens. You should go home now, Miss Beaufort. We shall call you if there is any change.'

'I don't think she had any family,' Sarah said in a tone of distress. 'Please, you will let me know how she is? I shall want to visit her when she is well enough.'

'Yes, of course. I think she owes her life to you, Miss Beaufort. If she had lain where she was for any length of time it would probably have been the finish of her.'

'I went through because I heard something and I was afraid she might be hurt,' Sarah said. 'It was just what anyone would have done.'

The doctor smiled and walked away, leaving Sarah and Larch together. 'I don't think many would have kept their heads the way you did,' he said. 'When you found her lying there like that and then the intruder rushed at you . . . it's a wonder you weren't killed too!'

'The police said that I had been lucky, but I think whoever it was just wanted to get away,' Sarah said. 'I can't tell you whether it was a man or a woman – all I saw was a devil mask and a long black robe.'

'You're joking!' Larch stared at her in disbelief, his eyes narrowing as he saw her expression. 'No, you aren't, are you?'

'I wouldn't make a game of it,' Sarah said as they walked outside. It felt cold and she shivered. The horror of what she had seen had just begun to catch up with her. 'It happened too fast for me to be scared, Larch. One moment I was thinking about getting help and then this . . . figure rushed out of the back room, pushed me to my knees and went through the shop. As soon as I could gather my wits I followed. The door-bell was still clanging the way it does when someone has gone out, but I looked through the window and couldn't see anyone. I couldn't think how that could be and it was scary, but when the ambulance came I saw that there was a side entrance next door to the house just past the shop. I think whoever it was must have gone in there, waited until I went back in to phone for the police and then gone on again.'

'Whoever it was probably took off the gown and the mask,' Larch said. 'He or she must have known of the side entrance – may have used it to put on the gown and mask before entering the shop. It's weird, Sarah. I don't know what Ben is going to make of this.' He looked at her ruefully. 'We both thought it would be perfectly safe for you to visit Mrs Roberts, but it looks as if you were the one in at the deep end.'

'Yes,' Sarah said and felt goosebumps rise on her arms. 'I certainly didn't expect that.' She slid inside the car when he opened the door for her. As he got into the driving seat, she turned to look at him. 'But I haven't told you what Mrs Roberts told me just before she passed out.'

'Go on then,' he said. 'Was it important?'

'It could be very important if she remembers when she wakes up,' Sarah said. 'She told me that she knows who the killer is, and then she said, "Morna was . . ." and that's all she managed before she lost consciousness.'

'My God! I hope the police have someone sitting outside her room,' Larch said. 'Obviously she had been gossiping about what she knew and the killer got to hear of it – that's why he tried to murder her too. He would probably have got away with it if you hadn't turned up when you did.'

'Yes, perhaps,' Sarah said, feeling a little sick. The first two murders had been discovered by other people, and she'd only heard about them later, but this brought home how nasty it really was. 'I'm so glad I was there, Larch. If I hadn't gone in when I did, she might have been dead by now.'

'Yes, of course.' Larch was thoughtful as he drove towards his own home. He wasn't going to say anything to Sarah, because he didn't want to frighten her, but if the murderer had heard Mrs Roberts tell her that she knew the name of Morna's killer, it could spell danger for Sarah. 'I'm taking you to my home first. Ben will want to speak to you, and you can ring Amelia from there.'

'I rang her from the hospital,' Sarah said. 'I told her I had found Mrs Roberts but I didn't say anything about the rest of it, and I would rather you didn't.'

'No, of course not. She won't hear it from me, and I dare say the police won't be giving details to the newspapers – I hope not anyway. You don't want them bothering you.'

'I can't think of anything I would like less,' Sarah said. She realized that he was upset by what had happened, and decided to change the subject. 'So how did you get on with Jethro Scaffry?'

'Couldn't find him,' Larch said and made a wry face. 'That seems to be my luck. Ronnie ran off again and Jethro seems to have vanished. Morna's caravan is still there though – and there was something curious . . .'

'About the caravan?'

'A bit more than that,' Larch said. 'I saw someone walking away before I got there. He didn't see me, but I saw him and his face was like a thundercloud. I waited until he'd gone and then went into the van; it had been turned over, everything tossed on the floor as if someone had been searching for something.'

'Whoever it was must have thought Morna had something that they wanted,' Sarah said. 'Who did you see walking away?'

'Sir James Beecham. I mean, he has a perfect right to be in the woods; they belong to him. Yet I know he came from the caravan because I saw him leaving it.'

'Do you think he was the one who ransacked the place?'

'I have no idea,' Larch said. 'He might have found it that way, as I did – but it could have been him. Besides, if he wasn't looking for something why would he have gone there?'

'Yes, he must have had a good reason, mustn't he?' Sarah was thoughtful for a moment. 'Did you have a look around yourself?'

'I wouldn't have known what to look for, Sarah. Even if I'd found it I probably wouldn't have realized what it was. Only the person who did that knows what they were looking for.'

'Yes, I suppose so,' Sarah said, though she thought she would have looked if she'd been there. 'Well, at least it's another piece in the puzzle. You must tell Ben exactly what you saw. I'm looking forward to hearing what he has found out, aren't you?'

'Are you sure you feel up to it? I know it's what we arranged, but you've had a nasty shock.'

'Yes, it was unpleasant,' Sarah said. It had been horrible but everything had happened so fast that she hadn't felt anything at the time. It was only now that the horror of it all was beginning to register. 'But I still want to hear what Ben has to say, and I want to hear what he thinks when we tell him our news.'

Sarah had a nasty feeling that Sir James was connected to the murders. All the little bits and pieces were making it seem that he might be the culprit. She had thought that there might be two murderers, but after the attack on Mrs Roberts she had changed her mind.

Seven

'Forgive me for sending you there,' Ben said when they were seated in front of a nice warm fire, with a plate of delicious sandwiches, a Georgian silver coffeepot and a decanter of fine sherry on the table in front of them. 'I thought she might have something to tell you, because she clearly likes to gossip, but I didn't expect you to find an attempted murder in process.'

'It's just as well I did go,' Sarah said. 'The murderer might have managed to finish the job if I hadn't turned up. The policeman who arrived with the ambulance told me they would have someone guarding her twenty-four hours a day. If she recovers her senses, she may be able to tell us what she knows.'

'Well, I may be able to supply a piece of the jigsaw,' Ben said. 'You told me that she said, "Morna was . . .", didn't you?' Sarah nodded. 'I think she may have been trying to say that Morna was carrying a child. The police surgeon has done some examinations, and I have been told that she was about three months gone.'

'Morna was having a baby?' Sarah stared at him. 'That's terrible! I never thought of anything like that. Who would do such a thing? To kill a mother and child – that makes it a double murder.'

'Yes, it does,' Ben said grimly.

Sarah felt sick. 'I imagined she had been killed because she knew something about Miss Bates's murder – although I did wonder if there might be some other reason. Do you think it was because of the baby that she was killed?'

'A reluctant father?' Larch said. 'Could she have tried to blackmail whoever it was into marrying her?'

'Or giving her a lot of money, perhaps?' Ben's gaze narrowed. 'That is a motive I've come across more times than you can imagine. The only thing that doesn't quite fit is the devil mask and the long black gown. Why did the murderer dress up like that to attempt to silence Mrs Roberts? He or she must have heard her speak of Morna. But almost anyone could have been in the shop and heard her gossiping. I doubt she could have kept it to herself if she thought she knew something important.'

'But why didn't she tell the police?' Larch asked.

'She may have been thinking of blackmail,' Ben said. 'Or perhaps she didn't realize how important it was at the time. She may have known that Morna was pregnant, but not who the father – or the killer – was, until that person attacked her.'

'Larch saw Sir James coming from Morna's caravan,' Sarah said. 'Do you think he had been looking for something that might connect him to her?'

'You think he might be the father of her child?' Larch looked astonished. 'Good grief, he's old enough to be Morna's father.'

'That doesn't rule him out,' Ben said. 'I didn't manage to see him today, so I shall certainly be asking him about it when I call in the morning. I've telephoned to make an appointment.'

'Did you speak to Miss Bates's brother?' Sarah asked.

'Yes. I had to track him down at his place of work, and that was very interesting. He works in the library in Norwich – not the lending library, but one of the records offices. They keep ancient maps and records of sales and land ownership there – it's a sort of local version of the land registry.'

Larch raised his brows. 'What did he have to say for himself?'

'He didn't want to talk to me at first, but I persuaded him to think about it. He asked me if I thought his sister might have been trying to blackmail someone, and then he told me that he had discovered something about the land at Thorny Woods.'

'The land where they want to build those houses?'

'Yes, I imagine so,' Ben replied. 'He found something in the old records and didn't know what he ought to do about it. He mentioned it to his sister, but hasn't done anything more since then. He was a bit anxious about it and I think he suspects that she might have attempted to blackmail someone – possibly Sir James. I told him that he should report his findings to the proper person, and he says that he will get the proof and send it to your father.'

'My father?' Larch stared at him, bewildered. 'I don't understand – why my father?'

'Because, if his assumptions are correct, that piece of land
belongs to your father rather than Sir James Beecham. The
woods have grown out over the original boundary, and the
land they now cover was originally part of your great, great
grandfather's estate.'

'Surely that can't be true? Father must have deeds and maps.
He would know if the land belonged to him.'

'Well, apparently things were done haphazardly in the old
days. The deeds to that particular piece of land may have got
lost under a pile of old documents at the lawyers, and the
wood has encroached slowly, I should imagine.'

'Good grief!' Larch exclaimed. 'Sir James stands to make
several thousand pounds from the sale of that land and it may
not be his legally. I should think that would be reason enough
for murder!'

'Well, it certainly looks that way,' Ben said. 'But only if
Mr Bates has his information correct, and if your father is
prepared to take the case to court. It might cost a considerable
amount of money to prove it, and in the end it might just be
a misunderstanding of an old map.'

'Yes, I shouldn't be at all surprised if it were,' Larch said.
'But it will be interesting to see the documents Mr Bates has
access to. I'm sure Father would be delighted if it were true.
He could make certain that the wood was safe then.'

'If Keith Bates discovered this, wouldn't others have done
so?' Sarah asked. 'Perhaps Sir James has been blackmailed
by someone who works in the council offices.'

'Yes, that might be the case,' Ben said. 'If he paid that man
off and then perhaps had another blackmail letter from Miss
Bates . . . he might have felt that enough was enough.'

'That would be sufficient to make someone think of murder,'
Larch said, looking struck. 'And he is known for his temper.'

'It looks as if a visit to that gentleman could be very
worthwhile,' Ben said. 'But you will be wanting to know
about Ronnie?' He smiled at Sarah. 'You'll be happy to hear
that I was able to talk to him, and I agree with you.
The psychiatrist was of the same opinion, and the police
have changed their minds about him being the murderer. The
attack on Mrs Roberts helped his cause, because Ronnie was

still in custody. I understand they are going to let him come home tomorrow.'

'That's wonderful!' Sarah said, feeling relieved. 'It was a miscarriage of justice, arresting him like that.'

'Yes, that was the opinion of most of us, poor lad,' Ben said. 'He did see Morna that night, though. She took him into her caravan, gave him something to eat and then sent him off. Apparently, Jethro took him off to a hut he often uses himself, and the two of them spent the night there. His story gives Jethro an alibi and if Jethro confirms it they are both in the clear as far as Morna's murder is concerned.'

'If we could find Jethro we could tell him that,' Larch said. 'But for the moment he seems to have disappeared . . .'

'You killed her, didn't you?' Jethro Scaffry confronted the man. 'The police are bloody idiots if they believe that Ronnie Miller did it just because he left his spade outside her caravan. I know what you've been up to and I know that you killed her, because she was having your baby! You carried on with her and then when she told you she was pregnant, you didn't want to know.'

'Prove it, can you?' the accused sneered. 'Your sister was nothing but a whore and I'd had enough of her threats so I clouted her a bit, but I didn't kill her. She wanted five hundred pounds. I told her to whistle for it and she said that she would go to my uncle. He might have paid her to keep her quiet for the sake of the family name, but I don't give a shit. Go to the police if you dare; they damned well can't pin it on me, because I was nowhere near her that night.' In fact he'd raped her, because he was angry, but he comforted himself with the thought that she'd deserved it.

'I know it was you. I've seen what you and your posh friends get up to in the woods. Maybe you don't care about your family name, but you've been stealing cats to slaughter the poor beasts.' Jethro's expression was scornful. 'Mad as hatters you lot are, thinkin' you can conjure up the devil. I've watched your rituals and I know things the police would be interested in. One of them girls you had last summer weren't no more than twelve.'

Simon Beecham reached for the fork he had been using to lift some shrubs for transplanting. He made a threatening gesture towards Jethro.

'You open your mouth about that and you're dead,' he said, his expression suddenly malicious. 'I had a fling with Morna but I didn't kill her – and if you tell anyone about that business you're finished, take my word for it.'

Jethro scowled. If he knew for sure that Simon Beecham was the murderer he would kill him. He knew that Morna had been messing around with him for some months. He'd seen the bugger coming from her caravan more than once, and he'd known what was going on, but he hadn't done anything about it. Thorny Woods was the first place they'd been allowed to settle for more than a few days, and he hadn't wanted to cause trouble. Now he wished he'd thrashed the bugger the first time he'd seen him.

'Watch your step,' he muttered as he backed off. 'I'm goin' ter be watchin' you, and I ain't finished with you yet. If I find out it was you, the police will have a job putting all the bits together.'

'Remember what I said. Go near the police and you're dead!'

Simon held his fork at the ready until the gypsy jumped into his decrepit old van and drove off, then he hurried inside his cottage to make a phone call.

'Thank you for telling me,' Sarah said, and replaced the receiver. She went through to the parlour where her grandmother was doing *The Times* crossword puzzle. Amelia laid the paper down and looked at her expectantly. 'Mrs Roberts has come through the night but she's still unconscious.'

'Yes, well, after being attacked like that, you must expect it, Sarah. She is lucky to be alive.'

'I know. It was horrid, Gran. Hearing about Miss Bates and Morna was bad enough, but finding Mrs Roberts like that . . .'

Amelia looked concerned. 'It's a great pity it had to be you. I'm glad that you found her for her sake, but I am afraid it may give you nightmares.'

'No, it's all right, Gran. I couldn't sleep much last night but it was because I was thinking about that poor woman. I can't imagine how she is going to look after her shop if she is ill for a long time. And she certainly won't be well enough to come home for some weeks – even if she survives.'

'We should miss her and her shop,' Amelia said, her expression thoughtful. 'But perhaps her sister will come and stay for a while.'

'Does she have a sister?' Sarah was surprised.

'Yes, I believe she lives in Devon or somewhere down that way. The police will let her know I expect. So you can stop worrying, Sarah. Think about yourself instead.'

'There isn't much to think about for the moment. I've been looking in the papers for advertisements for auditions, but there hasn't been anything suitable.'

'Perhaps there will be something in the post. Why don't you collect it for us, Sarah? I think the post boy is about to put the letters through.'

'How do you know that, Gran?'

Amelia smiled and shook her head. 'Instinct? I've no idea but something tells me – and it tells me that Mrs Roberts will be fine.'

'I hope you're right.'

Sarah went through into the hall. There were five letters lying on the mat. One was for her, three for her grandmother and one for Miss Janet Bates.

'Now isn't that just too bad,' Amelia exclaimed when Sarah showed her. 'What ought we to do with it? I suppose it should go to her brother but we don't have his address. You could put it through her door, Sarah.'

'I think I shall give it to Mr Marshall,' Sarah said. 'He will know what to do with it.'

'Now why didn't I think of that?' Amelia asked. 'Open your letter, dearest. It might be important.'

Sarah sat down at the pretty little mahogany writing desk near the window and slit the envelope. It had come from one of the girls she'd made friends with at Bournemouth and was about an audition. 'It's from Mary Jennings,' she said. 'There's an audition for a show and it's . . .' She turned the page and gave a little cry of surprise. 'It's on a cruise ship going to New York, Gran! Mary says they are looking for girls who can sing and also dance a bit. She is going to audition herself, and suggests that I meet her in London.'

'Didn't I tell you something might be in the post? When does she want you to meet her?'

'The audition is at the end of next week, and the cruise

leaves at the end of November. It would mean that I would be away for Christmas and I promised Daddy I would go to him if I could.'

'If you get the job I'll go and stay with him,' Amelia promised. 'I should telephone your friend straight away and let her know you are coming.'

'She isn't on the telephone,' Sarah said, 'but I think I shall write and tell her I'll be there. It was good of her to let me know, and I ought to try, didn't I?'

'Yes, of course.' Amelia smiled at her. 'Write the letter now and then Andrews will take you down to the village to post it. If you are thinking of visiting Mrs Roberts this afternoon, I might come with you. We could do a little shopping and have tea out.'

'That sounds lovely,' Sarah said. 'Yes, I think that would be a good idea. It will take our minds off things . . .'

'It was good of you to see me, Sir James,' Ben said as he was shown into the book-lined study. It had bookshelves on three walls, and large French windows that overlooked the park, a handsome room with solid antique furniture. 'I imagine you know why I am here?'

The two men sized each other up in silence. Sir James was tall and well built, dressed in an expensive tailored suit, Ben Marshall of a much leaner though wiry set and wearing grey slacks and a thick tweed jacket with leather patches on the elbows.

'Something to do with these wretched murders, I suppose. It is getting serious now. I dare say the local police could do with some help.'

'My inquiries are informal,' Ben said with an easy smile. 'If this was official my colleagues from Norwich would be here – but I thought you might be able to give me some pointers?'

'Of course. Glad to help if I can,' Sir James said, and there was a note of real anger in his voice. 'I shall not be satisfied until you catch the bastard who killed that girl – Miss Bates too, of course. And he's had a go at Mrs Roberts, I understand? That woman is a terrible gossip – nevertheless, this cannot be allowed to go on.'

'I quite agree with you,' Ben said, and sat at his host's

request. 'We have a few leads. Nothing concrete yet though, I'm afraid.'

'I thought the police had arrested Ronnie Miller?'

'Yes, but they should be bringing him home sometime today. It really wasn't an option to keep him longer, sir. He may have the mind of a child, but he seems harmless. Might get a bit out of control if he has a few drinks, but the local landlord knows not to give him more than one beer shandy.'

'I see . . .' Sir James frowned. 'I was hoping it might be cleared up quickly, but if it wasn't Miller . . .'

'I think you can rule him out, sir. I wondered if you had seen any strangers in the village recently?'

'Strangers? No, I don't think so. I'm out quite a bit on estate business. We've got a bit of bother on over this planning business . . . I don't think I've seen anything unusual at all.'

'You haven't had anyone making threats to you personally?'

Sir James's expression suddenly became wary and angry. 'No, not at all. If I had, I can't see that it would have any bearing on the case, Mr Marshall.'

'Oh, you never know, one thing leads to another.'

'I'm not sure I like where you are going, sir.'

'I'm not going anywhere in particular just yet. So, no strangers – but that would mean we were looking for someone local. Not a very pleasant thought, sir.'

'It certainly isn't,' Sir James said. 'If you want me to account for my movements, I was at meetings most of the day that Miss Bates was killed, and I am not in the habit of walking the woods at night.'

'It might be a bit embarrassing – not to say dangerous from what I hear,' Ben Marshall said. 'I understand there are some odd things going on. I'm surprised that you haven't cracked down on it, sir.'

'It's a bit of harmless nonsense. A few idiots with more time than sense playing at being druids – a fertility thing I'm told. I thought it would be a waste of the police's valuable time.'

'You don't think it might be something more sinister – devil worship perhaps? Those cats must have been slaughtered for some ghastly ritual.'

'Yes, well, that was unpleasant,' Sir James said, looking awkward. 'But I think that has stopped now.'

'Had a word with someone, did you?'

'Yes, as a matter of fact I did. Is this relevant, Mr Marshall?'

'Yes, it might be. The murders might be connected, though I don't know why or how.'

'Stuff and nonsense! These people – druids or whatever they call themselves – are a bunch of idiots, but they wouldn't do anything like that! You're barking up the wrong tree.'

'You know someone connected to this business?'

'I might.' Sir James glared at him. 'If you have an accusation to make, come out and make it!'

'I beg your pardon, sir. It's just that I am trying to sort things out in my mind.' Ben smiled pleasantly and stood up. 'Forgive me, Sir James, I must ask you and then we can finish this – did you have anything to do with the murder of Miss Janet Bates or Miss Morna Scaffry?'

'Certainly not! I thought this was an unofficial inquiry?'

'Yes, sir, it is. I am merely helping out a friend. Thank you for your patience. Don't worry, I shall see myself out.'

As he went into the hall, he saw a woman in a wheelchair. She had faded gold hair, a sweet face and dark blue eyes. She smiled at him as he stopped to speak to her.

'Mr Marshall?' She offered her hand, on which were several expensive diamond rings. 'You came to see my husband about the murders? It is terrible that this should be happening here. Have you discovered any important clues as yet?'

'No, not many,' Ben said and smiled back at her. She must have been lovely when she was younger. 'I don't suppose you have any to offer me, Lady Beecham?'

'I rarely go out. Most of my time is spent here at the house or in the gardens. But I can see the woods from my window and I know that there are sometimes lights there at night . . . both flickering and steady. I wish someone could stop what is going on there, Mr Marshall. It would be a great pity if these incidents continued unchecked.'

'Yes, indeed it would,' Ben agreed. 'We shall have to see what we can do about it – when we have the murderer under lock and key.'

'You may find that one leads to the other,' she said and wheeled her chair about, leaving him staring after her.

Now what did she know that she wasn't saying? Ben wondered about it as he left. He was certain that Sir James was guilty of something and that he had lied to him.

Larch had spent the morning in his studio. He stood back and looked at his most recent work, a portrait from memory. He sighed because he knew it wasn't nearly good enough. If he wanted to paint her, he should ask Sarah to sit for him.

Perhaps he just wasn't a portrait painter. He knew some of his landscapes were good. He had been asked to hold a show on more than one occasion, but he hadn't produced anything he thought good enough. The trouble was he was striving for something that wasn't there yet. What he needed was some time away from the familiarity of his home – somewhere the scenery was exotic and presented a challenge.

Artists needed that challenge, but Larch didn't know that he wanted to be that dedicated, or even if he was good enough to put his art first. There was another side of him, and that side of him wanted something entirely different.

Wiping his brushes, he smiled wryly as he looked at the portrait. Even if he were ready to settle down, he was pretty sure that Sarah wasn't . . .

Sarah and her grandmother visited Mrs Roberts at the hospital. She was still unconscious and under constant observation. It was easy to see that she was very ill, because of all the hospital paraphernalia, and they were only allowed to stay a few minutes. However, they took her some flowers, because it would cheer her up if she woke and saw them.

After leaving the hospital, they went shopping in a large department store, indulging in a spending spree. Then they walked up the hill and gazed into the windows of the antique shops. Norwich had quite a few cobbled streets and parts of it were still reminiscent of the prosperous wool town it had been centuries earlier, with timbered buildings and a tiny part of the ancient town wall still standing.

It was dark by the time they got home, and Millie told them that Mr Marshall had telephoned earlier to say that he wouldn't be able to see Sarah that evening.

'Also, Captain Meadows rang to say that he has an appointment this evening, but he would like to take you out to lunch tomorrow – "as a reward for protecting him from the flesh eater" he said, miss.' Millie pulled a face. 'I don't know if I've got that right, but I think that's what he said.'

'Yes, I understand the message,' Sarah said and smiled. 'Don't look so worried, Millie. It is just Captain Meadows's little joke. Nothing sinister or unpleasant.'

'Oh, I see.' The housekeeper's plump face creased in a smile. 'Up to his usual tricks, was he? Shall I bring a pot of tea through, Mrs Beaufort?'

'Yes, thank you,' Amelia replied. 'In about half an hour please, Millie.' She glanced at Sarah as they went through to the parlour. 'What was all that about?'

'Larch was cornered the other day when we went out to tea. It appears that he agreed to look at someone's work, another artist. She plays bridge with you sometimes. Madeline, I think her name is, though I don't think Larch mentioned her surname.'

'Madeline Lewis-Brown,' Amelia said. 'You need say no more, Sarah. I understand what he means perfectly.'

'Poor Larch,' Sarah laughed as she remembered the look in his eyes. 'I think she frightened the life out of him. I promised I would go and protect him.'

'Yes, you should, and it will be nice for you to go out with him, dearest. You always get on so splendidly together.'

'Yes, we do, ever since we were children and I came to visit in the school holidays. I thought he had changed when he first came back after the war, Gran, but he seems to be getting over it now.'

'That was a terrible experience for any young man,' her grandmother said. 'He was only nineteen when he joined the army, Sarah, and he saw things that no one ought to see.'

'Yes, I know. He never talks about it, but I think it is the reason why he can't seem to take anything seriously.'

'Except his painting.'

'Yes, perhaps. He is so talented, but he doesn't know it, Gran. He is always striving for something better . . . something beyond the horizon.'

'That is a good thing for an artist, isn't it?'

'Yes, I expect so,' Sarah said. 'Would you mind if I disappeared upstairs for a while, Gran? I should like to wash my hair.'

'Come down and have some supper when you've had your bath,' Amelia said. 'We'll talk for a while, and then we might both have an early night . . .'

'Yes, of course, Gran,' Sarah said and smiled at her. 'That sounds a lovely way to finish off our day . . .'

Eight

'Ronnie, what are you doing?' Mrs Miller went to the back door of her cottage and looked out at her son. It was dark except for the light from the oil lamp he had lit earlier, and too cold for him to sit out here. He had been messing around with his spade ever since the police brought it back. 'Haven't you finished that yet? I've got some cake for your tea. Come in now, there's a good lad.'

Ronnie looked round at her, his eyes vacant. He had been working on his spade for ages, making it really sharp. Cut through the earth like butter that spade would, just the way he liked it. And gardening was the one thing he really understood.

'Got to go to work in the morning,' he said. 'Miss Bates will wonder where I've been.'

'Miss Bates is dead.' Mrs Miller sighed. She had tried to explain it to him so many times. 'You can't go there any more, Ronnie. You will have to find a new job – if anyone will have you.'

She felt angry over the way the police had behaved, dragging her son off twice as if he were a dangerous criminal. Ronnie hadn't been the same since. Some of the time she didn't think he even heard her. He seemed miles away, lost in thought.

It was disgusting the way people treated the lad, she thought, conveniently forgetting the countless times she had laid her stick across his backside. She'd only done it to discipline him, to keep him safe, because the great daft lump would get into trouble if she let him have his way. But the police had finished his prospects of getting a job locally.

And no one had considered what that might mean for her. She was a widow on a small income, and Ronnie's money had come in handy. Miss Bates had been very generous giving him five shillings a week. She would have to find herself a small job, just for a few hours a day. She might ask down at the post office when Mrs Roberts got back from hospital. At least her Ronnie couldn't be blamed for that; he had been in police custody.

'Are you coming in?' she asked.

'You go in, Ma,' Ronnie said. 'I'll be in for me tea in a minute.'

Mrs Miller smiled. Sometimes, when he spoke like that, she could almost think he was normal – whatever being normal meant. The people who were committing these murders – were they normal? She wondered about it as she went in and cut her son a large slice of seed cake. He deserved a bit of spoiling. It wasn't his fault that the police had got it all wrong – a miscarriage of justice, that's what it had been. That nice Captain Meadows was right.

Glancing out of the window a few minutes later, she saw that the oil lamp was still by the bench, but Ronnie had gone. She went to the door and called him, but there was no answer. She sighed as she returned to the warmth of the kitchen. Her son would never have gone off like that until all this happened. Ronnie had changed and it frightened her, because she wasn't sure why he seemed so different.

Ronnie had locked his spade in the garden shed before he left. He didn't want the police to take it again. He wasn't sure why they had taken him off like that, but it had upset him, made him angry. They had asked him all those questions, shouting at him, frightening him. The last one had been better, though. Mr Ben Marshall. He had told Ronnie to call him Ben and he'd smiled, asking him what happened the night he was in the woods.

Ronnie frowned as he remembered. He had gone to the caravan and Morna had let him in. She had made a fuss of him because he was so wet, and she'd given him a mug of hot tea laced with something stronger.

'That will make you feel better, love,' she'd said.

'What is it?' Ronnie licked his lips, because he'd never tasted anything like this before.

'Best whisky,' Morna said, and chuckled as she saw that he was enjoying himself. 'Jethro says it fell off the back of a lorry. I expect he nicked it, but who cares? It's good when you're chilled right through. I get chilled sometimes standing on the market.'

'You sell heather,' Ronnie said and finished his tea. He looked hopefully as Morna refilled the mug but she didn't put any more of that nice stuff in. Still, he could feel it warming him inside. Morna was wearing a full skirt that swished as she moved about the caravan and a blouse that dipped low at the front, showing her plump breasts. He thought how pretty she looked, and reached out to touch her arm as she brushed past him. Her skin felt lovely and she smelled like flowers. 'You're pretty, you are.'

'And I think you are a little drunk,' Morna said and laughed. 'My fault, Ronnie. I don't mind you touchin' my arm, but don't go getting ideas, will you?'

Ronnie stared at her. He had no idea what she meant. He just thought she was pretty, but his head was beginning to spin a bit and he giggled as she ran her hand over his hair. He put his large hand over her wrist, and a feeling of excitement surged through him as he saw how fair her skin was compared to his. He wasn't sure what he wanted, but he knew that it was something to do with the way her skin felt and her scent.

At that moment the door of the caravan opened and Jethro came in. He raised his brows as he saw Ronnie, and glared at his sister.

'Taking a risk, aren't you?'

'He's harmless enough.'

Jethro's eyes glinted with scorn. 'Not if he's been drinking, Morna. He's a man not a boy.'

'I can handle him.'

'It looks like it.' He turned to Ronnie. 'You can't stay here tonight, lad. I'll take you with me. Come on, we'll go now.'

Ronnie had been disappointed, but he raised no protest because he liked Jethro almost as much as Morna.

'All right,' he'd said. 'Where are we going?'

'I'll show you.' Jethro grinned at him. 'It's a secret, but you can keep secrets, can't you, lad?'

'Yeah,' Ronnie said. He thought Jethro meant he wasn't to tell anyone. He grinned at Morna and followed her brother obediently down the steps of the caravan. It was cold out but it had stopped raining.

They seemed to walk for quite a long time, and then Ronnie saw the wooden hut. Jethro unlocked the door and they went in. It was filled with boxes of stuff, some of it cases of the liquid Morna had put into his tea. Jethro laughed as he saw him looking at it with anticipation.

'Given you a taste for the good stuff, has she? Well, it won't hurt for once. I'll open a bottle and we'll both have a snifter. It'll help us sleep.'

Ronnie remembered drinking the good stuff from a tin mug, but nothing more after that until the morning. Jethro had given him a shake, waking him to a mug of tea and a piece of bread and cheese. He'd had a stinking headache, but he hadn't associated it with the drink he had enjoyed so much the night before. It was just one of the bad heads he sometimes had.

'Get off home now, lad,' Jethro said. 'Your mother will be waiting.'

Ronnie finished his breakfast and left the hut. He couldn't remember why he was in the woods, and he was afraid his mother would take her stick to him again. It was some minutes after he left the hut that he saw something white lying on the ground. He walked up to it, staring down at the body of a naked lady. It was only when he realized that it was Morna that he bent down to touch her. He touched her face first, and then her breasts, her shoulders and then her face again, wondering at how cold she was.

He had tried to make her wake up, because it was cold and she ought not to be lying there like that, but when he shook her, her head just fell to one side. Ronnie suddenly realized it was like Miss Bates all over again, and he backed away, then turned and started to run.

After that the police had come and taken him away again. They had told him that Morna was dead, and his mother kept saying Miss Bates was dead, but he wasn't sure what that meant. He thought if he went back to her van, Morna might give him some more of that stuff he liked. If not, he might go to Jethro's hut and see if there were any bottles left inside . . .

'You look wonderful,' Larch said when Sarah invited him in the next morning. 'That colour suits you – and your hair is pretty.'

Sarah felt the colour rising in her cheeks. Larch wasn't
given to compliments as a rule. 'Thank you. I washed my hair
last night and it went well this morning. Would you like
coffee?'

'No, I don't think so. I would rather get this visit over and
done with, Sarah. I really don't want to go at all, but I gave
my word at a weak moment and I suppose I had better keep
it.'

'Is Madeline a professional artist?' Sarah asked, after calling
goodbye to her grandmother, picking up her jacket and following
Larch outside.

'I don't know all that much about her,' Larch confessed.
'She moved into her cottage at Thorny March a few years
back and she sells a few pictures in a shop at Blakeney I
think. Some of her work is of the Norfolk Coast, I believe,
and the holidaymakers buy it during the summer – but I
imagine she has money. Those lapis lazuli beads she wears
are good quality, as is her other jewellery. I think she has been
married, but I've never seen her husband.'

'Perhaps she ate him like black widow spiders do,' Sarah
said and giggled as she saw Larch's expression.

'I wouldn't be at all surprised,' Larch said, and grinned
back at her. She had such an impish look about her at that
moment and it made him feel happy to be alive. 'I'm glad
that you are coming with me, Sarah – but then I always enjoy
being with you. We have fun, don't we?'

'Yes, we always have,' she said. 'I haven't told you yet, but
I'm going for an audition in London next week. It's for a job
on a cruise ship leaving for New York at the end of November.
I think it gets back sometime in January.'

'That will be an experience for you.' Larch concentrated
on the road. Thorny March was a couple of miles past Thorny
village, and the roads were narrow and twisty. Cars had to
pull over into little stopping places if another happened to
come in the opposite direction. 'I've been thinking of going
abroad for a few months myself. I need to stretch myself as
an artist if I'm ever going to be any good.'

'Oh . . . that is a good idea,' Sarah said, though it wasn't
quite what she was thinking. 'I hope you won't disappear for
ever.'

'I shouldn't think so for a moment,' Larch said. 'We're

nearly there. I think Madeline's cottage is just around this bend. I telephoned earlier and said I was coming. She said she would be here . . .' He wasn't sure why he had changed the subject, except that he was afraid to say what was really on his mind.

He pulled the car to a halt in a lay-by just down from the cottage, because the road was too narrow to park right outside. Then he got out and went round to open Sarah's door for her. He gave her his hand, smiling down at her, his heart jerking.

'Shall we go and see what the lady has to say?'

'I'm not an expert on art like you,' Sarah said, 'but I know what I like – and I like your pictures, Larch. You haven't shown me your new stuff yet.'

'I will soon,' he promised.

They went round to the back of the cottage. Madeline's studio was in her large garden and she had told Larch that he would find her there.

She came to the door as they approached, her eyes moving past him to settle on Sarah with evident annoyance. 'I didn't know you were bringing Sarah,' she said.

'Oh, we have an appointment later so it saved time,' Larch replied easily. 'Besides, Sarah has a good eye and you wanted an opinion, didn't you?'

Madeline hadn't wanted any such thing as Larch already knew, but she had no alternative but to smile and invite them both in. There was a strong smell of turpentine and paint. Examples of her work hung from every available space on the upper walls and were piled up against the bottom half. She had three easels and there was an unfinished painting on each of them. Larch approached the first easel and stood staring at it thoughtfully.

Sarah took one look and decided that it wasn't her kind of thing, though she could see it was well executed. It was very stylized stuff, and as she wandered away she could see that much of it was very similar: pretty pictures of Norfolk cottages; pictures of beaches with fishing nets, boats and the sea; some of Blakeney Point, others of Old Hunstanton, Cromer and Snettisham.

Larch was giving Madeline his professional opinion. She could see that Madeline was pleased that she had left them to it, and she continued to walk around the studio looking at various pictures. At one end there were some larger canvases facing the wall. Curious, she pulled one back and stared as she saw something very different. These pictures were not at all like the others. They seemed to be much darker, painted in a bolder style, the paint much thicker, and were of flames, with figures dancing in the background.

Fascinated, Sarah moved another two canvases and discovered similar pictures, but one was rather shocking for it portrayed a naked girl lying on the ground and a man bending over her. He was sexually aroused and intent on plundering the girl, who looked very young. She pulled it forward quickly, her cheeks warm, and stared at the picture behind it. This time it portrayed the naked man alone, his body painted with blue streaks, his hair long and wild, his eyes staring as if in some kind of a trance. His pose with his arms held up to the sky, as if in some unholy prayer, was enough to make her shiver. Especially, when she saw the devil mask lying at his feet.

'What are you doing?' Madeline's voice was sharp and angry. 'Please do not touch those pictures. They are not for sale and are very private.'

Sarah flushed with embarrassment, aware that she had seen something she was not supposed to. She moved away instantly.

'I'm sorry. I didn't realize.'

Madeline's gaze narrowed. 'They were commissioned for someone. He asked me not to show them. Please do not talk about what you have seen.'

'No, of course not,' Sarah said. 'But they were rather good, I thought.'

Madeline was silent, her eyes glinting now, as if Sarah's praise had amused her. 'Liked them, did you? Well, well, now that is a surprise.'

'Are you hiding secrets from me?' Larch asked her. 'Or am I allowed to see?'

'I would rather you didn't,' Madeline said, bestowing a sweet smile on him. 'They aren't finished yet, which is why they are still here. Besides, they were a private commission and I ought not to have left them where they could be seen. It wasn't Sarah's fault, it was mine.'

'I am sorry. I should have asked first,' Sarah said. 'I think you must be very proud to be able to paint so well . . .' She said it to ease things but saw that Madeline liked being praised.

'That picture of a cottage is very nice. I might buy it for Gran's birthday.'

'Let me give it to you,' Madeline said. 'Just to show that there are no hard feelings.'

'Oh no, I couldn't . . .'

'I'll buy it,' Larch said and took out his wallet. 'I think you said most of these sell for five pounds?'

'Yes, but I would rather give it to Sarah.'

'We'll pay for it,' Larch said. 'And now we ought to be going. I think you have good commercial talent, Madeline.'

Sarah saw the fury in Madeline's eyes and the way her hands clenched at her sides. It was obvious that she thought Larch's comment was a deadly insult. Sarah was glad when they were sitting in the car once more. He tossed the painting carelessly on to the back seat.

'I trust you didn't really want that picture?'

'You know I didn't. Gran would hate it. I just wanted to cover my mistake.'

Larch frowned as he released the brake. 'What was so special about those pictures?'

'One was of a very young girl lying naked on the ground with a sexually aroused naked man bending over her, another was of the same man standing by a fire with his arms outstretched. They had dark backgrounds and orange flames and were startling. As different from her other stuff as it is possible to be.'

'Sounds fascinating. Where do you think she got her inspiration from?'

'I don't know . . . unless . . .' Sarah shot a look at him as they reached a wider stretch of road. 'Unless it was from experience, in the woods, perhaps? One of the figures in the background was wearing a devil mask, and I'm not sure but I think I may have seen the man in her painting who was not masked.'

Larch swerved to avoid a pheasant that had started up in front of the car. He pulled into a lay-by and switched off, turning to look at her.

'Who was he?'

'I can't be certain – but I think it might be Simon Beecham.'

'Good grief!' Larch pursed his lips. 'If you're right . . . it explains why Sir James hasn't called the police in to stop all that stuff going on in his woods. If that got out it would cause a terrible scandal.'

'Yes, it might,' Sarah agreed. 'Do you think Madeline is a part of all that too?'

'Yes, it wouldn't surprise me. There is something of the nymphomaniac about her. I've always thought so.'

'If she has the paintings, might she also have a gown and mask – or would that belong to someone else?'

'You mean the man who plays the part of the devil in their rituals?' Larch nodded, his eyes narrowed. 'I should think that likely, and if I'm right that means—'

'If Morna was having his child rather than Sir James's, he might have killed her to keep it quiet. He could have been the one who attacked Mrs Roberts.'

'Yes,' Larch agreed. 'That sounds very possible, Sarah. I shall report to Ben this evening and tell him what you've discovered – but in the meantime, I suggest we go and have our lunch.'

It was quite late when Ben returned to the house that evening, but Larch had sat up for him and was lounging by a flickering fire reading a book. He smiled at Ben as he entered and offered him a nightcap.

'I don't mind if I do – just a small one,' Ben said and sat down, stretching out his legs as Larch went to pour him the whisky. 'Thank you. What kind of a day did you have?'

'Rather a productive one. At least, it was Sarah who made the discovery, as always.'

Ben arched his brows. 'Don't tell me there's another dead body?'

'No, but something equally as interesting,' Larch said. 'Sarah and I went to see Madeline Lewis-Brown, an artist who lives in Thorny March. She had asked me to give an opinion on her work. I was reluctant to go because quite honestly I think what she really wanted was to seduce me.'

Ben laughed. 'Maneater, is she?'

'Sarah compared her to a black widow spider and I think that about sums her up.'

'That girl of yours has a keen eye.'

'Yes,' Larch said. 'Not that she's my girlfriend in that way.'

'For the moment perhaps.' Ben smiled easily. 'So what did she see that she ought not to have done?'

'Some rather explicit paintings of naked men and women

dancing round a fire in the woods. She said that one of them was of a man about to have sexual relations with a young girl, and there was a devil mask in some of the paintings.'

'That accords very well with what you've told me of the lady so far. It seems that she is a member of our little band of devil-worshippers, doesn't it – and I think I know another.' Ben frowned. 'I have a hunch that Simon Beecham may be one of the members – perhaps even the pivotal member if those pictures happen to be of him. It sounds as if he might be the high priest of this cult.'

'How did you know? Sarah said that the man in the picture might be him, but she doesn't know him and wasn't sure. She has seen him twice before but never to speak to.'

'When I interviewed Sir James this morning I suspected that he might be protecting someone. He isn't the kind of man to put up with that sort of thing going on, particularly on his land, which means there had to be a good reason for his forbearance. It makes sense if his nephew was involved – and it explains the quarrel you overheard that day.'

'I don't imagine his forbearance was out of family love,' Larch said. 'Family pride might have something to do with it, though I think there may be something else behind it. Sir James was ranting at him that day at the Chestnuts and Simon appeared to threaten his uncle. Sarah had pushed the window open so that we could hear, and like an idiot I closed it before we heard any more.'

Ben looked thoughtful. 'I am certain both Sir James and his nephew may be mixed up in this business somehow. I'm not sure that either of them are murderers, but they certainly have something to hide.'

'Yes, I think that is a fair assumption,' Larch said, and then recalled the letter Sarah had given him. 'This was delivered to the dower house this morning. Rather than push it through Miss Bates's letterbox, Sarah thought you might know what to do with it.'

Ben took the letter and stared at it for a moment, and then he took a small penknife from his pocket and slit it open. He unfolded the single sheet of paper and whistled between his teeth.

'It's a bank statement. It may surprise you to know that Janet Bates had thirty thousand pounds in her account.'

'That is a lot of money,' Larch said. 'You wouldn't think she had that kind of money from the way she lived. Could it have been from blackmail, do you think?'

'That is something I intend to find out,' Ben said. 'I have discovered the name of her solicitor. Tomorrow I'm going to ask him about the will, who benefits – and if he knows where her money came from.'

'It looks as if she might have been blackmailing someone, but one shouldn't jump to conclusions.'

'You know, I think Sarah may be right when she says there is more than one murderer,' Ben said. 'But we are getting closer, Larch. At least we have more clues than the police have, though of course I shall share our findings with them as soon as I think I know where all this is leading.'

'You don't yet?'

'Not for certain. I may be a little closer when I've had a talk to Simon Beecham – and possibly Madeline Lewis-Brown . . .'

Nine

Sarah rang the hospital again the next morning and received the welcome news that Mrs Roberts had recovered consciousness. She was told that the postmistress was still very ill, but they were now hopeful of a full recovery. Feeling relieved, Sarah asked Andrews if he would drive her into Norwich so that she could visit her.

Mrs Roberts was lying with her eyes closed when Sarah went into the side ward, and she looked so fragile that Sarah hesitated, wondering if it would be better to go away again, but then she opened her eyes and looked at Sarah.

'Sarah,' she said in a faint whispery voice unlike her usual confident tones. 'They tell me I owe my life to you . . .' Tears trickled down her cheeks. 'Thank you, my dear . . .'

Sarah sat on the chair next to the bed. 'I only did what anyone would in the circumstances, Mrs Roberts. I was very worried about you.'

'They tell me someone attacked me,' Mrs Roberts said and wrinkled her brow as if distressed. 'A nice policeman came earlier and asked me some questions, but I told him I can't recall anything about it. That is so foolish of me, isn't it? I can remember most things, but not what happened that morning . . .'

'I think it happens sometimes after a bang on the head,' Sarah said. She thought it might be just as well, because if Mrs Roberts had been able to name her attacker that person might have had another go at her. 'I'm just glad that this time whoever it was didn't succeed.'

Mrs Roberts looked a bit upset. 'Do you think it was to do with those awful murders? I thought that perhaps someone had tried to rob me.'

'I hadn't considered that,' Sarah said, looking thoughtful. 'I suppose it might have been that – but surely a thief would have taken what he wanted and run away?' And he was unlikely to have been wearing a black gown and a devil mask, she thought.

'I am not certain which is worse. It is all so horrible. I am not sure I shall feel safe living at the shop alone in future.'

'Perhaps your sister might come and stay?'

'Yes, I know Jilly will come and see me as soon as she can, and she might stay on for a while. We are quite fond of each other but we've always led separate lives.'

'Well, perhaps you can find someone to help you for a few hours in the shop. I am sure there must be people who would like to earn a little money.'

'Yes, perhaps. I shall have to see.' She still looked upset. 'I might sell the shop and retire. Jilly has been on at me to do it for ages, and perhaps I shall.'

'Everyone will miss you,' Sarah said.

'Oh, the shop won't close,' Mrs Roberts said with a faint smile. 'I could have sold it ages ago but I didn't want to. I like talking to people and I thought I should miss it.'

'I should think you might,' Sarah said. 'All this business is so unfortunate and it's a pity it happened, but you mustn't let it make you afraid of life.'

'I can't understand why I was attacked,' Mrs Roberts said, a little tearful again. 'It isn't as if I know anything about the murders.'

'Perhaps you know something without realizing that you know,' Sarah suggested. 'You speak to so many people, Mrs Roberts. You may have mentioned something quite innocently.'

'Yes, perhaps.' She sighed and put a hand to her bandaged head. 'I wish I could recall what happened, but that morning is a blank. Oh well, I mustn't worry over it, so the doctors say. It was so sweet of you to come, Sarah dear. I know you and your grandmother called yesterday to bring me those flowers.'

'We have been very concerned for you. I was so pleased this morning when they told me you were recovering.'

'Yes, well, it looks as if I have been lucky,' Mrs Roberts said. 'And that won't please whoever it was that tried to kill me – will it?'

'That is why you have a very nice police constable sitting outside your door, Mrs Roberts. He will be there until they have sorted all this unpleasant stuff out.'

'And that can't be soon enough for me!'

Sarah agreed and decided to change the subject. She told Mrs Roberts that she was going to London in a few days for an audition for another job, and the postmistress smiled.

'I do hope you get it, my dear. You certainly deserve it.'

'Thank you. I hope I do, but I expect there will be a lot of girls after the jobs, because it's rather glamorous, isn't it?' The idea of working on a cruise ship to New York had a strong appeal.

They talked about all sorts of things after that, Mrs Roberts telling her something of her life before she married Mr Roberts, and what it was like to be in service. Sarah felt happier about the postmistress's frame of mind when she left twenty minutes or so later.

'Good luck with your job,' Mrs Roberts said as Sarah prepared to leave. 'But you watch yourself with the men on board, Sarah. Rich men always think they can do what they want with girls – like poor Morna. Morna was having a baby, you know. I think it may have been the father who killed her, because she told me he had refused to give her any money.'

'Oh . . .' Sarah's eyes narrowed, because it had come out so unexpectedly. 'I suppose she didn't tell you who he was?'

'No, she stopped short of that . . .' She hesitated and frowned. 'I suspect someone but can't say, because I don't know for sure.'

'Yes, I see. Quite right. Well, I expect the police will be trying to discover who he is and then they will question him.'

'All they seem to do is waste their time arresting poor Ronnie Miller,' Mrs Roberts said, and looked strange as if something had come to her quite suddenly. 'I was saying that to someone and . . . then I can't remember anything more.'

'It will probably come back to you,' Sarah said and smiled at her. 'Don't worry about it, Mrs Roberts. I expect the police will catch him very soon now.'

She was thoughtful as she left the hospital. If Mrs Roberts had insinuated that she knew the identity of the man who had fathered Morna's child, it might possibly have been the reason for the attack on her. But then again, it might have been for a totally different reason.

*   *   *

Ben stopped his car in the drive that led up to the nursery office. It was a rather muddy track, and he grimaced as he got out and put his foot in a puddle. It had been raining for most of the night. He could see a large greenhouse ahead, and a brick-built office with glass windows that looked out on the drive. Away to his right there were some acres of small trees, and larger ones beyond. On his right there were small shrubs and roses. A man was pruning the roses, and Ben hesitated before approaching him.

'Is Mr Simon Beecham anywhere about?' he asked.

'He might be. Who wants to see him?'

'I'm Ben Marshall, a friend of Sir William Meadows.'

'You're the one poking his nose into other people's business, then,' the man said and scowled at him. He clipped savagely at a rose bush. 'As I have it, you retired from the force last year. Who gave you the right to be asking questions?'

'I am working in a private capacity,' Ben said easily. 'But I do have the full approval of the Norwich police. This case is a bit off their patch so they asked if I would work with them.'

'Oh . . .' The man straightened up from his work, clutching his pruning shears in his right hand. 'I suppose I'd better talk to you then or we shall have those idiots out here again.'

'I wouldn't call them that, Mr Beecham, though I know they wasted time arresting Ronnie Miller.'

'You don't think he killed her then?'

'Morna Scaffry – or Miss Bates?'

'Either,' Simon said and shrugged, as if it were all the same to him. 'Shall we go into the office? It's time for a break anyway. Sometimes I wish I'd chosen an indoor occupation, especially when it is wet and cold.'

'Not too cold today, is it?'

'It's wet and uncomfortable and you soon turn cold,' Simon said as he went into his office. A pretty woman was typing but he bent his head and whispered something in her ear and she left, glancing at Ben nervously. 'Ally will bring us a mug of coffee. You wanted to ask me some questions I believe?'

'Yes, if you wouldn't mind answering them?'

'And if I say no? I suppose you will send someone with a warrant? I might as well get it over with. Yes, I did know

Morna, and I did have a relationship with her for a while. She tried to blame me for the child she was having, but that was a lie.'

'Can you be sure of that?'

'Pretty sure,' Simon said. 'I had the mumps badly as a young man and I've been told it is unlikely I shall father a child.'

'Ah, I see,' Ben said. 'Would I be able to get confirmation of this from your doctor, sir?'

'Possibly. It isn't set in concrete, but it is unlikely. She asked me for money and I told her to get lost. She threatened to go to my uncle. I have no idea whether or not she did, but I doubt if he would kill her. He was more likely to have given her the money to keep her quiet. I've never known him to let gypsies stay on his land before, but he told his gamekeepers to leave them alone. I haven't the faintest idea why.'

'Are you suggesting some kind of a relationship between Morna and your uncle, sir?'

'I have no idea. I'm just telling you because you obviously suspect me of killing her. I gave her a good slapping a week or so earlier, but I didn't kill her. That is all I have to say on the matter, and if you have any more questions I should like a formal meeting with my solicitor present.'

'I don't think we are anywhere near an arrest just yet,' Ben said, 'though the police may wish to interview you on other matters. It has come to my attention that you may have been involved in some sort of pagan rites in the woods. These activities sometimes involve the mutilation of animals.'

'I have never killed a cat in my life, and I deny being involved in any such group. I'm very busy, Mr Marshall, and if you don't mind I should like to get on with my work.'

He left the office abruptly just as the girl brought a tray of coffee and biscuits. She looked startled as she put the tray down.

'I thought Mr Beecham wanted his coffee?'

'I expect he will come back when I've gone,' Ben told her with a smile. 'Don't worry about it, I'm leaving now.'

'He's been in a mood for the past couple of weeks or so,' Ally said. 'I've never known him to be so short-tempered.'

'I dare say he has something on his mind,' Ben said as he left.

He was thoughtful as he walked back to his car, taking care to avoid the puddle as he got back inside. Simon Beecham was on edge over something. He had answered the questions about Morna calmly enough, but the nerves had cut in as soon as Ben had mentioned the pagan rites in the woods. And he'd lied! He knew all about what was going on there and it worried him.

Ben wasn't sure whether or not he believed Simon about not being able to father a child. He had obviously had an affair with Morna, and she had accused him of fathering her baby, asking him for money. He wondered if she had also asked Sir James, and what the outcome had been.

Would he have paid her in cash, and if so – where was the money?

He knew that the police had searched her caravan but he also knew that someone else had done that first. His colleagues hadn't found any money, but he would talk to them again and see if a bank book of any kind had come to light. Gypsies didn't often put their money in banks, but you never knew for sure.

Meanwhile, he had decided to pop home for a quick visit. Cathy had phoned him earlier in the day with a report on the cats. Something she'd said had made him a bit concerned about one of the cats, and he was sure his wife wasn't telling him something concerning his prize female. Besides, he wanted to have a look at some of his old case notes. Something at the back of his mind was bugging him and he wasn't sure why . . .

Andrews found the wreath lying outside the front door when he opened up the next morning. He stared at it for a moment, then went back into the house to fetch his gardening gloves before picking it up. It was made of dark green laurel leaves and tied with black ribbons, and a message was attached. He swore beneath his breath as he read what it said.

It was addressed to Sarah and warned that she might not see the next wreath delivered to her. The threat was obvious, and Andrews hesitated over what to do about it. He had no intention of telling Mrs Beaufort or Sarah about the wretched thing, but he ought to let Captain Meadows know.

*   *   *

Madeline Lewis-Brown glanced round as the door of her studio opened that afternoon, a frown on her face, but it disappeared as she saw who it was and she smiled.

'Darling, I wondered how long it would be before you came to see me. It's ages since we spent any time together. I haven't finished your painting yet. Are you going to pose for me today?'

'No, I'm not,' Simon said and glared at her. 'I was a bloody fool to let you persuade me into it in the first place – any of it. I've come to ask you to destroy those pictures. That damned ex-police inspector has started sniffing around, and I don't want him to find them. They could incriminate me, and I have no intention of going to prison for having sexual relations with underage girls.'

'Don't look so outraged, Simon,' Madeline said, a dangerous gleam in her eyes. 'You loved every minute of what we did, don't pretend to be righteous now.'

'I was out of my head with those damned drugs you gave me. And the girl was out cold. She probably didn't even know what was going on, poor bitch. I only got involved with it through you, Maddy, and I wish I hadn't. I was a bloody fool. I think Marshall suspects I killed Morna!'

'You didn't, did you?' Madeline's eyes narrowed as she looked at him, faintly amused by his outburst. 'No, I thought not. Who is being a silly boy then?'

'Don't talk to me that way,' he muttered. He moved back as she reached out to touch him. 'Stop that! I'm not in the mood for sex at the moment.'

'You seldom are these days,' Madeline said. 'It takes some of Maddy's special drink to get you going, doesn't it, darling – but how you love it then! You're a veritable god then, my precious. It's a pity to waste all that energy on those virgins who don't appreciate you for what you are. Shall I make you a nice drink now?'

'I told you I don't want that! I've finished with all that stuff and I want you to burn those paintings.' He walked to the end of the studio and started pulling them out, throwing them down in a careless heap.

'What do you think you are doing with those?' she asked, her voice sharp and angry. 'They took me hours to paint and they are some of the best things I've ever done. I'm certainly not going to destroy them.'

'I'll burn them myself!'

'Leave them alone! They belong to me, not you, Simon. If you destroy them you will regret it.'

Something in her voice made Simon look at her. Her eyes were glittering the way they did sometimes when they were in the woods, and he felt chilled, mesmerized. She was so dominating, and he had been drawn into her circle like a fluttering moth to the flame.

'If the police get them I'm done for.'

'Silly boy, Simon. As if I would let anyone harm you. You know that I love you. I need you, Simon. We all need you. You are our love god. Without you the ceremonies would be useless.' Her eyes seemed to be sapping his will. 'Leave the paintings alone. I will get rid of them my way, and no one else will see them. I promise you it will be all right.'

Simon went to her. Sometimes it seemed as if he had no will of his own when she commanded him. He was her slave, hers to do with as she would. He had tried to break free before, but she would not let him go.

'You've got to protect me, Maddy,' he said and let her lead him through into the back room where the couch was. 'I don't want to go to prison. I might even hang . . .'

'Why should you, my darling? You've done nothing wrong,' Madeline said. 'Now, I am going to give you one of my special drinks and then you will forget all about this nasty business . . .'

The shed in the woods had a new lock on it and Ronnie couldn't get in. He pulled at it but it refused to break and he turned away, feeling annoyed. He had helped himself to the good stuff one night, and it had made him feel wonderful. Now he wanted more. He couldn't sleep without it, because he had nightmares. He kept seeing Miss Bates lying on the floor and Morna spread out on the ground with no clothes on. The pictures frightened him.

He had been back to Morna's caravan to look for her a couple of times but she wasn't there. Miss Bates wasn't at her house either. His mother had told him they were dead, but he still wasn't sure what that meant – unless it was that they had gone away.

He decided he would go to Morna's caravan and see if she

had come back. She might have some of the good stuff there, and she might give him some of it, because she was nice.

When he got to the caravan, he saw that Jethro was sitting outside by a fire. He stared at him eagerly as the gypsy looked up and nodded to him to sit down.

'Is Morna here?'

'Morna is dead,' Jethro said and scowled.

'What does that mean?'

'You poor bugger,' Jethro said. It didn't matter how often you told Ronnie something – it seemed as if he couldn't get it straight in his head. 'It means she has gone away.'

'Will she come back?'

'She can't, Ronnie. She's buried in the earth six feet down, the silly bitch. I warned her about him, but she wouldn't listen.'

'I don't think I like her being down there.' Ronnie felt all mixed up and angry. Morna had been nice to him. 'Why is she buried?'

'Because that bugger done for her,' Jethro said. 'He had been havin' it off with her, Ronnie. And then when he got tired of it, the bugger killed her, and that's why she's buried and can't come back again.'

Ronnie remembered how cold Morna had been lying on the ground, and her face had looked funny. 'Does it hurt to be killed?'

'Yes, it hurts,' Jethro said angrily. 'One of these days I'm going to hurt him. I'll make him sorry for what he done to her!'

'Do you know who killed her?' Ronnie asked, because he was beginning to feel very angry inside. Morna had been so soft to touch and so nice, and he didn't like the idea of somebody hurting her. She had gone away because of it, and he didn't like that either. He wanted her to come back but she couldn't because she was buried deep in the earth. Now that was something that Ronnie did understand. He had buried the roots of plants and bulbs – but people shouldn't be buried.

'I reckon it was Simon Beecham,' Jethro snarled, his eyes glittering. 'Stands to reason it was that bugger, and as soon as I can prove it I'm going to teach him a few lessons.'

'Simon Beecham . . .' Ronnie thought about it. He didn't forget names, and he knew Sir James Beecham, because he had worked up at his house, doing jobs for Harold Jackson. 'Does he live up at the big house?'

'Nah, his uncle wouldn't have him, especially if he knew all I know,' Jethro said. 'He's got a nursery for trees and things just through Thorny village.'

Ronnie thought he knew where that was, because he'd been to fetch some trees with Mr Jackson. He was the head groom up at the big house, and he sometimes gave Ronnie a morning's work cleaning the stables and spreading the muck on the gardens. Ronnie remembered that on one occasion he'd helped to plant big trees they had fetched from the nursery. So he knew where it was, because he didn't forget things like that.

'Want a drop of this, do you?' Jethro pulled out a bottle of the good stuff and showed him. 'Here, have as much as you want. It don't mean much to me now. I schemed and pinched things for money for Morna. She wanted a flower shop and somewhere nice to live. I was saving up for it for her, but she had money of her own – five hundred pounds in a post office book. What do you think of that? I know what I think. Someone gave her money to keep her quiet, but then he decided that she couldn't be trusted so he killed her.'

Ronnie took a swig from the bottle Jethro had given him. He could feel the fiery liquid warming his belly and he grinned.

'We should kill him,' he said, repeating innocently what he'd heard without understanding what it meant. 'The bugger what hurt her.'

'Yeah, that's just what we ought to do,' Jethro said. 'Go on, drink up, lad. Plenty more where that came from.'

'I shall miss you,' Larch said. He had come to the station to see Sarah off. 'But I hope you get the job. It will be a wonderful experience for you.'

'Yes, it would be lovely. You will telephone me and let me know if anything happens, won't you?'

'Yes, of course, though it all seems to have gone a bit quiet at the moment, that's why Ben went home to see to his cats. He rang me earlier, said he's working on several ideas. I think he has made up his mind who the murderer is, but has to find a way of proving it.'

'He thinks it's Simon, doesn't he? At least we know that

he might be the father of Morna's child, though he told Ben it wasn't possible.'

'He could be lying. Ben hasn't found any medical evidence to support that yet.'

'Well, you can tell me everything when I get back,' Sarah said and leaned forward to kiss him on the cheek. As she did so, he turned his head and their lips met. It surprised her, and she felt a rather nice tingling sensation. 'Larch . . .'

'Have a good time and take care of yourself,' he said and looked a little embarrassed. The guard blew the whistle at that moment. 'You had better get on the train, Sarah. Let me know the time of your arrival when you come home and I'll pick you up.'

'Yes, all right,' she said and jumped up the step into the corridor. 'Take care, Larch. You won't do anything silly while I'm away?'

'Nothing ever happens to me. You are the one who makes all the discoveries, Sarah. I shall see you when you get back.'

'Yes, of course. Bye, then . . .' She stood at the window and waved to him until she could no longer see him standing on the platform, then went into the carriage and sat down.

She opened her detective story and began to read it. In the story the detective made lots of discoveries that led him to the murderer. She wasn't certain that anything they had discovered so far had the slightest bearing on the murders at Beecham Thorny.

Larch was relieved that Sarah was going to be away from Beecham Thorny for a few days. Andrews had phoned him about the wreath and he'd telephoned Ben to pass the information on.

'Don't tell her,' Ben said. 'It may just be someone playing a nasty practical joke, but keep an eye on her.'

'She's going to London for a few days, to do some auditions.'

'Ah, good thing,' Ben said. 'It will be nice for her to get away, and she'll be safe there. If that wreath is connected to the murders it means that she has been treading on someone's toes.'

'Well, I expect everyone knows she found Mrs Roberts – and then there was the episode of those paintings. Do you think . . .'

'Perhaps,' Ben said. 'I am doing some research at the moment. I don't want to say anything just yet, but I may be on to something important . . .'

Larch wondered exactly what Ben meant. He hadn't liked to push him, and it wasn't so important because Sarah was away for the moment – but his remarks were very thought-provoking.

He hadn't a clue as to what was going on himself, but he would be very relieved when this business was over. At first it had seemed amusing to try and find out what they could, but with the second murder he had become more uncomfortable, and after the threat to Sarah he was beginning to feel very worried.

Ten

'Thank you. We'll let you know, Sarah. Leave your telephone number with Liz, please, and ask her to send the next girl on.'

Sarah walked off the stage, sure that she had failed her audition. She pulled a face at her friend Mary, who was standing with a crowd of other young hopefuls waiting backstage.

'I only sang a couple of verses so that's probably it. Some of the girls were given twice as long.'

'Shame,' Mary said. 'Never mind, you may find something else. Talk to Liz. She was telling me about two other auditions that are being held this week.'

'Right, thanks.' Mary's name had been called. Sarah wished her friend luck and went to talk to the woman who was looking after the girls that morning.

'How did you get on, love?'

Liz Rankin was a small, grey-haired lady with years of experience in the business. She'd held various jobs from dresser to continuity and had comforted hundreds of tearful girls when things turned sour.

'They said to leave my telephone number with you.'

'Did they?' Liz smiled. 'Well, that's hopeful. It means you're on their list of possibilities.'

'Really? They had me off so quickly that I thought it was hopeless.'

'No, that's not so. If you were out they wouldn't ask for a telephone number.'

'Fingers crossed then.'

Sarah walked away to look at the wall of fame. The theatre had been used as a venue for all kinds of productions over the years, and there was a mass of photographs and posters of artistes who had played or sung on stage.

Quite a few were faces Sarah knew well but some of them were of artistes she had never heard of let alone seen on stage. She walked slowly down the line, looking at the faces and costumes, some of decades earlier that she found fascinating: Sarah Bernhardt, Marie Lloyd and Mrs Patrick Campbell amongst them. Suddenly, she stopped in front of a photograph of Shirley Anne Asbury. She had been lovely, a bright, eager young woman with a wonderful smile.

'Some of them are long dead,' Liz said, coming to stand just behind her. 'You're looking at Shirley Anne Asbury. I remember her well. She was lovely, wasn't she? It was tragic the way it all went wrong for her.'

Sarah turned to face her. 'Did you know her well?'

'Yes, quite well. I was the wardrobe mistress when she was appearing in a play here. Lovely actress, she was. It wasn't surprising that all the men were after her.'

'What happened to her?'

'There was a scandal – not when she was here, but a couple of years later. A young man was killed after a party in the South of France, at a villa where she was the guest of honour. The papers said he was either drunk when he fell from that hotel balcony – or he was pushed. Some of them hinted that Shirley Anne's lover pushed him. There had been an argument over her during the evening and the two of them fought. The young one – only nineteen, as I recall – he went off by himself and the police found him splattered over the patio beneath her balcony the next morning.'

'That was very sad, but I don't see why she had to give up her career. She was poised on the verge of stardom, wasn't she?'

'You've heard her story then?' Liz frowned. 'I'm not sure what made her give up. I believe she was terribly distressed over what had happened. She started drinking and she couldn't remember her lines – and then she just walked out of the production she was in, which did her reputation a lot of harm. She disappeared for a long time. There were wild rumours. But then it came out that she'd had a child – a daughter – and that someone had snatched the baby.'

'Oh no! How awful for her! Her career was over and she had lost her child.'

'There was worse,' Liz said. 'Some people thought the baby

was dead – that she might have murdered it by suffocation and then got rid of the body. The nurse stood by her, swearing that the child had been taken from its pram in the garden, and her dresser said that Shirley adored the baby, but it had all been kept secret. The name of its father, everything. That seemed to make the scandal worse, as if there had to be some dark mystery behind it. There had been some talk of Shirley making a comeback, but that stopped it. After that she started drinking for real and ended up in a home for the mentally unstable.'

'Is she still alive?'

'I'm not sure. I believe her dresser had some money left to her and she went off somewhere. I think the baby's nurse hung around for a while.' Liz shrugged. 'Why do you ask?'

'Just interested. I'm researching something about the theatre and silent film stars. I should like to know more. Is there anyone who would know?'

'Her dresser might. Let me think, yes I remember – she was called Janet. Janet Bates.'

'Really?' Sarah felt a flicker of excitement and spoke without thinking. 'Janet was murdered three weeks ago.'

Liz stared at her. 'Is that why you want to know if Shirley Anne is still alive? Janet adored her. She would have done anything for her – at least when I knew her. I always wondered why Janet left her after she got the money.'

'Do you know where the money came from?'

'No idea. I thought it might be an inheritance but I couldn't say.'

At that moment, Mary came bouncing back to join them. Her face was flushed, her eyes bright with excitement.

'I'm in,' she said. 'They told me to tell you, Liz.'

'I thought you would be,' Liz said and smiled. 'Come with me, Mary. I'll fill you in on all the details.'

Sarah watched as they went off to Liz's office. She felt a little pang of envy that her friend had been taken just like that, though she was pleased for her. But her own disappointment meant little beside the interesting story Liz had related.

Janet Bates had been Shirley Anne Asbury's dresser for some years. It wasn't surprising that she had had so many pictures of her. Sarah was thoughtful as she waited for her friend to return. She couldn't help wondering if the old scandal had any bearing on Janet Bates's murder.

'Cheer up,' Mary said as she came back. 'You still have a chance of getting in. And tomorrow there's an audition for a musical at a big theatre in London. We'll go and put our names down now.'

'But you've already been picked for the cruise.'

'I might get the musical too,' Mary said. 'I know which I should prefer. Come on, I'm starving. Let's have coffee and an iced bun first – and then you can tell me what's on your mind.'

'What are you doing, Ronnie?' His mother looked at him from the back door of her cottage. He had been sitting there for ages, sharpening his spade over and over again. 'It's nearly time for your tea. Are you coming in? I've made some of your favourite seed cake.'

Ronnie didn't turn his head to look at her. He was less inclined to do what she told him, and he had become surly of late. Sometimes when he looked at her she felt a shiver of fear trickle down her spine. She didn't know what had happened to him, but he wasn't the great daft lad she had loved and cared for all these years.

'I'm having my tea,' she said. 'Please yourself if you come or not. I shan't wait for you. Surely that spade is sharp enough by now? You hardly ever use it these days.'

Ronnie sometimes did a little work in their garden, but only if she nagged him into it. He was sleeping late in the mornings, and sometimes he didn't come home all night. She wondered where he stayed on those nights, but even though she'd threatened to take her stick to him he hadn't told her when she asked. And when she'd got the stick out from the corner, he had grabbed hold of it.

'No, Ma,' he'd said and there was a glitter in his eyes that chilled her. 'No more.'

She had looked at him for a few seconds and she hadn't liked what she saw. She had been afraid of what he might do if she tried to beat him the way she had countless times in the past. She'd done it for his own good, of course, but she couldn't expect him to understand.

Ronnie had certainly changed and she had no idea why.

* * *

Simon answered the telephone reluctantly. He was pretty sure he knew who was ringing. He didn't want to speak to her, and yet a little voice at the back of his head warned of the consequences if he didn't.

'Yes, Simon Beecham here?'

'Just connecting you,' came the operator's voice.

'You know we have a little gathering planned for this evening, don't you, darling?'

'It's too cold for that sort of stuff tonight.'

'Not in the woods. At my house.'

'I can't make it. I have a prior appointment.'

'Well, you had better get out of it then. We need you here. Don't let me down, Simon. If you do you will be sorry.'

The receiver went down with a bang. Simon winced, feeling angry and yet nervous. It wasn't the first time he'd tried to get out, but he was caught tight. If he hadn't taken part in that ceremony with the girl who was underage, he would have told the rest of them to get lost ages ago. There were too many witnesses, and they would all do what Madeline wanted, because she had something on most of them. If he told her to go to hell he might end up being arrested for having sexual relations with a fifteen-year-old girl. Something he couldn't even remember doing, because he'd been off his head on that damned drug.

The irritation kept nagging at him as he took a bath and dressed for the evening. Madeline was becoming a nuisance. If he had the courage he would teach her a lesson, the way he had done with Morna Scaffry. He frowned as he thought about Morna. She had made him angry that day, going on and on about the baby and wanting money, and he had been almost certain that the child wasn't his, and he'd hated her because she had been with someone else. If he'd thought it was really his . . .

He felt a pang of remorse because of the way he'd treated her that last time, and regret that she'd been so brutally murdered. He supposed that he'd cared for Morna as much as anyone in his life, but she'd made him angry. Not angry enough to kill her though. Quite honestly, he was a bit squeamish about things like that. It was Madeline who sacrificed the animals, using some kind of anaesthetic to knock them out first. If he hadn't been drugged out of his head he didn't think he could have stood that bit.

The sex had been exciting in the beginning. That was what had drawn him into it. He'd never been much good with girls of his own class. Morna had been different. She was a gypsy and that made him feel a bit superior. Then Madeline had come into his life and swept him into the muddy waters of devil rites and the kind of sexual activity that he could hardly have imagined.

She was right. He had loved it at the beginning, but now it frightened him. He was frightened of what was happening to him, to his mind and his body. He was no longer able to perform in normal situations. That damned stuff Maddy gave him had taken him over.

It was dark outside because there was no moon, the clouds having obscured it. He left the house, treading carefully as he made his way towards his car. Maddy would be annoyed if he arrived with mud on his shoes, and he didn't want to upset her too much just yet.

He had almost reached his car when a dark shape loomed up out of the blackness, startling him.

'What the . . .?' he said, just as the hard object came crashing down on his skull, felling him. Mercifully he had lost consciousness when the blade of a sharp instrument was driven down on his throat, severing his head almost completely from his body, blood oozing on to the gravel drive.

At that moment the moon sailed out from behind the clouds, and the murderer looked down, smiling. For a moment the avenger stood staring at Simon's lifeless body before turning away.

It would be good to welcome Sarah home with some flowers, Larch thought. She was arriving later that morning, and from her telephone call she was a bit despondent. Apparently, she'd auditioned for two jobs and at both of them she had been told to leave her phone number, but as yet she hadn't heard anything. Yes, flowers would cheer her up, he decided.

He drew up outside the nursery and was walking up the gravel drive just as the screaming started. Seeing the young girl standing near the house, he quickened his pace, because he could just glimpse something lying on the ground and he thought it might be a body.

'Hello . . .?' he called. 'Is something . . .' the words died on his lips as he saw the mutilated body lying there and felt sick. 'My God! When did this happen?'

'I don't kn-know . . .' Ally said, stumbling over her words as she tried to answer him. 'I came a few minutes ago and found him lying here.' She was shaking, hysterical as she started to sob wildly. 'It's horrible . . . horrible! Who would do such a thing?'

'I don't know. It's a wretched thing for you to find.'

As she turned to him, Larch put his arms about her, holding her as she sobbed for a while, and then she pushed away from him, gazing up at him with fear in her eyes.

'Who are you?'

'Captain Meadows. My father is Sir William, the local JP – we live over the way at Thorny Hall. I came to buy some flowers, but forget about that. We have to telephone the police. Have you the key to your office?'

'Yes.' She nodded, wiping her face with the clean white handkerchief he gave her. 'Yes. Simon thought it was best for me to be able to lock up or get in . . .' She swallowed hard. 'Shall I telephone them – or shall you?'

'I'll do it,' Larch said. 'There's someone else I need to ring – Ben Marshall.'

'I remember he came here. Simon was in a foul mood after he left.'

'Mr Marshall is ex-Scotland Yard. He has been investigating these murders. But I'll telephone the Norwich police first and then Ben. Fortunately, he returned last night.'

Larch made the necessary calls. Ally was sitting down at her desk, still looking very pale.

'I don't know what I should have done if you hadn't come.' She twisted the handkerchief in her hands nervously. 'It was such a shock. I just started screaming.'

'Anyone would,' Larch said. 'I've never seen anything as nasty in civilian life. Killing someone is bad enough, but to . . .' He shook his head. The sight had turned his stomach sour, though he'd seen worse during the war.

'I don't know what to do. Should I carry on here or go home?'

'I think you must stay here until the police come,' he replied, 'but after that . . .' He sighed with relief as he heard a car engine, and then a door slamming as Ben got out and came towards them.

'Stay in the office, both of you,' he said. 'The police will want to search for clues, but I'm just going to have a quick look before they get here.' Ben was as good as his word. He returned in a couple of minutes looking grave. 'That's nasty. It was you who found the body, Ally?'

'Yes, sir. I had just come into work. I opened the office but then I saw something lying near the house and I went to look . . .'

'And I turned up a few seconds after,' Larch said. 'I came to buy some flowers for Sarah. She's coming home this morning.'

'Good thing you were here,' Ben said. He smiled gently at Ally. 'Is there anything else you can tell me? Any strange phone calls, anything different these past few days?'

'No, not really,' she replied. 'Simon has been in an awful mood for a couple of weeks or so . . .' She hesitated and then frowned. 'Sometimes he seemed nervous, especially after you spoke to him. He was very short with me, which is unusual – but I think he was worried about something.'

'Yes, I imagine he might have been,' Ben said and nodded to himself. 'Well, the police may be a while coming, Ally. I think you could go home, my dear. One of my colleagues will probably want to interview you, so leave me your name and address. This is just a caution, but don't leave the village for the moment, please.'

She stared at him in horror. 'You don't think I could do something like that?'

'No, I am quite certain you didn't,' Ben replied and smiled. 'It is just that you may be needed again. You see, you may remember something that you can't think of at the moment – something that might help us sort this mystery out.'

Ally wrote her own address down, and Ben handed her a small piece of paper with two telephone numbers. 'This is where I am staying for the moment, and this is my home number. Even if you don't think of anything for a week or two I want you to ring me when it happens.'

'Yes, sir,' she said, looking doubtful. 'But I don't think I shall remember.'

'Are you all right to get home?' Larch asked. 'I could take you and come back later.'

'No, thank you, Captain Meadows,' she said. 'I have my

bicycle. If I leave it here I've got to come back and fetch it, and I don't think I want to. I don't think I want to come back here ever.'

'No, I can quite understand that,' Ben said. 'Off you go then, Ally. I may come to see you myself another day.'

He watched as she went out, fetched her bicycle from behind the office and peddled off as fast as she could.

'What a terrible shock for the poor girl,' he remarked to Larch. 'A nasty business. It must have taken some force to sever the head like that. Whoever did it meant business.'

'Yes, you're right. It puts a new complexion on the case, doesn't it? I mean, I thought you were considering Simon Beecham as the murderer?'

'I considered him, but I wasn't ever very much inclined. I think our Simon was a bit of a coward at heart. He was involved in some pretty murky stuff that might have landed him in trouble with the police, but I somehow don't see him as murdering Morna Scaffry or Miss Bates.'

'Was he killed because he knew something about it – could he have known who the murderer was?'

'He might. At the moment I am as stuck for clues as you are, Larch. For one thing there is no murder weapon that I can see – so that means the murderer took it with him.'

'You think it was a man then?'

'Almost certainly,' Ben said. 'The force used to achieve such a clean cut would need a man's strength – which rather messes up my theory. I had a woman down for Morna's murder.'

'A woman?' Larch was startled. 'Really? I would never have thought that. I mean, she was naked and that suggests a sexual motive, doesn't it?'

'It was probably intended to look that way. Or perhaps she was set upon in her bed and escaped into the woods but got caught again. She might have been stripped after she was killed. Inspector Morrison thought her body had been moved, because there were marks on her heels, as if she had been dragged. He believes she could have been killed in the caravan – hence the mess.'

'Is that what you think?'

'It's one theory,' Ben said. 'Or it could have gone something like this . . .' He wrinkled his brow in thought. 'She may have left the caravan dressed only in some flimsy night attire, perhaps because she heard something. The murderer seized the chance presented, killed her and then her clothes were removed to make it look as if it were a different type of crime.'

'So that would make it premeditated rather than something done in anger?'

'Oh, yes, I am pretty sure the killer plans his or her next move,' Ben replied. 'Morna's murder was for a reason, as was that of Miss Bates – though I can't find the connection. And I certainly have no idea why Simon was killed at the moment. Indeed, his murder makes nonsense of the theory I had almost settled on. I was thinking about talking to Morrison about bringing someone in for questioning – but now I'm not sure.'

'I can't make head or tail of it all. At the start I thought it must be easy enough to discover the culprit but it just keeps getting more and more tangled.'

It was half an hour before the police arrived. They asked Larch a few questions, which he answered with one eye on his watch, knowing that he was going to be very late picking Sarah up from the station.

When he finally got away, he drove immediately to the station but the train from London had arrived and departed before he got there. He looked for Sarah in the small waiting room but there was no sign of her, and he realized that she must have decided to find some other way of reaching the dower house. He frowned as he went back to the car and set off for Beecham Thorny. It was a nuisance that he had been so long delayed, and he hadn't even managed to get Sarah the flowers he'd been going to buy her.

As he drove through the main street, he saw that the village shop was open for business and wondered who was looking after it since Mrs Roberts was still in the hospital.

Sarah had waited several minutes for Larch to arrive, but when he didn't she telephoned her grandmother's house. Millie answered and told her that Andrews had taken Amelia visiting. Replacing the telephone, Sarah hesitated but decided against phoning Larch's home. He was unlikely to have forgotten her, which meant he was busy doing something more important.

The station at Thorny Junction was midway between the two villages, and it wasn't really that far to walk, especially as the sun had decided to come through. Even though it was the end of October now, it was really quite pleasant. The fresh air would do Sarah good, drive away some of the gloom that had been hanging over her since she'd left town. She'd gone with high hopes, but she hadn't heard from either of the auditions, which probably meant that she hadn't made the grade.

Her disappointment was considerable, but she tried to put it from her mind, and, as she walked past the village shop, she was intrigued to see that it was open for business. She decided to pop in and say hello, because it must be Jilly, Mrs Roberts's sister.

The shop was empty of customers, but a rather plump lady was busily dusting some of the shelves. She turned and beamed at Sarah.

'What can I do for you, my dear?' She had a broad Devon accent and her voice was warm and friendly.

'I just came in to say hello,' Sarah told her. 'I thought it couldn't be Mrs Roberts because Gran told me she isn't expected home for a few days yet.'

'Will you be Sarah, then?' Jilly asked and smiled as Sarah nodded. 'Well, there's a love. Betty told me you were in London trying for a new job. She's that lucky to be alive, and it's all down to you. We're both so grateful to you, my lovey.'

'Really, I did very little,' Sarah said and blushed. 'But I'm glad I came to see her just the same. If I hadn't . . .'

'The murderer would have finished her off,' Jilly said. 'We had a do like this where I live a few years back. I told Betty at the time that the police never got the ones behind it – all that devil worship going on and they arrested one man. There was a pack of them, you mark my words.'

'You had some murders where you live?' Sarah stared at her, feeling a prickling sensation at the nape of her neck. 'And you think it was to do with the practice of pagan rites or devil worship?'

'It was devil worship where I come from,' Jilly said, and pulled a face. 'Pack of silly idiots we all thought at the beginning, behaving like children they were. We didn't know what was happening to the cats for a while, but then the murders started and the police told us it was some sort of black cult. They arrested one man for the murders, but we all thought there was more to it.'

'I wonder . . .' Sarah shook her head. 'You mustn't tell anyone else about this – for your own sake. I shall tell Mr Marshall. He is a retired Scotland Yard inspector and he may come to talk to you about this – but please don't mention it to anyone else, will you?'

'In case they try to kill me?' Jilly looked belligerent. 'They can try, lovey, but they won't find me so easy to get rid of!'

'But just in case, please?'

'Ah well, I dare say you're right,' Jilly said. 'You send the gentleman along as you said, and I'll watch out for anything suspicious. You get a lot of folk in a shop, lovey, and you never know what I might see.'

'That's why you have to be so careful,' Sarah said.

She smiled and left the shop. The village was almost deserted except for a dog nosing in the gutters and a child playing with a hoop. As she left the village, starting to climb the hill towards the Manor, she saw a black car coming very fast in her direction. For some reason she sensed that it was coming straight at her, and she jumped off the road on to the grass verge just as it swept by, narrowly missing her.

Sarah was so shocked that it took a moment to realize what had happened. The driver of the car had meant to knock her down! And whoever it was had been wearing a mask over his or her face. The realization that an attempt to kill her had been made caused her to feel sick, and so it was not until she tried to walk on that she realized she had wrenched the heel from her right shoe.

Her ankle felt a little sore but she discovered that she could walk easily enough. Fortunately, she had another pair of shoes in the bag she was carrying, and it was a moment's work to get them out and change. She had just started to walk up the hill again when she heard a car coming behind her, and looked nervously over her shoulder, wondering if the driver had returned for another try. She was relieved when she saw it was Larch.

He pulled up, stopped the engine and came to her, picking up her bag. 'I am sorry I was late,' he said. 'Something came up and I couldn't get away.'

'I should have rung for a taxi,' she said, and he realized that she looked pale. 'Did you see that black car – the one that tried to knock me down?'

'Knock you down? You're not serious? Sarah! When did it happen?'

'Just a moment or so ago. I was walking up the hill and I saw it coming towards me. At first I didn't think anything of it, but then I sensed that it was gathering speed and I jumped on the grass verge. The driver swerved towards me but then went on by.'

'Did you see who was driving it?'

'Whoever it was had a devil mask on – just like the one I saw when I found Mrs Roberts.'

'My God!' Larch said, and now he looked white himself. 'It can't have been planned, Sarah, because no one could have known you would be here – but someone saw you and took a chance.'

'Yes, perhaps. But the car could only have come from Gran's or the Manor . . .'

'Get in the car,' Larch said. 'I'll telephone Ben when we get home, and we'll see if anyone saw anything at the dower house.'

'Gran and Andrews are out. Millie is the only one there at the moment. I hope nothing has happened to her . . .'

'I can't see why anyone would want to hurt Millie,' Larch said. 'Someone thinks you know too much, Sarah. You are going to have to be very careful from now on.' He looked anxious. 'This whole business is getting very nasty.'

'Has something else happened?' She saw the doubt in his face. 'You must tell me, Larch. We have to talk about these things – and I've got something to tell you and Ben.'

'We'll talk when Ben arrives,' Larch said. 'I need to hear what he has to say about all this . . .'

In the event, Amelia arrived first and asked Larch to stay for lunch. He refused, pleading a prior engagement and, as Sarah walked to the door with him, told her that he would pick her up that evening.

'We'll talk to Ben at my house,' he said. 'It's best that Amelia doesn't know what happened earlier.'

'Yes, I agree. I'll tell you both my news then.'

'We shall both have to be patient,' Larch said, pulling a wry face. 'You'd better go back with Amelia. You may be hearing some unpleasant news later.'

Sarah raised her brows but he shook his head and went off. She returned to her grandmother feeling a little annoyed that he hadn't told her something that was obviously important.

'Did you have a lovely time with your friend?' Amelia went into the parlour. Mr Tibbs followed, mewing plaintively as he wound himself about her ankles. 'You foolish animal,' she scolded affectionately. She looked at her granddaughter. 'It's a pity you didn't get either of those jobs, but I'm sure something will turn up soon.'

'Yes, perhaps,' Sarah said. 'And yes, I did have fun with Mary.'

'They held Morna Scaffry's funeral while you were away. I sent some flowers from us both, Sarah, and Andrews took me. It was quite surprising, because the church was full. And there were so many flowers. I went to look at them afterwards and . . .' She hesitated and then, 'A few mourners followed the coffin outside and when I went to look at the flowers I saw Sir James Beecham and a woman talking . . .'

Sarah sensed her uncertainty. 'It wasn't Lady Beecham?'

'No. It would have been difficult for her to take her wheelchair round to the graveyard, and as far as I can recall she wasn't in church. He certainly was, and this woman . . .' Sarah raised her brows. 'It was odd because I remembered Larch saying about the woman driving a car very fast from the direction of the Manor the night you came home . . .'

'Was the woman at the church wearing a fur coat and dark glasses?'

'Yes – and an expensive silk scarf over her head. She looked most upset, and she stood talking to Sir James for a while before she left – in a black car as it happened. Although she wasn't driving it. Another woman was driving. She was wearing a plain grey coat and a black felt hat. I didn't really notice her until she was driving away . . .'

'Yes, it is a little odd,' Sarah said. She was trying to make sense of something in her head but at the moment it didn't fit. If the woman had been at Miss Bates's funeral it might have helped fill in the pieces of the jigsaw, but the gypsy girl could have nothing to do with the old scandal concerning Shirley Anne Asbury. 'I wouldn't have expected Sir James to be there – and who was the woman in the fur coat? He obviously knew her.'

'Quite well I should think.'

'Did you mention this to anyone else?'

'No, I wasn't sure what it meant, if anything,' Amelia said. 'Besides, you were in London and Mr Marshall had gone home to see about his cats – but you might mention it to him when you see him, my dear. He may think it unimportant, but I know he likes to be told little things like that.'

'Yes, he does, and of course I shall tell him,' Sarah said and smiled at her. 'I visited Fortnum and Mason and bought you some of your favourite biscuits and chocolates, Gran. Shall we have lunch now? And then you can settle down and indulge yourself.'

'And you can tell me all about the things you did in town,' her grandmother said with a loving smile. 'And what you were whispering about to Larch in the hall . . .'

Eleven

'How are you, Sarah?' Ben asked, giving her an anxious look as she entered the small sitting room that evening. 'I was distressed to hear what Larch had to say about that incident with the car. I don't suppose you had time to get many details, did you?'

'No, I'm afraid I didn't think about it,' Sarah admitted and sat down on the sofa, opposite a welcoming fire. 'It was such a shock and all I could think about was getting out of the way. I can tell you it was black and a saloon car but that's all I can remember. I do know that whoever was driving had on one of those peculiar masks.'

'Well, that is something I suppose,' Ben said, 'though a large number of cars on the road these days are black so it doesn't narrow the field much. It sounds as if it might have been a member of the pagan group, though there are probably quite a few of them.'

'Only one that has reason to bear a grudge against Sarah,' Larch said. 'I know for a fact that Madeline sometimes drives a black car. I'm not saying it was her, but it is the sort of spiteful thing she might do on impulse.'

'Then I shall certainly pay her a little visit tomorrow.' Ben looked thoughtful. 'But I think we had better fill Sarah in on what happened this morning. Would you rather do that, Larch?'

Larch nodded, a reluctant expression in his eyes. 'Perhaps I should. I haven't been looking forward to telling you this, Sarah, because it is rather gruesome. It's the reason I was late coming to pick you up. I called at the Beecham Nursery to buy flowers and heard screaming. The young woman who works there had found Simon's body.'

'Simon Beecham has been murdered?' Things just seemed to get worse and worse! Sarah had been almost convinced that Simon had killed Morna because the girl was blackmailing him, but this had turned her theory on its head. 'How did he die?' She saw that Larch was hesitating. 'You must tell me all of it, Larch. It won't upset me.'

'The police seem to think that someone knocked him out and then . . . chopped through his neck almost severing his head . . .' Larch stopped as he saw the colour leave her face. 'I would rather have kept it from you, Sarah. The police aren't releasing details just yet, but I expect it will get out soon enough.'

'That is absolutely horrible!' Sarah said, and was glad that she was sitting down. 'Have you any idea who could have done it?'

'The weapon must have been very sharp,' Ben said, frowning, 'and it was used with some force. I think the killer must have been a man, and it was quite deliberate. I should say the motive might well have been revenge in this instance.'

'Revenge for Morna's murder?' Sarah asked. 'Because he killed her?'

'It may have been because someone believed that he was responsible.'

'But you don't think so?'

'Simon was a suspect, but in my opinion he wasn't the murderer,' Ben said. 'I have my suspicions, but this latest murder seems to rule my theory out – unless, it was a revenge killing by someone else.'

'So the person who killed Morna is not the person who killed Simon, but the killer thinks he murdered her,' Sarah said, working it out aloud. 'Why do you think Morna was killed if it wasn't for blackmailing Simon?'

'That may well have been the motive,' Ben told her. 'I have been working on the theory that Morna was killed to protect Simon . . . perhaps jealousy may have played a part in it, too.'

'You're saying . . .' Sarah looked at him, her eyes widening in shock. 'You think Madeline Lewis-Brown killed Morna, don't you?'

'I think there is a strong possibility. Simon's murder threw me for a while, and then I realized that it didn't have to be the same person behind both. If Madeline killed Morna, it was possibly to protect Simon from blackmail, possibly from jealousy. However, we suspected Simon of the murder for a while and it may be that others did too, and that they – or he

– decided to take revenge. It might seem to whomever it was that the police weren't doing anything about Morna's murder, perhaps because she was a gypsy.'

'What made you suspect Madeline of her murder?' Sarah asked. 'Was it those pictures I saw?'

'Yes, that made me wonder just what she was up to,' Ben said. 'But I have been trying to remember something ever since I arrived. I passed the Chestnuts that first afternoon, because I had taken a wrong turning, and I caught a glimpse of a woman I seemed to remember. It was at the back of my mind and I just couldn't think what was eluding me, but then you told me about Madeline Lewis-Brown, and it triggered something in my memory. You see, there was this other case about five years ago in Devon —'

'The police arrested one man for the murders, which were rather nasty, but the locals thought there was a lot more to it, didn't they?' Sarah smiled as Ben stared at her. 'Mrs Roberts's sister, Jilly, told me. She comes from Devon and says she knew something was going on. I told her not to talk about it and said you would call on her.'

'Let's hope that she followed your advice for her own sake. I shall call on her tomorrow, before I visit Mrs Lewis-Brown.' He looked thoughtful. 'I believe it may have been Madeline who tried to run you down, Sarah. She must have seen you from the top of the hill and taken a chance. As Larch said, it couldn't have been premeditated, because no one knew you would be there at the time.'

'Yes, I'm sure it was an impulse,' Sarah agreed. 'Whoever it was may not even have meant to kill me, simply to frighten me.'

'If Mrs Lewis-Brown killed Morna out of a mistaken desire to protect Simon, she is possibly very angry with you,' Ben said. 'And if she is the lady I think she could be, she may have been involved in some very nasty things over a period of years. Remember that someone tried to silence Mrs Roberts – possibly because she was hinting that she knew who had fathered Morna's unborn child.'

'Yes, I see.' Sarah felt a little shiver run down her spine. 'But Madeline wouldn't have killed Simon, would she? If she murdered Morna to protect him or from jealousy over their affair, she wouldn't kill him.'

'As I said, I think it needed a man's strength,' Ben said and looked serious. 'That was a very nasty affair, Sarah.'

'Do you have any suspects?'

'Morna's brother is the obvious one. I believe Jethro has been heard berating Simon Beecham, and he clearly had the motive.'

'You think that he believed Simon was her killer?' Larch said, and looked thoughtful. 'I've seen him with Ronnie Miller recently . . .'

Ben looked at him sharply. 'What are you thinking?'

'I'm not sure really, but something Ronnie's mother said to me yesterday made me wonder. Whoever killed Simon used something very sharp and it took a lot of force . . . like a spade cutting through earth . . .' Larch hesitated, clearly uncertain in his mind. 'Mrs Miller said that Ronnie is always sharpening his spade these days and that he is hardly ever home. She thought that he had been drinking spirits and she wondered where he got the money.'

'You think that Jethro might have put him up to it?' Ben nodded. 'It is possible – and it is just possible that a sharp spade was used to kill Simon – but do we think that Ronnie could have done it?'

'I thought he might have used his spade to kill Miss Bates's cat,' Larch said. 'But I wouldn't have thought him capable of murder and yet . . . it was so very violent. Someone who struck out in rage might have done it, I suppose, someone who didn't truly understand what he was doing. If he knew and liked Morna, believed that Simon had killed her—'

'Jethro might have incited him to do it,' Ben said, looking thoughtful. 'Yes, it might have been the pair of them. It certainly bears thinking about. Or it might have been Madeline if she had fallen out with him. I am not sure that she would have the strength – but she can't be ruled out at this stage.'

'You don't think it might have been Sir James?' Sarah asked. 'I'm sure he is involved in all this somehow.'

'I don't see it as his type of killing,' Ben said. 'I believe he might shoot someone if he was angry enough – but not brutally murder someone like this.'

'So you have suspects for two of the murders. But where is the connection to Miss Bates?'

'Now there you have me. It could be blackmail, because

she had discovered what was going on in the woods and threatened to go to the police.'

'Yes, I suppose so,' Sarah agreed. She had been going to
tell Ben what she'd discovered about the old scandal, and
about the woman with Sir James Beecham at Morna's funeral,
but hesitated, because it would only muddy the waters. He
had his theories and if he was right she must be wrong. 'So
what do you intend doing next? Are you going to speak to
the police about your theory?'

'Not until after I've spoken to Madeline Lewis-Brown,' Ben
said. 'If she is the woman I think then I shall ask her a few
questions about the shenanigans in the woods, but I'll leave
it to Morrison to arrest her. I don't have the proof I need as
yet, but she may break down under interrogation.'

'I doubt it,' Larch said. 'She doesn't strike me as the type
to panic. But those pictures will go some way to proving that
she was involved and hopefully the police may find something more.'

'Well, we can only hope for a speedy end to the case,' Ben
said. 'One thing I would ask, Sarah, is that you be very careful
until we have this lady under lock and key. Whether or not
she is our murderer, she might be spiteful enough to harm
you in some way if she got the chance.'

'Yes, of course.' Sarah shuddered. 'It has all been most
unpleasant. I feel so sorry for Miss Bates and all the others.
I mean, if Simon Beecham didn't kill Morna, well, he didn't
deserve to die that way. It was a horrible thing to happen even
if he was guilty, but if he was innocent – it was wicked.'

Ben telephoned that evening to make a couple of appoint-
ments for the next day. Jilly Bullock was delighted he had
phoned and said she would look forward to seeing him the
next morning. However, Madeline's answer was very different.

'What do you want?' she asked in a waspish tone. 'I am
very busy. I don't have time for this sort of thing.'

'It's just a few questions,' Ben said. 'I really do need to
talk to you, Mrs Lewis-Brown. It is quite important.'

'Oh, very well,' she said. 'But I have to go out later so be
here at ten o'clock sharp and don't expect me to give you
more than half an hour.'

'I dare say it won't take long,' Ben said. 'I'll be on time,

Mrs Lewis-Brown. Thank you for seeing me.' He pulled a face as he replaced the receiver, because it wasn't going to be a pleasant interview. He didn't have the authority to make it official so he would have to tread carefully, but to his mind a lot of the clues he'd received so far seemed to point in Madeline's direction, at least as far as the gypsy girl's murder was concerned.

Madeline was fuming when she replaced the receiver. What did that damned snoop want to poke his nose in for? She wasn't in the mood for talking to him, but she hadn't dared to refuse.

Simon's murder had upset her, and she wasn't easily upset. But she wasn't the only one. Most of the others had been scared off and were saying it was time to cool things for a bit. But then, most of them had been in it for a laugh, only interested in the sexual side of the rituals.

Madeline had enjoyed the power it gave her over them, and she'd used her power to good effect for the past few years, but this latest murder had frightened the rest of them more than she did, despite what she knew about their private lives. A wry smile touched her lips. Maybe she would move on soon. It might be time for a new name and a new identity, though she had been doing rather well with her paintings.

She decided to go out to the studio. She would hold her nerve for the time being, because she had settled here. Besides, that interfering fool probably didn't know anything important. As a rule she found it easy to run rings round most people. She decided she would wait until she'd talked to Mr Marshall before moving on.

She had been working for an hour or so when the door of her studio opened and someone entered. Busy with her work, she was annoyed and didn't look up immediately.

'I thought I told you tomorrow morning—'

'It's me, Maddy . . .' a voice said and Madeline laid down her paintbrush, coming out from behind the easel. Her expression didn't change, though she knew her visitor well. 'You don't look very pleased to see me?'

'Last time you were here you took some things that belong to me.'

'Borrowed them. What's wrong with you? I've brought them back, so don't look so annoyed.'

'It's not really you,' Madeline said. 'It's that damned ex-Scotland Yard inspector. He has been poking his nose into all kinds of things and now he wants to talk to me, says he has a few questions to ask me. I may have to move on . . .'

'What kind of questions?'

'Oh, come and have a drink,' Madeline said. 'This picture isn't working for me anyway. I'm too upset over Simon. I still can't understand why anyone would want to kill him.'

'Maybe someone didn't like him?'

'I think it was to do with that girl who was killed,' Madeline said. 'Someone thought he killed her but it wasn't him.' She poured wine into two glasses and set them down. 'I'm drinking too much but I feel bloody awful . . .'

'Sit down,' her visitor said. 'What you need is something to clear your head. I've got a nice little pill here that will make you feel much better, Maddy.'

'What is it?' Madeline was vaguely interested because she was always interested in trying something new. She sat down on the sofa. It was comforting not to be alone, because she was still grieving for the man she had loved in her own way.

'It's just a little pick me up. I've got two – one for you and one for me . . . they will dissolve in the wine and you won't taste a thing, but I promise it will make you forget all your troubles. Don't I always help you out when you're in trouble?'

'You're having one too?' Maddy nodded as she watched the pills being dropped into the wine glasses, and accepted her glass. She trusted her visitor completely.

She lifted her glass and drank it straight down, waiting for her visitor to do the same, but the other glass was being poured down the little sink she used to wash her brushes and something was happening to her. She gasped as her sight became hazy and her head started spinning.

'What have you done to me?'

'Just what I promised. All your troubles are over, Maddy. You won't have to talk to that nasty policeman, and that means you can't tell him anything you shouldn't. And now I'm going to leave you to sleep.'

Maddy's head had fallen back, the glass dropping from her hand to the floor. She wasn't listening any more. She was dead. That was the thing about cyanide, it was very quick and therefore relatively painless – better than some poisons, which took a long time to work. Maddy hadn't suffered too much. The observer washed the second glass and polished it clean with a dry cloth, then replaced it on the sideboard.

Walking over to where Madeline lay, the murderer stood looking down for a moment and then smiled. 'You always had your way, didn't you, Maddy darling? Well, this time I decided it wasn't going to happen.'

The murderer bent down and removed the string of lapis lazuli beads from around Madeline's neck, slipping them into a coat pocket. They were valuable and it was nice to have something to remember those you had once cared for by. The murderer turned and walked out of the studio. A black car was parked outside. It was exactly like Madeline's except for the number plate.

'It's funny you should have telephoned last evening,' Jilly said to Ben that morning. He was her only customer and she had been dusting when he entered. 'I was thinking about telephoning Sarah Beaufort, because I've seen her – the woman I mentioned to Sarah. Well, I didn't actually say, but I hinted that I might know something. '

'You've seen someone you know?' Ben looked at her through narrowed eyes. 'A woman you believe might have been involved in some murders in your village a few years back?'

'Yes, that's right, lovey,' Jilly said, thinking what a nice, clever man he was. 'All that nasty business with devil worship and the murders. See all sorts of things in my business and that's a fact. I ran a little teashop then, though I gave it up last year, got too much for me.'

'Yes, things catch up with one, don't they?' Ben looked at her expectantly. 'You were saying? You've seen someone?'

'She came into the shop yesterday afternoon, not long after Sarah left – parked her car just outside. Black it was and a saloon. American make, I think, but a few years old.' She smiled in triumph, proud of her powers of recall. 'I knew her as soon as she came in. I don't know what she calls herself now, but she was called Madeline Browning then. She has dyed her hair red. It used to be a chestnut brown but she has used henna on it to make it a brighter red. I might not have been sure if she hadn't been wearing those lapis lazuli beads, but I remember them.'

'You have remarkable powers of observation,' Ben said approvingly. 'Did she know you?'

'No, I don't think so. She wouldn't have noticed me when she used to come in with her friend in the old days, all wrapped up in him she was – he was the one you arrested for those murders.' Jilly nodded, looking pleased with herself. 'I always thought she must have been involved as well, because she led him about by the nose. You could see it in his manner – he was bewitched by her. I thought when the police arrested him they would have her too, but they didn't.'

'That may be because she had disappeared,' Ben said. 'There was no real proof, nothing to connect her to the murders, and the local force thought he might have killed her too. He was questioned about it but denied it. Besides, he had confessed to the other murders and refused to name anyone else, said it was all down to him.'

Ben had had his doubts at the time, but as merely an observer he had not been able to do much other than offer an opinion to the local force – much as he was doing now. Except that in this case Morrison was grateful for his help and was giving him a free hand.

'Well, he would, wouldn't he?' Jilly said. 'Mad for her he was. Anyone could see it. If you ask me, she was the one behind the whole thing. He was probably protecting her.'

'Yes, you may well be right,' Ben said. 'But we shall have to see what comes of it this time. Thank you very much for your information, Mrs . . .?'

'Oh, call me Jilly. Everyone does. Jilly Bullock, and it's Miss. I've never been married.'

Ben smiled, tipped his hat to her and left the shop. Everything was falling into place very nicely. Having unearthed his old case notes, he had thought Madeline Lewis-Brown might be the Mrs Browning who had gone missing some years earlier, and it had seemed to fit.

She was a very clever woman and it might not have occurred to him to suspect her if she hadn't made one mistake. The wreath meant for Sarah had alerted him, because it was so personal. It had to be connected to the discovery of the paintings, and that had put the suspicion firmly on Madeline Lewis-Brown – or whatever her real name was.

The old saying that hell hath no fury like a woman scorned

held true in this case. Madeline had been angry because Larch had taken Sarah to her studio, and because she had discovered the paintings – but primarily because Larch had seemed to find her work wanting in real talent. Anger had made her careless. A little thing, perhaps, but enough to give Ben one of his famous hunches.

He decided to give Morrison a call and tell him that he was about to interview the lady, because they didn't want her to slip away as she had the last time.

Thorny March was a little off the beaten track and it took Ben a while to find the right road, and then it was so narrow that he wondered if he had taken a wrong turning after all. He wished that he had asked Larch to accompany him, but he had considered that this first interview with Madeline Lewis-Brown ought to be on a one-to-one basis.

Seeing a black saloon car coming towards him, he drew over into a stopping place and waited for it to pass; he recognized the driver as Sir James Beecham and nodded to him. Then he drove on, parking in the lay-by that Larch had told him about. He got out of the car and locked it, walking up to the front door of the cottage, which was hinged in the middle and studded with iron.

Ben rang the bell several times but there was no answer, so he walked around to the back of the house, noticing that there were three laurel bushes growing by the side wall. Easy enough to make up the wreath that had been sent to Sarah if one already had the materials to hand.

The door to the studio was open wide. It was a very cold day and Ben didn't think he would want to work with the door open when it was this cold. He was feeling icy, his stomach churning as he walked slowly towards the small, brick-built building. Something was wrong here! The studio had skylights, which on a summer's day would let in the kind of light an artist needed, he supposed, but there wasn't much light today, because the sky was grey. He would have thought that electric lights would be needed on such a dull day, but there were none showing.

'Mrs Lewis-Brown?' he called, and knocked the door. 'I am calling to make a few inquiries as we arranged . . . Ben Marshall . . .' There was no answer so he went inside the studio.

His nerve ends were tingling and his nose itched: classic symptoms that something was wrong. He could see three easels with paintings on each of them and a lot more paintings stacked around the room, but there was no one about.

'Madeline . . . are you here?'

Ben let his gaze travel around the studio, noticing that a paintbrush had been abandoned with its tip still loaded with paint, which was now dried, which was surprising for a professional artist. His gaze settled at last on the door that clearly led to a back room. He walked towards it, knocked again and waited, then turned the handle and went in. His eyes were immediately drawn to the woman lying on the sofa. Her head was back, her eyes closed, but he knew immediately that she wasn't asleep.

'Good grief!' he said, and crossed the room swiftly. He suspected even without touching her that she was dead, but felt for a pulse. It was just possible that he might be in time, though he sensed that it was too late. She was very cold and he judged that she had been dead for several hours, possibly since the previous night. He looked for signs of a struggle. There were none. An empty wine glass lay on the floor close to her. It had cracked as if it had dropped from her hand. He noticed a certain pinkish look about her skin. Ben bent down to pick the glass up, wrapping it about with his handkerchief. He sniffed at it and caught the distinctive smell of cyanide. Not everyone was able to pick that out, but he had a nose for it. It was a tasteless, quick-acting poison readily available in the form of rat poison. He replaced the glass where he had found it.

It looked as if Madeline had panicked after he telephoned her the previous evening and committed suicide, but where was the note? He searched for it on the sofa, sideboard and the various tables and chests in what had obviously been Madeline's private room. She washed her brushes here and sat down for a drink when she needed a break from work.

After a fruitless search, he decided that she hadn't bothered to leave a note, though he discovered a black gown and a devil mask lying on a cane chair. They looked as if they had been thrown down, and he wondered that she had chosen to leave them lying there. Yet perhaps they were her way of confessing, at least to the charge of devil worship and all the unsavoury stuff that had gone with it.

Ben picked up the telephone receiver, putting a call through to Inspector Morrison in Norwich. He was aware of dissatisfaction. It would have been good to have made the arrest – even better if Madeline Lewis-Brown had confessed to her crimes, because he was certain in his own mind that she had killed Morna Scaffry. He believed that she had been behind the attempt on Mrs Roberts – and the wreath that had been sent to Sarah.

Well, at least there would be no more spiteful attempts to frighten Sarah, he thought. They still had Simon Beecham's murder to clear up, but on the surface this seemed to be pretty straightforward.

'I'm not surprised she took her own life,' Amelia said when Larch told them the news that evening. 'If she murdered poor Morna Scaffry and did all those horrid things she must have known that time was running out for her.'

'I certainly didn't suspect Madeline Lewis-Brown of murder until Ben told us his theory,' Sarah said, 'though I knew she must have been concerned in that other stuff in the woods.' She looked at Larch. 'Have the police found anything about all that at her cottage?'

'Yes, I think she had kept a kind of diary listing names, dates and rituals. It was a dangerous thing to do, but Ben says she had got away with it before and thought she could laugh at the police. She didn't leave a suicide note or a confession so it's still all speculation as far as the murders go, but Inspector Morrison seems to agree that she was the one. As far as he is concerned Morna's murder is down to Madeline Lewis-Brown. They are still looking for the connection to Janet Bates. Morrison thinks it must be blackmail, though the money was a legacy, left to her by someone she had looked after for a few years.'

'Would that be Shirley Anne Asbury?' Sarah asked. 'I know Janet was her dresser for some years . . .'

'I'm not sure,' Larch said, 'but it hardly matters now. Thank goodness this is all over and we can get back to normal.' He smiled at her. 'There's a dance on at the Chestnuts this weekend – would you like to go?'

'Yes, very much,' Sarah said. She wasn't sure why but a little voice was nagging at the back of her mind, telling her that the mystery was only half solved. 'What does Ben say about Simon Beecham's murder?'

'Morrison thinks it is probably down to Jethro Scaffry and Ben isn't disagreeing, though he isn't too sure. Anyway, he thinks the murders are over now. Jethro might have killed the man he believed had murdered his sister, but there's no reason for him to kill anyone else. Besides, the police will probably have him arrested before long. They're already searching for him – and Ronnie Miller, who has gone missing again.'

'Yes, poor Ronnie,' Sarah said. 'I can't help thinking he has been dragged into something he doesn't understand.'

'Yes. I can't help feeling sorry for him too,' Larch said. 'Especially if Jethro encouraged him to do something he would never have thought of doing for himself. But it may have nothing to do with him. Just because it looks as if Simon may have been killed with a spade, it doesn't mean it was Ronnie's.'

'No, of course not.' Sarah frowned at the idea, because it was unpleasant. 'I don't think he would be capable of planning a murder, Larch. If it wasn't Mrs Lewis-Brown, I think it more likely that Morna was killed by her brother. I saw them arguing once and I should imagine he has a violent temper.' She looked at her grandmother. 'Or . . .' She broke off because she couldn't suggest that it might have been Sir James in front of Amelia.

'Well, the police will sort it out now,' Amelia said. 'And the sooner the better. I don't mind admitting that I have been very worried about this whole thing. It has been most unpleasant. At least now we can enjoy our lives again. It's my bridge afternoon tomorrow, and I think I shall go. I had decided not to but there seems no reason to cry off now – thanks to Mr Marshall.'

'Ben says he couldn't have done it without Sarah,' Larch said, and smiled at her.

Sarah laughed and shook her head. 'That's nonsense, Larch. I've been working on very different theories.' Larch raised his brows but she shook her head. 'No, it was all in my head and it doesn't matter now. I am just so glad that Ben has solved the mystery.'

'Well, there is still Simon's murder to solve,' Larch said, 'but that looks straightforward. With any luck, the police will have it all sewn up in a matter of hours.'

'Yes, I'm sure they will,' Sarah said. 'Anyway, let's talk about something else. What are you going to do for Christmas, Larch?'

'I haven't the faintest idea,' he said. 'That's ages away yet – why?'

'Oh, I might go and stay with Daddy,' Sarah said, 'and I wondered if you might like to come too.'

'Well, I'm not sure,' he said, and rubbed the bridge of his nose. 'You won't mind if I give it a little thought?'

'No, of course not,' she said, though she did mind. She had hoped he would say yes immediately. 'What kind of a dance is it tomorrow – ballroom or modern?'

'I expect there will be a bit of both,' Larch said. 'You know, the usual thing, Sarah.' He glanced at his watch. 'I think I had better go. Ben intends to leave in the morning and I promised to have a drink with him this evening. Would you like to come, Sarah?'

'No, I don't think so,' she said, because her feelings were a little hurt. 'I'll see you tomorrow, Larch.'

'Yes, of course. Goodnight, Sarah – Amelia, you can stop worrying now.'

'Thank you for coming to tell us,' Amelia said. 'Sarah will see you to the door, won't you, my dear?'

'Yes, of course.' Sarah jumped up and led the way through to the hall. 'Give my regards to Ben,' she said, half regretting her decision not to go with him. 'Thank him for all he has done.'

'I'll tell him,' Larch said. 'I think he wants to get back to his cats – his wife rang about a problem apparently.'

'Oh . . . well, I suppose he needs something to fill his time. He was too young to retire really.'

'I'll tell him you said that,' Larch said. 'I'll pick you up tomorrow.'

'Lovely.' Sarah waved as he went out and got into the car, then returned to the front parlour and looked at her grand-mother. 'Shall we have a game of chess?'

'I think a game of chess would be very nice, my dear. Why didn't you go with Larch? You would have enjoyed yourself.'

'I didn't feel like it,' Sarah said. 'Besides, I like being with you and I've been out most of the time since I came to stay.'

'Well, that's how it should be. You are young, Sarah. I like to think of you having a good time.'

'I'm going out with Larch tomorrow evening,' Sarah said. 'And now that these murders have been solved I shall visit a few friends.'

'Lady Beecham invited us to dinner at the Manor next week,' Amelia said. 'It won't be quite your sort of thing, but I think we should go.'

'Oh yes, of course,' Sarah said. 'Sir James did mention an invitation but I thought after Simon . . . but perhaps they are trying to behave as normally as possible. Have you heard when the funeral will be?'

'Oh, in a week or so I suppose,' Amelia said. 'Now that it's all cleared up there's no need for the police to delay it, is there?'

'I shouldn't think so,' Sarah said and began to set out the chess pieces. She wished that she could feel as certain as the others that the murders had been cleared up.

She still had some lingering doubts and questions that needed to be answered, but Larch had seemed so sure it was all over, she hadn't felt inclined to raise her doubts; besides, she didn't want to upset Amelia when she probably had it all wrong in her head. After all, it wasn't really up to her to solve the murders, and what had started out almost as a game had become much more serious.

Ronnie was so cold. He kept shivering and he felt unwell. He needed some of the good stuff inside him, and he was hoping that Jethro would be at the caravan. He had been feeling awful for a couple of days now, terrible pictures of something bad in his head, pictures that frightened him. He wasn't sure what they meant, but he knew that he didn't like them. If he drank enough of the good stuff he would be all right again. The pictures would go and he would be able to sleep.

When he reached the spot in the woods where Morna's caravan was always parked, he was startled to see that it had gone. For a moment he thought he must have mistaken his way, but he could see where the grass was flattened and discoloured from being beneath the caravan for a long time.

He removed his cap, scratching his head as he tried to think what had happened. Jethro hadn't said anything to him about going away. It made him frightened, because there were quite a few things he couldn't remember now, blank patches in his mind that he couldn't trace.

Perhaps Morna had come back and taken her caravan away. Vaguely, he remembered Jethro telling him that she was buried in the earth, but maybe she had got out again. Ronnie was glad if Morna wasn't buried any more, but he wished the caravan was still here, because he was shivering a lot now and he needed some of the drink that put fire in his belly.

He remembered the hut where Jethro kept more of the good stuff, and he turned away, deciding to go and see if there was any left. Jethro had told him he was going to get more so perhaps it would be in the hut.

It was so bitterly cold. Ronnie could never remember feeling so ill. His teeth were chattering and he needed a drink. He put his head down against the flurry of snowflakes that had just begun to fall, trudging solidly towards the hut.

When he reached the hut, he discovered that the door was open. He went inside. It was dark but he could just make out shapes and saw there was a pile of sacks lying in a corner. All the cases of the good stuff had gone. He could feel the aching need in his belly, and the cold nipping at his fingers and toes.

Tears had started to run down his cheeks as he sat down on the pile of old sacks. He needed that drink so badly and he didn't know what to do. If he didn't get a drink the pictures would come back and they frightened him so much that he huddled up, his knees close to his chest, hugging himself.

He could see Miss Bates lying with the blood all around her, and the way the cat's head had come off when he chopped at it with his spade – and then there was Morna, lying there all white and cold, her face a funny blue colour. And then there was the other thing, but he didn't want to think about that . . .

Twelve

S arah looked out of the window. It had snowed during the night and a blanket of sparkling white covered lawns, trees and shrubs; but now the sun was out and the gradual thaw had set in. Some of the trees were dripping, and small green patches had begun to appear on the lawn. She hoped that with any luck it would clear the snow within a few hours, and decided to take a walk into the village.

'Wrap up well, dearest,' Amelia said when she told her where she was going. 'Andrews will take you if you like?'

'No, it's all right,' Sarah said. 'I fancy a nice walk. The fresh air will do me good.'

'Yes, I am sure it will.' Amelia was happy enough for her to go now that all the trouble had been cleared up. 'Be careful where you walk. It may be icy underfoot. You don't want to take a tumble.'

'I'm putting my rubber boots on. Don't worry, Gran. I shall be fine.'

It was surprising how warm it felt in the sun, though the wind was still bitter. Sarah was wearing several layers and a long pink scarf that wound around her face to keep out the cold, her hands thrust into matching pink mittens. She glanced at the woods as she passed them, thinking how pretty they looked with the glistening snow covering the branches. She had always loved the woods and she thought it would be foolish to fear them because of what had happened. Now that it was all over the villagers could get on with their lives as before. Larch had told her that the villagers were going to organize a variety of protest moves to stop planning going ahead for destruction of the woods. And his father was looking into the legal aspects now that there was some doubt about who owned the land in question.

She purchased some stamps in the post office and a bag

of Tom Thumb Drops, staying to chat to Jilly for some minutes.

'Betty should be coming home soon,' the friendly woman told her. 'We've decided to see how it goes. If she settles I shall move in with her and sell my place, but if she can't put up with it we shall sell this property and go back to Devon.' She frowned, lowering her voice to a whisper. 'Is it true that Mrs Lewis-Brown committed suicide?'

'I have heard something,' Sarah said. 'But I don't think anyone knows what happened for sure. Perhaps we ought not to say anything until the police have finished their investigation.'

'It was a bad business altogether,' Jilly said. 'But we shall all sleep easier at nights for it if you ask me.'

Sarah smiled but made no comment. She started to walk home, noticing that the street was deserted. It was becoming cold again now that the sun had disappeared. People were sensible to stay indoors.

As she neared Janet Bates's cottage, she saw that a small car was parked near by, and as she approached the cottage a man came out and called to her.

'Miss . . .' he said and waved at her. 'Just a moment.'

Sarah hesitated. Her heart jerked as she wondered what he had to say and prepared herself for an angry outburst. 'Yes – was there something I can do for you, Mr Bates?'

He looked a little awkward. 'You could start by forgiving me for my appalling rudeness the last time we met,' he said. 'I wasn't thinking straight. What I said was rude and uncalled for.'

Sarah felt a surge of relief and smiled at him. 'I expect you were under a strain. Have you come to clear the cottage out?'

'Yes, that was my original intention, but now I think I might keep it. Janet left me a lot of money. I don't really need to work any longer. I might be able to indulge my hobby.'

'Oh?' Sarah looked at him but waited, remembering that the wrong questions had upset him on a previous occasion.

'I like to write – detective stories,' he said. 'I've had a couple published in a magazine. I think that's what gave Janet the idea for her book . . .' He hesitated. 'Actually, that's what I wanted to talk to you about. You see, I've found her notebooks . . .'

'Really?' Sarah felt a flicker of excitement. 'I believe there were rather a lot of them, weren't there?'

'About sixty or so,' he replied, and pulled a wry face. 'She had hidden them in an old fireplace behind the sofa in her bedroom. Some of them are definitely the first chapters of a book, the others appear to be some sort of notes. They relate to the book but I'm not sure how . . .' Again he looked hesitant, almost shy. 'Would you have a look at them? I should like your opinion. I know it's an awful cheek after the way I behaved but I'm wondering if . . . if they are the reason she was murdered. Someone told me that you've been helping a private detective to solve the case?'

'That's not quite true,' Sarah replied. 'I made a few notes on things I observed but it seems that I got it all wrong. The police think they've solved the murders now – but I wouldn't mind having a look at some of the notes if you really want me to.'

'Yes, I do, please,' he said and looked bothered. 'I'm not sure whether I should give them to the police, you see. I can't believe Janet would blackmail anyone – but if the things she has written in her notes are true she could have blackmailed four or five people. I haven't looked at all of them yet.'

'Well, I'll certainly have a look for you,' Sarah said, and smiled at him. 'Would it be all right if I take a few home with me? I promise faithfully to bring them all back, and I shan't go to the police behind your back.'

'You're a good sport,' he said. 'If we can start over, I should like us to be friends. My name is Keith . . .'

'And I'm Sarah. Let's have a quick look at a few of them together, and then I'll take a pile home to go through more carefully.'

'Shall I put the kettle on?' he asked, and looked down as a ginger cat wrapped itself around his legs. 'I think this must have been one of Janet's cats. Someone must have taken it in and fed it, but it keeps trying to get into the cottage, and I don't want it to be shut in, because I'm not coming to live here for a week or two.'

'When will you be leaving here?'

'Tomorrow afternoon. I decided to sleep over, see how I feel. If I'm all right, I'll be back in a couple of weeks to stay.'

'I'll bring the books I take back in the morning,' Sarah said, and shivered in the cold wind. 'Do let's have that cup of tea. I'm freezing.'

*　　*　　*

Lady Meadows looked around as her son came into the parlour where she was sitting at her writing desk. She could see that he had been working and was pleased because he hadn't touched his painting for a few weeks.

'Mrs Miller telephoned an hour ago,' she said. 'She seems very worried about Ronnie, says he hasn't been home in a couple of days.'

'She told me that he had started staying out to all hours. I'll go over and have a word with her, but he may be hiding out if he thinks the police are looking for him again.'

'You won't go like that, dearest?'

Larch looked down at his paint-stained clothes, which were disreputable by any standards. 'No, perhaps I should change. It's cold out and it looks as if it might snow so I'll put my boots in the car just in case.'

His mother wondered what he meant but he had left the room so she returned to her letters.

Larch changed his painting clothes for a thick pullover, cords and a heavy tweed jacket. If Mrs Roberts was really worried he might have a look for Ronnie, because it was dreadful weather to be sleeping rough. It was likely that he might be with Jethro in the caravan, and of course at his age he had a perfect right to be there, but at least Larch would be able to set Mrs Miller's mind at rest.

He drove over to Mrs Miller's house, half expecting that Ronnie would have come home, drawn by the desire for a nice warm fire and some good food in his belly. However, when Mrs Miller opened the door to him, she looked so upset that he knew Ronnie was still missing.

'No sign of him then?' he asked.

'No, sir. I'm sorry to bother you, but you've taken an interest in him and I'm at my wits' end. It isn't like him to stay out in this weather. He has been going off more recently, and he's been drinking – whisky or something like that. It's changed him, Captain Meadows.'

'This has all happened since the police arrested him, hasn't it?'

'Yes . . . but I think there's more.' Mrs Miller looked odd. 'I think he saw Morna . . . before the police found her, lying there in the woods. He has been saying some strange things, muttering and sharpening that spade of his again and again.

And he's been hanging about with Jethro Scaffry. I'm really worried about him.'

'Have you seen Ronnie's spade recently?' Larch asked. 'Do you know if he has taken it with him?'

'I think he's lost it,' Mrs Miller said. 'He asked me if I'd seen it the other day. I told him I wouldn't want his spade and he glared at me, and then he went off. Two days ago that was . . .' She stared at him. 'Why do you ask, sir?'

'Oh, just an idle question,' Larch said. 'Listen, I'm going to take a look in the woods for him. If I find him I'll come and let you know, all right?'

'Do you think he's with that gypsy?'

'Perhaps,' Larch said. 'But try not to worry. If my search comes to nothing I'll alert the police.' The police were probably on the lookout for him already, but Larch considered that Mrs Miller had enough to worry about as it was.

He left her and drove back towards Thorny, and the section of the woods where Morna's caravan had been parked for some months. The sun had disappeared and the snow had just started to settle again as he pulled on his long rubber boots, putting an army overcoat on over his jacket. It was bitterly cold and he decided to make a quick search and then call in help if he drew a blank. He patted the pocket of his overcoat, feeling the reassuring bulk of his army pistol. Just in case there was trouble.

It took Larch only a few minutes to reach the spot where Morna Scaffry's caravan had been parked for the past year or so. He saw that it had gone and frowned. Jethro had probably taken fright after Simon's murder and done a bunk, but what of Ronnie – had he gone with Jethro or was he here somewhere in the woods?

It was a question of whether to go home and telephone for help at once or make a brief search of the area. Larch didn't particularly fancy staying out in this weather for long, but on the other hand he wouldn't give much for Ronnie's chances if he was hiding out somewhere nearby in these bitter conditions.

The woods weren't that huge. He could probably search this area pretty thoroughly. After all, there weren't that many places Ronnie could hide in this weather. It would have to be a hut of some kind . . . of course – the woodcutters' hut! Larch remembered it clearly. It had been used years ago when the wood was regularly coppiced, but that hadn't been done for a while now. There wasn't as much call for that kind of thing now. Not many people would know of the hut, but Larch had played there with other lads as a boy, and perhaps Jethro might have seen it on his travels . . . Ronnie might have gone there with the gypsy.

He set out in what he thought was the right direction, but he had only been walking for a matter of ten minutes when he saw the dark heap lying on the ground just ahead of him. He knew instinctively that it was Ronnie and quickened his stride. Had there been yet another murder? Bending over the humped figure, he looked for signs of violence but found none. Ronnie was freezing, his eyes shut and his face blue with cold, but he was still breathing.

Larch gave him a shake, hoping to wake him, but although the lad moaned he didn't open his eyes. It was obvious that he was very ill, which was hardly surprising since he must have been lying there for hours.

It was a case of leaving him there while Larch went to fetch help or getting him out himself. For a moment pictures flashed into Larch's mind, and suddenly he was on a battlefield in France and the guns were firing around him, flashes of light blinding him. He could smell the stench of burning and of death, and he was sick to his stomach with fear.

'Come on, Dickon,' he urged, speaking the words aloud without realizing. 'We've got to get out of here before they start firing again.' But Dickon couldn't move. His leg was shattered. Larch had done the only thing possible. He had picked up his friend and carried him over his shoulder, the weight of his inert body making him stumble as the guns started up again, explosions on all sides, the shrapnel flying past them as he carried the man the short distance back to their lines.

'Come on, old fellow,' Larch said as the pictures faded and the world lurched back into place. He bent to heave Ronnie's body up to a sitting position. He kept hoping that the lad would stir and make it easier, but his eyelids hardly flickered. 'I'll get you there somehow.'

It was a struggle to heave Ronnie into a position where he could put him over his shoulder. He was well built, heavier than Dickon had been, but slowly, painfully slowly, Larch managed to straighten up under his burden, and then he started to walk. One foot in front of the other, knees buckling under the weight, each step a struggle that was almost too much. It was France all over again, the heavy weight dragging him down, the bitter cold nipping at him, sapping his strength, and the fear.

Larch shut the pictures out of his mind. He'd thought he had driven them out for good. At first they had haunted him day and night but it was some months since he'd experienced one of his nightmares. He wasn't going to give in to them now. He forced his thoughts to return to the present. All that was over. It was important that he get Ronnie to a hospital as fast as he could.

Sarah spent the afternoon reading the notebooks. Keith Bates had let her bring ten of them home, and she discovered that she had been right to think that Janet had been with Shirley Anne Asbury at the time of the old scandal. Janet had noted her employer's distress at the death of the young man, and told of how Shirley Anne had started to drink, how she'd walked out of the production she was starring in and lost all hope of getting a decent part in a film again.

Janet had told how Shirley Anne had discovered that she was pregnant. She had been in turn elated and despondent, and it seemed that she had hoped she might persuade her lover to marry her but . . .

Turning the page, Sarah read that Shirley Anne's lover was married. He had promised to get a divorce and marry her, but then something had happened and he had broken his promise.

> *Shirley was devastated. She started drinking worse than ever and in the end we had to take the bottle away from her. We had to lock it up so that she couldn't get at it or she would have killed herself. We told her that she had to think of the child . . .*

Sarah turned the page again and discovered that it was the end of a notebook. She picked up the next one and looked eagerly for the story to continue, but the notes began again after a long period had elapsed. She frowned, because she had chosen the books at random, thinking that they would be in date order, but they weren't. She had read several that related to things before this one, and some of them contained material that might have been scandalous at the time and concerned people in the theatrical business, but would hardly be relevant now. Another book talked about Janet being left a lot of money by someone for whom she had worked years earlier.

Shirley asked me to stay on, but I told her I couldn't. It has been unbearable watching her destroy herself and after what happened when the child was snatched . . . I have decided to leave. She still has Agnes. Agnes will take care of her if she will let her – and it's time I started to look after myself. Besides, Agnes hates me now and it is best I go . . .

After that the notebook began to tell of Janet's move to lodgings at first, and then after some years to her own cottage. At first she wrote about enjoying her new life and the people she met, but then she began to note things she had seen. People having affairs; people being jealous of each other's garden produce and vandalizing it: petty, silly little incidents that could mean very little and were surely not a reason for murder. Sarah hunted for the book in between, the one that would have described the kidnapping of Shirley's child and her reaction, but it wasn't there. She felt frustrated but knew that she would have to wait for the next day to read it.

Coming towards the end of the most recent book, Janet had noted that she believed Simon Beecham was having an affair with Morna Scaffry. She had also noted that she believed he was concerned in the devil worship going on in the woods, and that Madeline Lewis-Brown was very much involved.

She isn't as clever as she thinks she is. Sometimes she says things and laughs because she thinks we don't know what she is – but I know. And I know something she would like to know too. She wants him. I've seen it in her face when she looks at him, but he doesn't want her. I think she is very much like her sister and I've never

forgotten what she did . . . if Madeline knew what I know
I'm not sure what she would do . . .

There the entry ended. Sarah frowned. Who was Madeline's sister and what had she done that had made Janet dislike her? It was such a nuisance to have only half the tale. She ought to have chosen the notebooks more carefully, but she'd wanted to cover as much time as possible so that she could venture an opinion on whether the books would be of help to the police. So far there wasn't very much, other than that entry about Madeline and Morna Scaffry.

Sarah frowned as she put the books to one side and went upstairs to get ready for the dance that evening. She would return them in the morning and ask Keith Bates if she could borrow some more.

Larch was twenty minutes late. Sarah had begun to wonder if something had happened, and gave him a worried look as she opened the door to him.

'I thought you weren't coming.'

'I almost didn't,' Larch said, and looked apologetic. 'I've been at the hospital most of the day. Ronnie Miller had been sleeping rough in this weather and he was in a bad state when I found him in the woods. The hospital says he has hypothermia and it may well turn to pneumonia.'

'Oh, that's a shame,' Sarah said. 'What made him go off like that?'

'He'd been missing for two days,' Larch said. 'He must have gone off the day after Simon's murder – and his mother says he has been behaving oddly for days now.'

'It sounds bad, doesn't it?' Sarah saw the signs of strain in Larch's face. 'It is a horrid night. Would you rather we didn't go to the dance? We could just stay here and have some supper by the fire.'

'How like you to offer,' Larch said. 'But I'm here now and I would rather we went. To be honest, Sarah, I've had enough of all this – I want us to go out and have a good time.'

'Yes, all right, we shall,' Sarah told him. She made up her mind that she wouldn't mention anything about Keith Bates and the notebooks. After all, they hadn't told her much she didn't know already, and Larch was right. The murders had overshadowed their lives for weeks. 'Let's say goodbye to Gran, and then we'll go.'

Sarah noticed that there was a light on in Janet Bates's cottage when they drove past. Larch didn't appear to notice. Glancing at his profile, Sarah saw a little nerve flicking at his temple. She sensed that something was bothering him, but she hesitated to ask. Larch had suffered from moods when he first came home after the war, sometimes retreating into silence for long periods. He had seemed to be over it recently, but she felt that his silence was one of those awkward ones that she had found disturbing previously.

However, when they got to the hotel, Larch seemed to shrug his despondent mood off and became the perfect escort. They had a wonderful dinner, getting up to dance at intervals during the meal, and then drifting into the main ballroom afterwards.

'This is fun,' Sarah told him when they returned to their seats after doing the now popular Charleston late in the evening. It was a lively dance, which had originated in America, and had caught on after being featured in a Broadway musical called *Runnin' Wild* the previous year. 'I didn't know you could dance like that, Larch.'

'Nor did I,' he admitted. 'It must be you or the wine or something.'

'Oh no, I think it is natural talent. When I was in Bournemouth we often went out on our nights off, and I danced with a lot of partners, but I think you were better than any of them.'

'Flatterer,' Larch teased. 'I suppose you had a lot of friends . . . men friends?'

'Yes, quite a few,' Sarah admitted, and then she caught something in his manner. 'But they were all just friends. We went out as a group, you see.'

'No one special then?'

'No. No one special . . .' She waited, hoping that he would go on but he didn't. 'When are you going to show me your latest paintings, Larch?'

'Oh . . . tomorrow if you like,' he said. 'I actually did some work this morning for the first time in weeks.' He gave her an oddly shy smile. 'I've been asked to give a show of my work, but I'm not sure I'm ready for it. I think

I need more experience – perhaps a more exotic location to paint.'

'I think your paintings are wonderful,' Sarah said. 'You paint local scenes but they are so real . . . so stark and lonely sometimes. Not in the least like Madeline's pretty cottages . . .' She stopped and shook her head in apology. 'Sorry, I didn't mean to bring that up.'

'We can't simply stop talking about it. It happened and so it is a part of our lives.' He pulled a wry face. 'I wonder what Ben is doing. He said that he was afraid his wife had let her tomcat in with his prize-winning female.'

'What kind of cats does he breed?'

'Mostly Siamese, I think,' Larch said. 'Not breeds I care for – give me a plain old tabby every time.'

'Miss Bates had a ginger tomcat,' Sarah said. 'I think it still goes back to the cottage. It was there this morning.'

'Someone is staying there,' Larch said with a little frown. 'I suppose it's her brother. I thought he intended to sell it.'

'I think he may have changed his mind,' Sarah said. It was on the tip of her tongue to tell him that she had spoken to Keith Bates that morning, but she decided against it as the band started to play the last waltz. 'Shall we dance this?' she asked. 'And then we ought to go. The roads may be treacherous if it has frozen hard again.'

'Yes, let's make the most of it,' Larch said, smiling as he took her hand. 'You may be off again soon and then it could be ages before we do this again.'

Sarah nodded. She had wondered if Larch would use the evening to bring them closer together, but if anything he seemed further away than he had for a long time.

Ben finished brushing one of the cats, taking a last look around at the cages before he locked up for the night. All the cats lived in large wire enclosures within a wooden shed, and each of them had an old armchair to use as a bed or a scratching post. His wife laughed at him for giving them such luxuries but he felt it was the least he could do. If it weren't for her tomcat he would take them into the house more often, but attempts to give his prize-winners more of a home life had led to disaster. At least they were warm and comfortable – pampered, Cathy said scathingly when she was in one of her moods. She had been in a mood since he got home, and he sensed she was hiding something from him.

He frowned as he locked up, leaving a small lamp burning so that the cats were not completely in the dark. He had always liked cats, and Siamese were such regal beings. They didn't particularly want to be one of the family like Cathy's Ginger, who believed that he ruled the roost. He suspected that Cathy's odd silence was to do with Ginger and he thought he might know what was troubling her. He had been expecting Bella to come into season at any time, and he was beginning to think she was pregnant. If Cathy had let one of the male cats in with Bella, he just hoped it wasn't Ginger.

'Everything all right?' his wife asked as he went into their sitting room. 'Bella all right?'

'Yes,' he said, and sat down in his favourite chair. 'You might as well tell me, Cathy – was it Ginger?'

She pulled a face and then shrugged. 'He kept following me into the cattery. He must have got into her cage when my back was turned . . .' She looked at him apologetically. 'I'm really sorry, Ben. I didn't do it deliberately and I know you were hoping for a good litter from her this time round.'

'Is that all that's been worrying you?' Ben asked. 'You're not angry with me because I went off the way I did?'

'Well, you are supposed to be retired,' Cathy said. 'And I worried that you might get caught up in it all again. There was a time when I hardly ever saw you. You were always working, out to all hours, never really off duty. And you did have a little health scare, even if you're fine now. I don't want anything to happen to you, Ben.'

'I've got more sense than to let it,' he said.

'Well, it's all over now, isn't it?'

'Yes . . . perhaps . . .'

'Ben!' Cathy stared at him in exasperation. 'I thought you told me the police had it all sewn up?'

'Well, it did look that way, but I've been having second thoughts since I got home. Something isn't right, Cathy. I can't put my finger on it, but it's bugging me.' He tapped his nose. 'I still believe that Morna Scaffry was killed by Madeline Lewis-Brown, and in her case it looked like a clear case of suicide – but something doesn't fit. I have a feeling that I've missed an important piece of the puzzle.'

'You're not going down there again?' Cathy pulled a face when he remained silent. 'Do you really have to?'

'Would you mind so very much?' Ben asked. 'If we got someone to come in and help with the cats you could come with me.'

'No, I don't think so, much too cold at this time of the year,' Cathy said. She shook her head at him. 'You are incorrigible, Ben Marshall. All right, go if you want to – but you can take me away for Christmas somewhere warm.'

'That's a promise, love,' he said. 'I'll get Ted Hughes to come in for the cats and we'll have a few days on the Riviera.' He grinned at her affectionately. 'I suppose you weren't thinking of making a cup of tea?'

'Yes, all right,' she said and got up. 'I was just about to suggest it myself.'

Ben frowned as his wife left the room. He wished he could get to the bottom of what was worrying him, but he had a feeling that somewhere along the line he had made a big mistake . . .

Sarah looked out of the window the next morning. The snow had almost gone, though it still lingered in sheltered spots, but the lawn was green again. She sighed, wondering why she was feeling a little down in the dumps. It had been a lovely evening at the Chestnuts, and yet she had sensed a withdrawal in Larch and she didn't know why.

She pushed her own feelings to the back of her mind as she remembered that she had promised to return Janet's note-books before Keith left. She would have to be fairly quick, because she had arranged to look at Larch's painting later that morning and he was collecting her at eleven.

Gathering up her bits and pieces she went out into the hall, calling out to her grandmother that she would only be gone a short time. Amelia didn't answer her, because she hadn't heard, but Sarah didn't realize that as she went out.

She walked as quickly as she could, because she wanted to look through more of the notebooks and there wasn't much time. Keith would want to leave soon.

The ground was slushy underfoot until she reached the main road, but she was wearing sensible boots and kept her footing as she negotiated the mud of a country lane.

When she reached the cottage, she saw that a note had been pinned on the door of Miss Bates's cottage and it was addressed to her. She opened it and read the few lines inside; it said that Keith had just popped down to the shop to get some milk and would only be a moment. He had left the door open for her to go in and keep warm until he returned.

Sarah smiled, thinking how different his attitude was now to when they'd first met. She entered the kitchen, which smelled of coffee and toast. The heat of the fire welcomed her and she went to warm her hands, before turning her attention to the pile of books lying on the scrubbed pine table. She was interested in two books in particular. One of them had been written up some years earlier, the other was quite recent. She bent her head, looking through them and discarding those she wasn't interested in for the moment.

Intent on her search she took no notice when she heard a slight sound, and then, as she suddenly realized there was someone behind her, she tried to turn her head just as a hand came over her nose and mouth. In the hand was a cloth of some kind and it had an unpleasant, pungent smell, but before she had time to associate the distinctive odour in her mind, the chloroform had done its work and she slumped back into the arms of the man who had drugged her.

He let her body sag, breaking her fall as she lost consciousness and leaving her to lie on the floor. There was something quite caring in the way he made sure she didn't fall and hurt herself. He frowned over her inert form for a moment, and then he scooped up the notebooks and stepped over Sarah's body, wrenching open the kitchen door and making good his escape.

'Wake up, Sarah!' she could hear the voice as from a distance and feel someone shaking her shoulder. 'Oh, my God! What the hell do I do? Sarah, please be all right! I dare not leave you to phone anyone. Don't die on me . . . please don't die!'

There was a frantic, wailing note to the man's voice and Sarah opened her eyes to find that Keith Bates was kneeling on the floor beside her. 'Oh, thank God! It gave me a hell of a fright when I came back and found you.'

Sarah made an attempt to sit up but her head was woozy and she felt sick. She closed her eyes and groaned, but on the second attempt she made it. Keith supported her when he saw that she was feeling rotten, and with a little help she managed to get to her feet and stumble to the chair by the fire, where she slumped down again.

'What happened?' she said. 'I can't remember . . .'

'I left the door unlocked for you while I went to the shop,' Keith told her. 'You came in and I think you must have been looking at the books on the table, and then . . . you'll have to tell me the rest, Sarah. I came back, found the books gone and you lying there. I thought you were dead.'

'I think . . .' Sarah's head was gradually clearing though she still felt groggy. 'I remember the smell of . . . chloroform. I think someone was here and . . . he put a hand over my nose and mouth. The chloroform knocked me out straight away.'

'Yes, it would. I've had that wretched stuff at the dentist's,' Keith said, 'and I know it makes you feel pretty awful for a while when you come round.' He fetched her a cup of water. 'Have a sip of this. The question is, why should someone attack you like that? Whoever it was couldn't have known you would be here . . . which means . . .'

'If you had been here you might have fared worse,' Sarah said, and felt cold all over. 'I seem to remember that he let me down gradually rather than letting me fall . . . but if you had been here instead of me . . .' She shuddered as she recalled what had happened to Janet Bates. 'I think whoever used chloroform on me may have been the same person who . . .'

'Killed my sister?' Keith went white and pulled out a chair from the kitchen table to sit down. 'That means he was after the books all the time, doesn't it?'

'Yes, it seems that way. But how could he know? How could he know that you had found them?'

'I might have mentioned it to the woman in the shop,' Keith said. 'I know I told her I was going to try and finish my sister's book and I bought some notebooks from her.'

'When did you tell her?'

'Last evening, after I'd spoken to you. I popped in and got chatting. She's very friendly and I'm sure I mentioned that I had found the notebooks.'

'Was anyone else there?'

'No – at least, someone came in towards the end of the time, but I don't think he heard me mention anything.'

'But Jilly could have told him,' Sarah said. 'It would be on her mind, and she must have thought that it was safe to talk about these things now . . .

'Did you recognize him?'

'Sorry, I didn't,' Keith said. 'But she would probably know. Not that it proves anything.'

'It might help,' Sarah said. Her mind was much clearer now but she was still feeling awful. 'Any chance of a cup of tea before I go home?'

'Yes, of course, and I'll take you in my car. You ought to ask the doctor to call, go to bed or something. I'm most awfully sorry, Sarah. I shouldn't have left the door unlocked, but I didn't want you to get cold.'

'I shall be all right in a little while. My head is beginning to clear now. At least he didn't knock me unconscious or . . .' She swallowed hard. 'I wonder why he didn't kill me? If he killed Janet . . . why not me?'

'Don't! I can't bear to think of it. I was terrified when I saw you lying there. If you'd been dead . . .' He had gone a ghastly putty colour. 'It doesn't bear thinking about.'

'Was I lucky or was there another reason?' Sarah frowned. After so many murders, why had she been spared? Why not simply knock her on the head with the poker and be done with it? 'The worst thing is that he took the notebooks.'

'He got most of them,' Keith said, 'but I kept a couple back to show you and they are still here. I hid them upstairs. I'll fetch them after we've had our tea. That's if you still want to see them?'

'Yes, please,' Sarah said, 'but that means you've lost most of Janet's work, doesn't it?'

'I don't think her book would have worked out,' he said. 'It might even have been libellous. I still think I'll try to write, but I'll stick to my detective stories. After all, I don't actually have to work at all thanks to Janet. It was lucky for me that she had someone trace me, because she need not have done. Janet was a very loyal person. She may have been nosy but if she cared about someone she never forgot them.' He got up and went over to fill the kettle with water. 'That was the interesting thing I wanted to share with you. It seems that she had employed a private detective to trace another child . . .'

Sarah was feeling a little less nauseous after her drink of water, and her head was clearing. 'Would that be Shirley Anne Asbury's daughter?'

'Yes.' Keith looked at her in surprise. 'How did you know that?'

'I didn't know she'd been trying to trace the child, but I did know that the baby was stolen from its pram some years ago – about seventeen years or so, I think.'

'Yes, that's right. It is all in Janet's notebooks, the ones I read. Apparently, the nurse put the pram outside in the garden and left the child while she went off somewhere. When she came back and the pram was empty, she claimed that she had asked Janet to keep an eye on the child. My sister says that was a lie. She quarrelled with the nurse. It was a very bitter quarrel and the reason she decided to leave her employment when her legacy came through. She thought that she was being blamed for the child's disappearance. She was bitter about that for a long time, because she believed it had made her friend turn against her. Apparently, Janet tried to contact her again a few years later and she snubbed her.'

'Yes, that makes sense of what I read,' Sarah agreed, a flicker of excitement overcoming the last remnants of lingering shock. She sat up straight in her chair and took the cup Keith offered her, sipping the strong sweet tea. 'This is just what I needed.'

'I would offer you something stronger but Janet never kept anything in the house and I'm not organized yet.'

'No, this is fine,' Sarah assured him. 'Did any of Janet's notes say that she thought she had found Shirley Anne's child?'

'Yes. That's it exactly. She was very excited about it. She said that she was going to reveal the truth in her book, and that it would serve Agnes right for lying about her. I think she was quite angry about the way she had been blamed for the abduction, and she wrote that she would punish the person responsible for turning Shirley Anne against her.'

'Did she say where the child was or what had happened to her?'

'No, strangely enough she didn't,' Keith said. 'At least, it wasn't in any of the books I read. I thought the latest was missing.'

'Isn't that always the way? Oh well, we have something to

go on. I shall have to give this some thought.' Sarah stood up, glancing at the kitchen mantle clock as she did so. 'Oh heavens, I shall be late. Someone is picking me up shortly.'

'Are you sure you feel well enough?' Keith asked. 'I'll run you home but I think you should have the doctor.'

'No, I'm fine now,' Sarah said. 'That horrid stuff knocked me out for a while but I shall be all right now.'

She spoke bravely but her knees felt a little bit wobbly. Pride made her keep her head up and say nothing, but she was glad to sit down again when she climbed into the car.

'When are you leaving?' she asked as Keith started the car.

'I don't think I ought to go just yet,' he replied. 'I think I should speak to the police or someone. After all, you could have been killed.'

'But I wasn't, and that is the curious thing,' Sarah said. 'Someone killed your sister because of something she knew – so, if it was the same person who took the notebooks, why didn't he kill me?'

'You're sure it was a man?'

'Yes, pretty sure,' Sarah said. 'I remember the hand over my mouth – it was a large hand. I'm sure it was a man.'

'Perhaps he wasn't the one who killed my sister.'

They had turned into her grandmother's driveway and she saw a car she recognized as belonging to Ben Marshall parked outside.

Sarah turned to look at Keith as he stopped the car. 'I think you've hit the nail right on the head,' she said. 'And if you wouldn't mind, I would like you to come in and speak to a friend of mine . . .'

Thirteen

'We were just beginning to worry about you,' Amelia said as Sarah entered the parlour with Keith behind her. 'You didn't tell me you were going out.'

'I did call out but perhaps you didn't hear. I was in a bit of a hurry because I wanted to take some of Janet's notebooks back . . .' She turned to Keith, beckoning him forward. 'This is Janet's brother and we have something to tell Ben. But if you don't mind, I need to sit down, I'm still feeling a bit woozy.'

'There!' Amelia cried, shooting a glance at Ben. 'I told you I thought something was wrong, didn't I? Did you have a fall, dearest?'

'Not exactly . . .' Sarah would have preferred not to tell Amelia all of it, but there was no way she could avoid it. She explained, making light of her feelings of shock and nausea. 'It wasn't so terrible, Gran,' she said as she saw Amelia's look. 'I've had that stuff at the dentist's. It just knocked me out for a while, that's all. He obviously didn't mean to hurt me, because he lowered me gradually rather than letting me fall – at least I seem to remember that, though it is all hazy.'

'You believe it was a man, Sarah?' Ben looked at her intently, eyes narrowed.

'Yes, I am fairly sure.' She glanced at Keith, who was still standing awkwardly. 'Please sit down, Keith.' She smiled at him. 'Keith came back and found me and we've had a cup of tea, so that's why I was a bit longer – but he didn't see anyone leaving. I thought it must be the same person who killed Janet, but then I wondered why he hadn't murdered me. Keith suggested that it might not be the same person.'

Keith blushed as Ben turned his direct gaze on him. 'We think whoever attacked Sarah wanted the exercise books, because he took them and left quickly.'

'When did you find the books?'

'Early yesterday. I saw Sarah on her way home and gave her some to read. She brought them back this morning and they were stolen with the others I'd left on the kitchen table – but I still have two or three I had hidden, because I wanted to keep them safe. I thought they might be important and I was going to show them to Sarah – but she knows what's in them now.'

'Who would know you had the books if you didn't discover them until yesterday?' Ben looked at Sarah. 'Did you tell anyone?'

'No, except Gran, of course – but Keith thinks he probably told Jilly last evening in the shop, and someone came in while he was there.'

'Did you know who it was?' Ben's eyes stabbed at Keith.

'He was tall, distinguished-looking, wearing a shooting jacket,' Keith said. 'But I don't know him.'

'Jilly might,' Sarah said, though the description might fit several of the farmers in the district. 'You could have a word with her, Ben – but we think we may know why the books were stolen. At least, it's one theory . . .' She hesitated and looked at Ben. 'I mean, I know you thought it was all over but . . .'

'You thought differently,' Ben said and nodded, because he had sensed it at the time but ignored the signs because he'd believed the case was solved. 'I should have asked you then instead of telling you it was all wrapped up, shouldn't I?'

'No, of course not. I think you were right about Madeline killing Morna, and I think it was as much from jealousy as anything else. If Simon was her high priest she would think he belonged to her.

'She fancied Larch too, and she was angry when he took me to her studio, especially when I discovered those paintings. If she thought Simon belonged to her, she might have killed Morna to get him back. And she might have tried to scare me that day in the car.

'I don't know why Simon was killed – unless it was because he was thought to have murdered Morna, which makes it a horrid miscarriage of justice, because like you I'm fairly certain it wasn't him. But I always felt that there were two different reasons for the murders. I don't think Janet blackmailed anyone. She didn't need money, and she was set on punishing the people who had blamed her for the tragic disappearance of Shirley Anne Asbury's child—'

'Hang on a minute,' Ben said. 'I'm afraid you've lost me there. Who is Shirley Anne Asbury?'

'She was a popular actress from the very early days of motion pictures,' Sarah said. 'I'm talking of the years from 1905 until probably 1909; she was from the era of Asta Nielsen and Max Linder. Her films were rather like the ones the French film maker Charles Pathé produced. Shirley disappeared from the scene about 1908, because of a suspicious death in the South of France, and by then she had had a child. A year or so after the birth, the baby was snatched from its pram and Shirley Anne's career was finished, because people remembered the suspicious death and whispered that she might have been concerned both with that and the disappearance of her child.'

'You've been busy. I didn't know any of this. I thought you were sharing everything with me?'

'Well, I didn't know any of it myself until I went to London for those auditions. I met someone there who knew Shirley Anne. She told me quite a bit about it, and then Keith supplied the missing pieces by finding Janet's notebooks.' She paused, then, 'We know that there was a nurse for the child and I think her name was Agnes, though I don't know her second name. Anyway, she left the pram in the garden and went off. When she returned the child was missing. She blamed Janet, said that she was supposed to be keeping an eye on the child. Janet said it was all lies but it turned Shirley Anne against her, and she decided to leave because she had been left some money.'

'My sister tried to make up the quarrel some years later – about the time she moved to Beecham Thorny, I think,' Keith said, 'but she was snubbed. Her letter was returned unanswered.'

'That would have upset her – or was she angry?' Ben was thoughtful. This was a whole new kettle of fish! And it put a new light on the proceedings.

'Janet hired a private detective to find me,' Keith said. 'He helped us become reunited about three and a half years ago. I think his success made her think he might find Shirley Anne's child.'

'That would be pretty difficult,' Ben said. 'I've had a few cases of a snatched child myself, and they either turn up almost immediately or that's it. A lot of years had passed since the child was snatched. I think his chances of finding her alive were slim.'

'Well, according to her notebooks he believed he had been successful. Janet was quite excited about it. She wrote that she was going to put it in her book, and that it would serve someone right for blaming her when the truth came out. We think she may have meant Agnes.'

'Yes, possibly,' Ben said. 'But what did she mean – it would serve Agnes right? Surely, it would lift a shadow for all concerned if the truth were discovered?'

'I haven't worked that bit out,' Sarah admitted. 'I have noticed that Janet tended to write her thoughts without always explaining them. She noted times and dates, also incidents, but her thoughts often left me wondering what she meant. And we think the latest book is probably missing. Keith couldn't find it and it wasn't amongst those I looked through.'

'This is fascinating stuff,' Ben said. 'Why didn't you mention any of it before this? It might have made a difference – a big difference.'

Sarah looked apologetic. 'Everything happened so fast. Simon Beecham had been killed by the time I came home from London, and the police were looking for his killer. It seemed as if it must be either Jethro or Ronnie – and I didn't want to muddy the waters, because you thought it was all sewn up. I was going to say something last night to Larch but . . .' she broke off as she heard his voice and then he came into the room. She jumped up and went to greet him. 'Come and meet Keith Bates,' she invited, 'and don't be cross but there's something we have to tell you . . .'

'What's wrong?' he asked, glancing at Keith, and then staring at Ben. 'Father said you had telephoned to say you were coming down, but I didn't realize you were here.'

'I wanted a word with Sarah. I'm afraid this business isn't quite over after all,' Ben said. 'Sarah was attacked this morning and she has been telling us some very interesting stuff about Janet Bates and Shirley Anne Asbury.'

'That's the woman in the photo we took from Janet's album,' Larch said, his brow arched at Sarah. 'You didn't tell me anything about her – other than her name.'

'I didn't know until I went to London,' Sarah said. She sensed that Larch wasn't pleased with her. 'When I came back there was all that business with Simon and Madeline's suicide . . .' her words trailed off, because she wasn't convinced that Madeline had killed herself, but she didn't want to say anything just yet. 'Anyway, Keith found Janet's notebooks. I read some and he read the others – and I was going to read some more but Keith went to the shop and left the door unlocked for me and . . .'

'You arranged to meet him? That was pretty stupid, wasn't it?'

'Hang on a minute,' Keith said defensively. 'I only went out for some milk. I shouldn't have left the door unlocked but I didn't want Sarah to get cold if she arrived before I got back – but when I came back she was lying on the floor . . .'

'Are you sure you didn't put her there? Give her a bang on the head, did you?'

'Larch!' Sarah said. 'That is most unfair. Keith helped me when he returned. Anyway, I wasn't hit over the head, I was rendered unconscious by a cloth with chloroform on it, and I'm perfectly all right now.'

'You might have been dead.' Larch gave her a furious look because the news had terrified him. 'Why the hell didn't you tell me any of this? I could have gone with you this morning and then it wouldn't have happened.'

'I would have told you, but you were upset after you took Ronnie to hospital, and – I thought it could wait. I wasn't sure it was important . . .' And she'd felt that he had somehow withdrawn from her, but she wasn't going to tell him that in front of everyone else.

Larch gave her a hard look and sat down. 'You'd better fill me in then, hadn't you?'

'I'll do that,' Ben said. He gave a brief résumé of everything that Sarah had told him. 'It looks as if Janet's murder might have been for a very different reason – which, if you recall, Sarah told us several times.'

'But why wasn't I murdered?' Sarah said. 'The man who used the chloroform on me could easily have killed me instead. And if he isn't the murderer – why did he want those notebooks, and who did kill her?'

'That is what I intend to find out,' Ben said. 'I shall have to go back over your original notes, Sarah. I must have missed something.'

'You mean the mystery woman?' Larch said. His expression told Sarah that he was still annoyed with her, but at least he was joining in now. 'The one who wore a fur coat, headscarf and dark glasses? I saw her driving from the Manor the night I came here, the night Sarah came back from Bournemouth – and Mrs Roberts saw her in her shop where she asked to buy a map.'

'And I saw her at Morna's funeral,' Amelia said, causing everyone to stare at her because she had been silent until now. 'She was talking to Sir James for a long time and another woman was sitting in the car waiting for her. I thought the one in the fur was rather attractive, though she appeared to be ill – at least she seemed fragile to me. The other woman was very different. I remember that she looked angry and . . . it is unkind of me to say, but she had a wart on her chin.'

'What colour car?' Larch and Ben asked at the same moment.

'Black, I think,' Amelia said, 'but then nine out of ten of my friends who own cars have black ones.'

'Yes,' Ben nodded gloomily. 'They are common enough these days. Perhaps I should go and have a word with Sir James. I think that that gentleman has more to do with this business than meets the eye.'

'Do you think he was the one who . . .' Sarah stopped and blushed. 'No, he couldn't have killed his nephew. That is too awful to contemplate.' She had always believed that he was deeply involved with what was going on here, but no one else seemed to agree and she might be wrong.

'Well, I shall pay him a visit this afternoon if he is at home,' Ben said. 'And I think we ought to ask Morrison to make inquiries concerning Miss Asbury and her companion – Agnes . . .' He looked at Keith. 'Are you intending to return to Norwich soon?'

'I was but I'm not sure now. Perhaps I should stay and look for that missing notebook?'

'I think it could be important,' Sarah said. 'If you want to go home I could look for it . . .'

'No!' Ben and Larch echoed each other.

'If you couldn't find what you needed in the stolen books, the chances are he won't either – which means he may try again,' Ben said and turned to Larch. 'Could you give Keith a hand? The sooner that notebook is found the better, in my opinion.'

'But I might think to look in places they wouldn't,' Sarah protested. 'It isn't fair to shut me out just because of what happened.'

'You were lucky this time,' Larch said and glared at her. 'Don't push your luck, Sarah. You might not be so lucky next time.'

'Well, I think you are both very mean,' she said, jumped up and ran out of the room. She was halfway up the stairs when she heard Larch call to her, but she was close to tears and didn't stop. It was ridiculous, but Larch's and Ben's concern for her had done what her attacker hadn't managed, and that was to upset her.

Larch returned to the sitting room. 'I'm afraid she's angry with us. I suppose she could have come with us as long as she wasn't left there alone.' He directed an accusing stare at Keith, who looked uncomfortable.

'Sarah won't say but she is more upset than she knows,' Amelia told him with a smile. 'She will probably have a good cry and a sleep, and when she wakes up she may feel better. You can come over again this evening, Larch. I am sure she will realize that you and Ben are only trying to protect her.'

'We haven't done much of a job as yet,' Ben said wryly. 'Sarah has discovered most of the clues for us so far and she has taken the brunt of it all – what with that car trying to knock her down, finding Mrs Roberts and now this . . .'

'She didn't tell me about the car,' Amelia said, and looked hard at him and then Larch. 'What else haven't I been told about?'

'Sarah didn't want you to worry. I think the car incident was only a warning, but of course I can't be sure.'

'Well, kindly tell me in future,' Amelia said. 'Sarah is my only grandchild and I don't want to lose her.'

Keith Bates stood up. 'I think I ought to be going now. I'll have a good look for the latest book, though that might have been taken earlier, of course. It wasn't in Janet's hiding place, but she could have shoved it somewhere quick – just to keep it out of the way . . .'

'Well, the police didn't find it,' Ben said and frowned. 'Mind you, they weren't looking for an exercise book.'

'There was a pencil on the table by the window upstairs,' Larch said, 'but no book. I thought it odd but I only glanced in because we shouldn't have been there and I felt guilty. We didn't know much about you then,' he added, looking at Keith. 'I'll come with you and we'll do a thorough search if you like.'

'Two of us will be better than one,' Keith said. 'I must admit it has made me a bit jumpy again.'

'My advice to you would be to keep your door locked when you are alone,' Ben said. 'Someone may have murdered your sister because of something she knew – and if they think you have discovered the secret – well, just be on your guard.' He sat on as Larch and Keith left together, each taking his own car.

'Keep an eye on Sarah, Mrs Beaufort. When she's feeling more herself she is likely to do anything. She will be cross because she thinks we are shutting her out, which isn't true, of course. I value her insight and I shall be talking to her again quite soon.'

'My granddaughter is very strong willed. I shall do my best to keep an eye on her, but if she takes something into her head . . .' Amelia shook her head and sighed. 'I've always admired her spirit, but this could be very dangerous – don't you think?'

'It depends what's going on,' Ben told her. 'To be honest, I haven't worked it out yet. I think Sir James may be mixed up in this – but I don't want to jump to conclusions. Sarah believes I was wrong about Madeline committing suicide, and she may be right.'

'Did Sarah say that?'

'She didn't have to,' Ben said wryly. 'I sensed it just now, though she was too polite to tell me I was wrong. I have been wrong before – and I've been having second thoughts myself. I wouldn't rule murder out completely.'

'Oh dear,' Amelia said. 'That means this is all still hanging over us, and I did hope it was over.'

'So did we all,' Ben said. 'Leave it to me, Mrs Beaufort. I promise you I shall get there in the end . . .'

Ben left the house and drove down to the village, deciding to pop into the shop. He was surprised to see that Mrs Roberts was back behind the counter.

'I didn't expect to see you here,' he said. 'Are you sure you should be working?'

'I'm fine now, and I've got Jilly to keep me company. She's going to stay with me and we'll run things between us.'

'Well, I'm glad you're feeling better.' Ben purchased a packet of cigarettes. He always felt able to think more clearly when he was smoking, though Cathy wanted him to give them up. He was about to turn away when he thought of something. 'Do you recall telling Sarah about a woman in a fur coat who came to buy a map from you?'

'Yes, I remember her – though I still can't remember who hit me.'

'Perhaps it's best you forget that bit,' Ben said. 'The woman who wanted the map – was she an attractive, rather fragile person?'

'No, not at all,' Mrs Roberts said. 'She had all the trappings of wealth but . . . I thought she was ugly, to tell the truth.'

'Did she have a wart on her chin by any chance?'

'I can't . . . No, not a wart. She had a bit of sticking plaster,' Mrs Roberts said. 'Yes, I do recall that now, though I'd forgotten until you mentioned it.'

'Well, you have been very helpful,' Ben said. 'I'm glad your sister is going to stay with you now.'

He was thoughtful as he went out. The mystery was still complicated, but he thought he might be beginning to see the way out of the maze.

'Andrews is going to drive me into the village,' Amelia said, standing outside the door of Sarah's room an hour or so later. 'Are you all right now, dearest?'

'Yes, I'm fine,' Sarah replied. 'I've been sleeping – don't worry about me, Gran.'

She got up after her grandmother had gone, going into the tiny bathroom attached to her room to splash her face with cold water. She was feeling better now, though still annoyed that her friends had tried to shut her out of the investigation. It wasn't fair, because she had come up with most of the clues for them. And she would have thought of looking in places that the two men probably wouldn't. Sighing, she tidied her hair and face and went downstairs just as the telephone started to ring.

'It's all right, Millie. I'll answer it.' She picked up the receiver. 'Sarah Beaufort here – may I help you?'

The operator's voice, then a click, then, 'Oh, Sarah, I'm glad I got you,' the woman's voice said. 'I heard something that I thought you would want to hear – about Shirley Anne Asbury, that is.'

'Is that you, Liz?' Sarah's heart raced wildly. 'I thought I recognized your voice. Thank you for ringing me. I am very interested in hearing what you have to say.'

'I rang round a few people after we talked that day and one of them has just rung me back with some interesting news – Shirley Anne is still alive. She was in a home for the mentally ill until a few months ago and then they discharged her. She has been living with her companion – Agnes Browning – and they aren't too far away from you. They have a cottage in a seaside place called Cley. On my map it looks as if it's just down the coast from where you are. I suppose it might be an hour's drive or a little more . . .'

'I know it quite well. My father took me there when I was a child. It has a high shingle beach, but you have to go down a long, narrow road between flat marshland to get there. That is so interesting, Liz. You don't know how helpful you've been.'

'There was just one more thing. Apparently, Shirley Anne has a terminal illness and she isn't expected to live more than a year at most – that was the reason she was allowed out into Agnes's care.'

'Oh, how awful for her. She has had a terrible life, so much tragedy,' Sarah said, feeling a rush of sympathy. 'I suppose you wouldn't have the address?'

'Yes, as a matter of fact I do – do you have a pencil and paper?'

'Yes, I have it here,' Sarah said and began to take down the details. 'Was there a phone number?'

'Yes, I can give you that too if you want?'

'Please!' Sarah wrote the number down, and then Liz said her doorbell was ringing. 'You must answer it. Thank you again for helping me.'

'Glad to be of help. Keep in touch – and there's another audition here next week. Come on Friday at eleven and you might be lucky.'

'Oh, thank you for telling me. I shall be there.'

Sarah replaced the receiver, and then picked it up and dialled the number she had been given. She pulled a face and looked at the address. It was indeed in the village of Cley, a short distance from Blakeney, and wouldn't take much more than an hour to get there by car. She hesitated for a moment and then rang Larch's home. His father answered.

'May I speak to Larch, please?'

'Sorry, Sarah. He isn't in – shall I ask him to ring you later?'

'Yes, please,' she replied. She replaced the receiver once more. She couldn't just sit here and do nothing. Perhaps she ought to walk down to Miss Bates's cottage and see if Larch was still there.

She ran down the stairs, her earlier mood evaporating as she put on her coat. She scribbled a note to her grandmother, telling her not to expect her home to lunch, and then took Amelia's bike from the shed, because the ice had gone now and it would be quicker to cycle than walk. She wanted to catch Larch before he left the cottage if she could. However, when she reached the bottom of the hill it was to see Larch's car disappearing in the distance.

'Bother!' she said. 'Bother, bother, bother!'

'Sarah!' Keith called to her and she saw he had come out of the cottage to greet her. 'If you wanted Larch he has just left. Can I help at all?'

'Did you find the notebook?'

'Well, we found one under a cushion on the sofa upstairs. It looks as if Janet put it there on impulse rather than hiding it. I think it has a bit about the child being taken all those years ago, and blames Agnes for neglecting to tell anyone she was going out that day, but I don't think it solves the mystery. Larch is going to give it to Ben later and see what he thinks.'

Sarah glanced at Keith's small Model T Ford and then gave him one of her brilliant smiles. 'I've just had a phone call from someone who knows where Shirley Anne lives these days. It isn't much more than an hour's drive – we could go in your car, Keith. If we could see Shirley, speak to her, we might be able to discover something important.'

'You mean go and snoop about?' Keith looked dubious. 'Do you think we ought to?'

'If you don't want to come I'll take Amelia's car when she comes back from shopping . . .' It was an idle threat because her grandmother would never agree.

'Do you want to go right now? I suppose we could – we might stop for a sandwich or something later . . .'

'I should be so grateful. And it isn't really all that far.'

'I know the way. I've been to Blakeney quite a bit in the summer, though not often to Cley.'

'Why don't you lock up and we'll go? It would be a nice run out in the car and you never know what we may find. Janet may even have told Shirley Anne about her discovery.'

'Well, if you really want to,' he said, thinking that he would like to put one over on the rather snooty Captain Meadows, who had been so very scathing about the way he'd gone out and left the cottage unlocked. 'It would be good to get this business settled once and for all.'

'Yes, that's what I think,' Sarah said, and rewarded him with another smile. 'After all, nothing terrible can happen if we stick together – can it?'

'It is very good of you to see me, sir,' Ben said as he was shown into Sir James's study. 'I just need to ask you a few questions if I may?'

'Well, I suppose I might as well allow it,' Sir James said, his brows meeting as he frowned. 'I can't help feeling that if I'd been more open with you last time my nephew might still be alive.'

Sir James had shadows beneath his eyes, as if he had not been sleeping well of late.

'I'm not sure if it would have made a difference, sir.' Ben wondered why his gut reaction was sympathy: he certainly deserved none if he had attacked Sarah. 'We think – and as yet this is not proven, you understand – but we think someone may have killed him as revenge for Morna Scaffry's murder.'

'Good grief!' Sir James sat down heavily, his face going

grey. 'You think that there was a connection . . .' He bowed his head, then raised it and looked at Ben. 'I imagined it was because of that dreadful woman and her coven.'

'In a way it was, because I believe she killed Morna.'

'She killed Morna? I – I thought it might have been my nephew.' A muffled groan issued from his lips. 'There is something I have to tell you, Mr Marshall. Morna Scaffry came here to see me the day before she died. She told me that Simon was the father of her child and asked me for money. Simon had refused to give her anything but I – I gave her five hundred pounds. It was in cash, because I always keep some by me for emergencies.

'I thought that she might have been killed for the money. That brother of hers . . . but then there was Simon. I wasn't sure whether or not he was involved. And then he was murdered too and I started to think it was because of the devil worship.'

Ben inclined his head. 'I may be proved wrong, but I believe you can put that idea out of your head, sir. We aren't sure who killed your nephew but the police want to interview Morna's brother; it may be that he did it out of revenge. Ronnie Miller may have been drawn into it as well, though we don't know that – and at the moment he is fighting for his life in hospital.'

'Yes, I heard about that, poor fellow,' Sir James said. 'Harmless lad I've always thought – bit surly at times but you can't blame him for that with the kind of life he's had. I don't know what more I can say . . .'

'As a matter of fact, I have come to talk to you about something else,' Ben told him. 'Do you know of or have you ever met a woman by the name of Shirley Anne Asbury? We have reason to believe that she may have had something to do with the murder of Miss Janet Bates.'

'No! No, that is a lie! Shirley wouldn't . . . she couldn't have done such a thing. Janet was devoted to her for years . . .' He bent his head, burying his face in his hands for a few moments, and then he looked up. 'I cannot continue to keep the secret, Mr Marshall. It's killing me . . .'

'Take your time, sir,' Ben said because he didn't like the look of the man's colour. 'No need to rush. Would you care for a drop of brandy?'

'Brandy won't help,' Sir James said, and reached for a little silver pillbox, popping a small pill into his mouth. 'They tell me it's my heart. Doesn't often trouble me, except when I'm under a strain.'

'Would you like to put this off until another time?'

'No, I think it's time I told someone.' His eyes had a queer, blind look as he stood up and walked over to the window, looking out at the gardens. 'When I was much younger I was in love with her – Shirley Anne. She was an actress with a good career ahead of her and I had not yet inherited this place, though I was married. It was not a good marriage and I became Shirley's lover . . .'

He paused and turned to look at Ben. 'There was another young idiot after her. He was always trying to get her alone and he kept asking her to marry him. Shirley gave me an ultimatum – get a divorce or she would marry Freddie. We were all in the south of France, and we had been drinking. He followed us upstairs to her room and we had an argument. He and I went out to the balcony to finish the quarrel and Shirley came out to us. She told us both that she'd had enough of our squabbling and he started crying. Before we could stop him, he climbed the railing and jumped.

'He was killed, of course. Shirley was devastated and Janet gave her something to make her sleep. We thought about moving the body but there was so much blood that it would have been obvious that he had fallen from Shirley's room so we . . . all went to bed and left him there.'

'You didn't call the police or an ambulance?'

'No. We made a pact to tell the police that we had no idea how he got there. It was the balcony to Shirley's sitting room not her bedroom – so we all pleaded ignorance. Shirley was in such a state that she had to be kept under sedation for some days, and by that time the police had decided that it was just an intoxicated idiot playing silly buggers. Janet told them that he had been drunk earlier and that Shirley had sent him away, which was true. She also said that she had heard him say he would kill himself if Shirley wouldn't have him – which may not have been true.'

'I see. So Shirley Anne had reason to be grateful to Janet?'

'Good lord, yes,' Sir James said. 'It was only after the other business that they fell out . . .'

'And what business was that?'

'Shirley was having my child,' Sir James said. 'We . . . had a daughter. She was about a year or so old when she was snatched from her pram, which had been left in the garden. Her nurse had gone out for the day but had asked Janet to watch her . . .' His voice shook. 'But she was taken . . . we all blamed Janet, though I've since wondered if it was truly her fault.'

'Did that upset you?' The look on Sir James's face was answer enough. 'You were upset when the child was snatched. And yet you didn't ask your wife for a divorce?'

'My wife had an accident at about that time. The doctors told us that she would be confined to a wheelchair for the rest of her life. As far as I was concerned that meant I could never leave her . . .' His face worked with grief. 'You'll never know what that cost me. I wanted children and Joyce couldn't have them . . . or any kind of marital relations. I told Shirley I would be a father to our daughter and then . . . she was snatched. That broke my heart, Mr Marshall. It finished Shirley. She tried to drink herself to death. She had lost everything: reputation, career, her lover and her child . . .'

'Yes, it must have been awful for her – for you too, sir. Children mean a lot and it's bad enough not having them; to lose one like that is tragic.'

'We tried to trace her. The police mounted a search but when no trace was found they suspected that Shirley might have smothered her and got rid of the body so that she could return to her career. It was a wicked lie, but I know for a fact that some of them believed it, though nothing was proven.'

'And did you never try to trace her yourself?'

'Yes, I employed someone but after five years of trying he told me the child was most probably dead.'

'Yes, I see.' Ben nodded his head. 'It must have been a shock when Miss Bates told you that she had succeeded where everyone else had failed. Did you think she was trying to blackmail you?'

Sir James sat down again. 'She didn't tell me. Janet wrote to Shirley, and she came here to tell me – but not until almost a week after Janet Bates was dead. She was worried that she would be connected to the murder because she knew that Janet had a lot of photographs and notebooks that might lead the police to her. And there was another reason . . .'

'Is that why you went to the cottage this morning? To try and recover them?'

'Yes . . .' Sir James looked sick. 'Is Sarah all right? I thought it must be Janet's brother when I went in and then I panicked when I saw her, because she would know me. So I used that wretched stuff, which I had taken along just in case – unforgivable, I know. I was desperate to get those damned notebooks and they are of no use whatsoever. There isn't a shred of evidence to prove what she told Shirley. If she has it, she hid it somewhere else.'

'You behaved despicably, Sir James. The police may have something to say about the drugging of Miss Beaufort and the theft – but that will be for them to decide. You were about to tell me something more?'

'Janet told Shirley that her private detective had traced our daughter. She said that she knew exactly what had happened to the child and that it was all going to come out in the book she was writing – and that once we knew the whole truth we would be sorry that we had accused her of neglect.'

'Did she mention the girl's name? She would have been about sixteen now, I imagine?'

'A few months more,' Sir James said and his face worked with grief once more. 'About the same age as Morna Scaffry . . .'

'Of course,' Ben said as a light flashed in his head. 'That's what all this has been about, isn't it? Janet believed that Morna Scaffry was your daughter.'

'Yes,' Sir James's hands had started to tremble as he agreed. 'When Shirley told me what Janet had told her, I guessed what she was getting at, but I couldn't believe it. She didn't say it right out, you see, just hinted. She said the child had been living with gypsies and that she had proof, because she had seen her several times. I realized that she must mean Morna Scaffry and I knew Simon was having a fling with the girl. He had asked me if the gypsies could stay in the woods for the time being, and I had agreed. The brother was an out-and-out scoundrel, into thieving as well as poaching if you ask me, but Morna was different . . . I bought some heather from her once and she reminded me of . . .'

'Did she remind you of Shirley Anne?'

'Yes . . .' A tear was trickling from the corner of Sir James's eye. 'There was something about her smile – but she didn't have Shirley's colouring . . . she had mine. I thought it was just wishful thinking. Wouldn't let myself believe that it could be our little Jane . . . but then when Shirley told me and Morna came to me in trouble . . . well, I gave her the money. I was still dubious, thought it was probably emotional blackmail, though Janet wasn't asking for money. She probably had more than Shirley. I wanted to believe it desperately . . . I told Morna she could come to me if she needed help when she had the child.'

'And then she was murdered.'

'You don't need to remind me!' His knuckles had turned white as his hand lay clenched on the desk. 'I haven't been able to sleep since then. Shirley didn't know where to find Morna – and I didn't tell her. God forgive me! If I had the poor girl might still have been alive. Shirley would have taken her home with her. But I wasn't convinced she was our daughter and I wanted to think things through. I knew where Janet kept her spare key and I was going to take a look for the proof, but then her brother turned up and the key wasn't there any more . . .'

'You could have broken in,' Ben said. 'Why leave it until now?'

'Everything happened too fast. I didn't know where to turn. I tried to find out more about her from Simon and we argued, and then he was killed. I thought it might have been one of the coven and I went to see Mrs Lewis-Brown, to ask her what she knew about it. She laughed in my face. That's when I picked up the chloroform, saw it there and took it.'

'Did you kill her? I saw you coming from that direction the morning I found her.'

'It wasn't then that I spoke to her. Besides, I thought she committed suicide? I did consider it because she was such a bitch, but I didn't touch her. After all, it wouldn't bring either of them back, would it?' He looked old and ill, his face ravaged by the strain of his confession. 'I have lost the daughter I hardly knew – if she really was our child, that is. I think the worst thing is not knowing. Shirley believes it, of course, and she is devastated all over again. She hasn't long to live, and I doubt I shall survive many years. Simon wasn't much, but at least he was blood kin. My wife has a cousin but no one close.' He shrugged. 'Not that there is all that much to leave anyone these days. You might as well know the whole. The estate is in debt and if I don't get that planning permission settled . . . but you don't want to know about any of that . . .'

'I see . . .' Ben frowned. 'Is that the whole of it, sir? You aren't keeping anything back?'

'If you think I know who killed Janet you're barking up the wrong tree, Marshall.' Sir James looked angry, his eyes narrowed. 'If I'd known that Mrs Lewis-Brown had killed Morna I would have killed her – and if I was sure that Morna's brother was behind Simon's murder I would shoot the legs from under him – but I can't help you with any of it. I only wish I could. You don't know how much I wish that I could bring Janet Bates back to life. If I'd known for sure that Morna was my daughter . . .' He shook his head. 'But I didn't and I can't do anything now, can I? It is far too late.'

'Yes, I'm afraid it is,' Ben said. 'If you had told me all this at the start we might have had something to go on – but you couldn't know what would happen.'

'What happens next?' Sir James asked. 'I shall be here if the police want to speak to me.'

'I'll think about what you've told me,' Ben said. 'I'm making no promises because what you did to Sarah this morning was despicable. That stuff can be dangerous if you don't know how to handle it – but if Sarah doesn't want it to go any further, well, we might not press charges. You will return Mr Bates's property to him, of course.'

'Yes. I wish I'd never taken the damned things. The woman was like a magpie hoarding her wretched secrets, but it was all a muddle as far as I was concerned.'

'Well, we'll leave it at that for the moment,' Ben said. 'Oh – whereabouts does Shirley Anne live these days?'

'She and Agnes share a cottage at Cley – that's not far from Blakeney.'

'Not far from here then?' Ben said, looking thoughtful. 'An hour's journey either way if you know the roads, I imagine?'

'If you're thinking that Shirley Anne killed Janet you are wrong.'

'Someone did, Sir James, and it wasn't you – but someone killed her and it may have had something to do with her claim to have discovered the truth about the disappearance of . . .'

Ben broke off as it came to him. 'What an idiot I am! It has to be the nurse, of course. What did you say her name was?'

'Agnes? But she has devoted herself to Shirley for years. Why should she want to kill Janet?'

'Because she lied about leaving the care of the baby to Janet perhaps – and Janet knew what had really happened.' Ben rubbed his nose because it had started to itch like mad. 'Shirley hasn't long to live. Is she going to leave what she has to Agnes by any chance?'

'Her name is Agnes Browning,' Sir James said, looking sick again. 'And I noticed when they came to the funeral that she is rather possessive of Shirley . . .'

'Agnes Browning?' The chills were running up and down Ben's spine. He knew he was on to something. 'Are you sure about that?'

'Yes, quite sure – why?'

'Do you know if she happened to have a sister – a younger sister?'

'I have no idea. What are you getting at?'

'It's just a hunch. But I think I ought to pay Shirley Anne and her companion a little visit . . . and if I'm right, the sooner I do it the better. We don't want any more murders. You might be next on the list yourself, Sir James.'

'Rubbish! Why should the woman want to kill me?'

Ben shrugged. 'Once someone like that starts it is like a drug, and they just keep on doing it. If I've got it right this time, she is a very dangerous woman.'

Fourteen

'I'm sorry we got lost back there,' Keith apologized. 'I came on the bus before and I thought I would remember, but I'd forgotten that turning.'

'Perhaps the bus went another way,' Sarah said. It had taken them well over an hour and a half to reach Cley village. Like a lot of the Norfolk villages on this part of the coast, it consisted in the main of cottages built of reddish brick with flint or stone interspersed. 'It doesn't much matter, but I am hungry. Shall we pop into that café and have a bun and some coffee?'

'Yes, that's a good idea,' Keith said. 'I thought about stopping ages back but wanted to make sure I could find the way here first.'

'Well, we are here now,' Sarah said, smiling at him. 'I would like to pick up a notebook and pen from the newsagent's, too, because I'm going to pretend to be a researcher.'

Keith pulled up in front of the café. 'That's a good idea. Shirley Anne was pretty famous in her day, and she will probably want to talk about her career.'

'I'm hoping that she will get on to more personal subjects after we've talked for a while. I've got a few ideas but they are all a bit vague. If Shirley Anne takes to us she may tell us more than she realizes.'

'Do you think she killed Janet because she was trying to blackmail her over something?'

'I think Janet probably wrote to her about the child. She had been wrongly accused of neglect according to her notebooks – and that is why she was determined to find out what had happened to the baby. She would have been so excited if she believed she had, and I am sure she must have written to Shirley Anne to tell her.'

'Yes, that makes sense.' Keith still looked doubtful. 'What

I can't see is why Shirley Anne would have wanted to kill her. I should have thought she would be so grateful that Janet had found her daughter.'

'I know the woman Larch and Mrs Roberts saw sounds as if it might have been Shirley Anne, but it could have been someone else.'

'I'm not sure I know what you mean?'

Sarah laughed. 'I only wish I did. I have an idea but I might be wrong. Let's go and have our coffee and then we'll talk. The wind is bitter out here.'

Ben arrived a few minutes after Amelia discovered the note from her granddaughter. She was hovering by the telephone wondering who best to ring when Millie opened the door to him, and she turned to him in relief.

'I was just wondering if you would be at the Meadows's house. I don't know what Sarah is up to now, but I must admit I'm worried. I have a horrible feeling she is heading into danger.'

She held the note out to him, which he read thoughtfully. 'Do you have any idea where she might have gone?'

'Millie said she took a phone call a few minutes before she left. She was in the kitchen most of the time, but she did hear Sarah repeating an address.' She looked at Millie, who had lingered in case she was needed. 'Where did you say it was?'

'I heard her say she knew it and that it wasn't far from Blakeney, Mrs Beaufort. She wrote it down but tore the paper off – you might see faint marks underneath if you look . . .'

'Millie's right,' Ben said and picked up the pad. He scribbled gently over it with a pencil and saw the impression of the word he had expected to find. 'I think I know exactly where she's going. Do you mind if I telephone Larch, Mrs Beaufort? I would like him to come with me, because Sarah could be in real danger this time.'

Amelia gestured towards the phone, waiting as Ben put through a call and arranged to pick Larch up on his way through the village.

'I should never have gone out and left her alone,' she said as he replaced the receiver. 'I've had an odd feeling all morning. She's found out who the murderer is, hasn't she?'

'Yes, and she has decided to go after her herself rather than coming to us – and that's because she thought we were shutting her out. It just shows that the road to hell is paved with good intentions. We should have involved her in the search for the notebooks.' He gave Amelia a rueful smile. 'We'll ring you as soon as we have any news.'

'Thank you, I should appreciate that.'

'I'll be on my way, and don't be too worried, Mrs Beaufort. Sarah is a resilient girl. I don't know how she plans to get there, but . . . Oh, lord, yes I do! She will have asked Keith Bates to take her and he'll do it. I think he's half in love with her already.'

'Yes, I noticed that,' Amelia said. 'But please go. She could be there already.'

Ben knew that Sarah and Keith were bound to get there ahead of them whatever he did. Larch had said he would be ready when Ben arrived to pick him up, but perhaps it might be as well to put a telephone call through to Morrison before they left . . .

'That must be the cottage,' Sarah said as they drew up opposite a red brick and Norfolk-cobbled house. There were heavy lace curtains at the windows, and a black car was parked beside the house. Sarah thought the car looked similar to the one that had tried to knock her down, but that didn't mean much. There were lots of Model T Ford cars around these days, and all of them black. 'You wait for me here, Keith. I don't think they'll let two of us in – but if I'm a long time come to the door and ring the bell.'

'You could say I was a photographer,' he suggested, feeling uneasy about letting her go alone. 'I've got my Brownie in the glove compartment.'

'I'll tell them my photographer is in the car. Don't worry, I'm not going to accuse anyone of murder. I'm here to do some research on Shirley Anne Asbury's career for my magazine.'

'Well, I shall give you twenty minutes and then I'll come and ring the bell.'

'Yes, all right. It's not that I don't want you with me, Keith. I'm really glad you came – but I have to get in there yet.'

'Yes, I know.' He had begun to wonder if he ought to have insisted that they speak to Ben Marshall before they came dashing down here, but it was a bit late for second thoughts.

Sarah got out of the car and walked across the road. On this part of the coast the wind was bitter at this time of year. Rosemary Cottage was on the outskirts of the village and it caught the full blast of the wind from the sea, as it blew across the flat marshland beyond the shingle beach. She walked up the path to the front door and knocked. From across the road Keith saw the lace curtains at the bedroom window twitch, though Sarah couldn't. She waited, shivering in the cold, and was just about to knock again when the door opened and a woman stood in the hall glaring at her.

'Yes? What do you want?'

Sarah knew at once that this wasn't Shirley Anne. Even the years couldn't have changed the once beautiful film star into an ugly monster like this. She was built more like a man than a woman with wide shoulders, a heavy, dumpy body, wiry grey hair and narrow-set eyes – and she had a wart on her chin.

'I am Sarah Beaufort. I am doing some research on early motion pictures and I should like to talk to Miss Asbury for a few minutes if I may, please?'

'Miss Asbury doesn't talk to newspaper reporters. Go away!'

'I'm not a reporter. I'm just doing research for . . .' Sarah put out a hand to stop the door being slammed in her face. 'Please. I just want to talk to Shirley Anne about the old days . . .'

'Who is it, Agnes?' a voice asked from somewhere behind the dragon.

'Just some nosy parker asking questions!'

'Miss Asbury,' Sarah called. 'I just want to ask you a few questions. I am a friend of Sir James Beecham . . .'

The door was firmly slammed in her face, but as she turned away it opened again and she saw a woman she recognized immediately standing there. Shirley Anne still retained the remnants of her beauty, though she looked fragile and ill, but when she smiled she might almost have been young again.

'Please come in, Sarah,' Shirley Anne said. 'That is your name, I believe? I must ask you to forgive Agnes. She was trying to protect me, but I'm afraid she was very rude.'

'Are you sure it is convenient?' Sarah could see the signs of illness in her face and suddenly felt that she ought not to be there, prying into something that was likely to cause this woman more distress.

'Yes, of course. I have so few visitors, my dear, and soon I shall not have any at all.'

She opened the door wide and Sarah followed her into a small but comfortable parlour. It was furnished in a way that suggested most of the things might have come from a second-hand shop, but had been tastefully arranged.

'This is a lovely room, Miss Asbury.'

'Do you like it?' Shirley Anne smiled and gestured to her to sit down. Sarah was startled because that smile had suddenly made everything click into place in her head. She knew who had committed the murders – all of them except perhaps Simon's – and why. 'I did my best to make it look nice, because it will be Agnes's home after I've gone. I've no one else to leave it to, and it isn't much for all she has done for me over the years. But as far as the furniture is concerned, it is surprising what you can buy quite cheaply second-hand.'

'It has a feel of the way things were at the end of the last century,' Sarah said, and took a deep breath because it was important not to let anyone guess what was in her mind. 'And a charm that makes you immediately at home. Some of these things must surely have been yours?'

'That is a lovely compliment – but why do you say some of the things must have been my own?'

'Because I recognize the pictures. I've seen several of them before. May I look more closely?'

'Yes, please do,' Shirley Anne said and sat down, watching Sarah as she moved about the room, picking up the photograph frames.

Sarah recognized photographs that she had seen in Janet Bates's album, and then she saw the art nouveau frame with the picture of two women standing together. She picked it up and looked at it, almost certain that it was the one she had seen on the table in Janet's parlour or its twin.

'This is a lovely frame. Is it by René Lalique?'

'Yes, it is,' Shirley said. 'It was given to me by a friend – a very dear friend . . .' A shadow passed across her face as Sarah set the frame down and then sat in the chair she had indicated earlier. 'You say you are a friend of James – you may have

known Janet. Perhaps you know that she . . .' Shirley smothered a sob. 'Forgive me, it upsets me to speak of it.'

'Yes, I did know Janet, and I know what happened to her.
She had a frame just like this – and she showed me some of
your photographs once because she knew that I wanted to
sing on stage.'

'Do you, my dear? How exciting! I wish you well in your
career – but you wanted to ask me some questions . . .'

'I did come here to ask questions, but if you feel it would
be too distressing for you . . .?'

'You're not really researching my early career, are you?'
Shirley looked at her in a slightly reproachful way. 'Why did
you really come? Is it because of Janet or . . .' she broke off,
visibly distressed.

'Janet tried to find your daughter, didn't she?' Sarah said,
because now she was here she might as well come out with
it. 'She wrote in her notebooks that her private detective had
succeeded where others had failed, but she didn't actually say
what he had discovered. Did she tell you?' Sarah saw the grief
flicker in her face. 'Yes, of course she did. It was the reason
she went to all that trouble, so that she could prove to you
that it wasn't her fault that the baby was snatched.'

'She told me . . .' Shirley Anne lifted her head. 'Janet's letter
told me that she was writing a book and that it would all come
out. She said that my daughter was alive and living near her
and that she knew her. She said that if I went to see her she
would tell me where she was and what she was called, but I
was ill, actually in hospital having some treatment, when I
received the letter and before I could visit her she had been
murdered. However, I went to see James soon after, and he
told me that she had hinted to him that he might already know
our daughter – you did know that he was the father of my
child?' Sarah shook her head and she smiled. 'Poor James.
He wanted to marry me but he was tied to his wife because
of the accident. She was stuck in that wheelchair and could
never give him a child and he adored our little Jane. It devastated us both when she was taken.'

'Janet gave Sir James a hint of the girl's identity?'

'She told him that he should pay some attention to Morna
Scaffry, and that he might discover something interesting if
he really looked at her.' The tears were slipping down her

cheeks now. 'I went to visit James about a week after . . . Janet was murdered. I told him about her letter and asked if he knew anything. He hesitated and then told me what Janet had said to him. Apparently, she took a letter that had been misdirected up to him, and she made all sorts of strange comments. He thought she had opened his letter and read it, and didn't take much notice of what she'd said – but then he saw the girl again and he said it gave him a shock, because he thought Morna looked like me when I was younger.'

'Yes, she did,' Sarah said. 'She didn't have your colouring, but she certainly had your smile. I noticed a likeness when I saw some pictures of you in the theatre in London – at least, I felt there was something familiar about you, but I couldn't place it and it was only when you smiled at me just now that I knew.'

'So you think she really was my daughter?' Shirley Anne's hand was trembling. 'Why would anyone kill her? Please, can you tell me that? It has been playing on my mind since she was murdered. I can't believe that I was so close to finding her.' She bent her head and covered her face with her hands as the tears flowed.

'I'm so sorry,' Sarah said and got up, going over to lay a hand on her shoulder. 'I didn't mean to upset you like this, but . . .'

'Leave her alone!' Agnes had returned with a tea trolley. She glared at Sarah. 'You're not wanted here. You've done enough damage. Coming here, upsetting her for nothing . . .'

'Yes, perhaps I should go. I am very sorry,' Sarah said. She was certain that she was face to face with a murderess but she had no real proof and that would be for the police to find.

'No, please don't go for the moment,' Shirley Anne said. She raised her head, giving Sarah a pleading look. 'At least have some tea with me. Tell me about Morna – did you know her well?'

'Not well, no,' Sarah said. 'But I bought some lucky heather from her in the spring and it brought me good fortune. I had seen her to talk to a few times and I liked her.'

'James said he liked her. He didn't believe Janet at first, you see, but then he began to think she might have been right.' Shirley had dried her tears now. 'Jane was snatched from the garden that day and it could have been gypsies. They came to the door a few days earlier and they might have come back and taken my baby.'

'Janet didn't tell you all of it. I wonder why? I read her notebooks and . . .'

There was a sudden crashing noise as Agnes dropped a cup on the tray and it smashed against the saucer. Both Sarah and Shirley Anne turned to look at her. She looked ashen.

'Is something wrong, Agnes?' Shirley asked.

Agnes stared at her, eyes bulging. 'Don't believe her,' she said. 'I know what she's going to tell you and it is a lie. The baby was in the pram when I went out. I didn't take her . . .'

'Nobody said . . .' Shirley Anne's eyes narrowed with suspicion, because the guilt was writ plain to see on Agnes's face. 'Oh, Agnes . . . you did, didn't you? You took my baby. You lied when you said you'd asked Janet to look out for her. You snatched my baby and you blamed Janet. Why? Why did you do that to me?'

'You wanted to return to the theatre,' Agnes said, her hands working at her sides. She was in distress, because it was Shirley who was accusing her – Shirley, the reason for her life these past years. 'The child was nothing but a nuisance. I thought if it were gone you would be free.'

'What exactly did you do?' Shirley Anne persisted in a soft voice. Her face was grey with grief, a little pulse beating at her temple. 'Did you abandon her or did you give her to the gypsies?'

'I left her in a blanket near where they were camping,' Agnes said. 'One of the women saw me and I knew she would take the child. I knew she would be safe – and that you would be free.'

'Oh Agnes . . .' Shirley said in that same soft tone. 'How could you think I wanted such a terrible thing? How could you hurt me like that? I thought you cared for me?'

'I did! I've cared for you all this time, haven't I? I loved you better than anyone. Better than that bitch Janet Bates. She told me all about it. She wrote to me and told me that the girl was living near her and that she was going to tell you when you went to see her. She said that it was time I told the truth about what had really happened that day.'

'And so you went to see her while Shirley Anne was in hospital, didn't you?' Sarah said, because it was all so clear in her head now and she had lost all caution. 'You wore Shirley Anne's clothes and a headscarf and glasses so that no one could see much of your face, but you had to go into the shop because you weren't sure of your way back to the coast road and you asked for a map.'

'It's all lies! Don't listen to her, Shirley. She doesn't know what she is saying.' Agnes was a ghastly putty colour. 'She's making it up. She doesn't know anything.'

'You killed Janet, didn't you?' Sarah went on, because the truth was written in Agnes's face. 'You thought she was trying to blackmail you but all she really wanted was for Shirley Anne to forgive her.'

'It wasn't fair,' Agnes said, and she was blubbering now, tears trickling down her face into her mouth. 'I've looked after you all this time, given my life to you – and she was going to take it all away from me. I knew you wouldn't want me around once she told you about me taking the baby and I . . . I killed her. I always hated her, snooping about, watching everyone. She told me she thought I'd taken the baby with me, but she didn't say anything at the time. I think she was afraid that you had agreed to it, that you had wanted the baby gone . . .'

'Of course I didn't! I loved Jane!' Shirley said, looking very fragile as she sat back in her chair. 'I need my pills – they're in that box on the side, Sarah. Just one of the pink ones, please.'

'I'll get it!' Agnes said, but Shirley shook her head.

'Never again, Agnes. Sarah will get it for me . . .' She closed her eyes. 'I don't think I want to see you again, Agnes. Please leave my house now . . .'

'No! Don't send me away! I don't want to leave you. Where shall I go – what shall I do?' Tears were trickling down Agnes's cheeks and her nose was red. 'Everything I've done was for you . . . it was all for you, to protect you. That girl was a gypsy. She would have taken everything you have and left you alone . . . I've always looked after you. I love you. You must know that I love you?'

'I don't think I care,' Shirley Anne said faintly as she swallowed the pill Sarah had given her. She turned her head to look at Agnes. 'Please tell me it wasn't you who killed Morna. Please spare me that . . .'

Agnes stared at her. 'I'm leaving. You can't make me admit to that! I killed Janet but I shan't admit to the rest . . .'

She turned and rushed from the room, the noise of her heavy footsteps on the stairs as she pounded up them. Sarah sat and held Shirley Anne's hand until a little colour came into her face.

'Do you want me to ring for the police?' she asked. 'She murdered Janet Bates and I think she may have attempted the murder of Mrs Roberts, too. I'm not sure about Morna. I think that may have been someone else, but I can't be certain. She may have committed all of them. I think she is out of her mind with jealousy.'

Shirley clung on to Sarah's hand. 'I can't take this in. It's all so horrible. It is bad enough if she killed Janet to stop her telling me all about the child, but if she killed others . . .'

'It may have been someone else – someone called Madeline Lewis-Brown.'

'But she . . .' Shirley's hands trembled. 'She is Agnes's younger sister . . .'

'Oh my God!' Sarah said. 'I hadn't realized that, but it explains quite a few things . . . how Agnes got the devil mask for instance . . .' Sarah saw that Shirley didn't understand and explained about finding Mrs Roberts and about the pagan rituals in the woods.

They heard the pounding of heavy feet coming down the stairs and then the front door opened and slammed again as Agnes went out. Shirley Anne shuddered, sitting with her head back against her chair, her eyes closed. She looked pale and vulnerable and Sarah's heart ached for her. What a terrible life she'd had all these years. And now this had happened when she was ill and needed friends about her.

'I am so sorry,' she said. 'I wish I could have spared you this last hurt, Shirley. How will you manage without her?'

'I suppose . . .' Shirley shook her head. 'I only have a few months left to me. I shall probably have to go into a nursing home.'

'Is there anything I can do for you? Anyone I can fetch to be with you?'

'I have no one. James will help me if I need help financially – but he has his wife to care for. He can't leave her.'

The doorbell had started to ring urgently. Sarah remembered that Keith was waiting for her outside.

'My friend is wondering what has happened to me,' she said. 'I think I had better let him in – if that's all right? I don't want to leave you here alone just yet . . .'

Shirley nodded and Sarah went to the door just as the bell started to ring again, discovering that not only Keith but Larch and Ben Marshall were standing there on the step.

'Thank God you're all right,' Keith said. 'When I saw that woman go rushing out with her suitcase I thought . . .' He looked a bit chastened, having felt the rough edge of Larch's tongue. 'I was just coming to see what was going on when your friends turned up.'

'Yes, I'm fine,' Sarah said. 'Please come in and meet Miss Asbury. Agnes has gone and I'm afraid she murdered your sister, Keith, though she denies killing Morna.' She looked at Ben. 'I believe that you will find that her sister is Madeline Lewis-Brown.'

'Yes, we know that,' Ben said. 'Sir James made a full confession. He was the one who drugged you – but he isn't a murderer. He's more of a victim than anything else. But you should have come to me, Sarah. It was madness to come haring down here yourself!'

'Well, perhaps it's as well I did,' Sarah said. 'I doubt Agnes would have confessed without some prompting from Shirley. It was the accusation in her eyes that got to her. I think she loves her to the point of obsession and it was fear of losing her approval that drove her to murder. But please come in and meet Shirley. We are just trying to work out what to do for the best. She isn't well, and ought not to be here alone for the time being.'

'No, certainly not,' Ben said, but Larch simply glared at Sarah. 'This must have been a terrible shock for her.'

'Yes, it has. Please come and say hello to her, Ben.'

The three men followed her into Shirley's parlour. Sarah gave a cry of distress when she saw that the sick woman had collapsed and lay in a little heap on the floor. She knelt beside her and Ben felt for a pulse.

'It is all right,' he said. 'The pulse is strong enough, but she has fainted. I think the best thing we can do is to send for an ambulance and let the hospital look after her for the moment. She'll be safe in there. I'll have a twenty-four-hour guard put on her room.'

'Perhaps I shouldn't have come . . .' Sarah's eyes were bright with tears. 'I didn't think what it might do to her . . .'

'I would have come in your place,' Ben said. 'Agnes Browning is a murderer – and she may have killed more than once.'

'Yes, she won't admit it, but I am sure she has. I think she killed Morna out of jealousy, because she knew that if Shirley Anne had her daughter she wouldn't need her – and perhaps she killed her sister too, because Madeline knew she had taken the gown and the devil mask. If it had all come out, Madeline might have betrayed her to save herself. I'm not sure which of them tried to run me down – it might have been either of them – but it hardly matters now.'

Larch was telephoning for an ambulance. He gave Sarah a cold look as she stood up. 'Are you coming home with us or with Keith?'

'I think I shall go to the hospital with Shirley Anne. I'll telephone Andrews when I'm ready to come home and he will fetch me.'

'Don't be so ridiculous,' Larch said. 'I have no intention of letting you stay here alone while that woman is still on the loose. If you're going to the hospital I shall come with you.'

'And I shall stay too,' Ben said. 'I'm going to ring Inspector Morrison and get some of the local force out here. We need to know a bit more about Agnes Browning if we're going to put her behind bars where she belongs . . .'

Fifteen

Sarah glanced sideways at Larch. She was increasingly aware of the silence, for he had hardly spoken during the last two hours as they sat waiting for the doctor to come and tell them whether or not Shirley Anne Asbury would recover her senses.

'I'm sorry,' Sarah ventured at last, because she was uncomfortable with the silence. 'I would have told you if I could but you had gone off somewhere. I had to come and discover whether my theory was right.'

'I hope you are satisfied now that you have.'

'Please don't! I feel badly enough as it is . . . I shall blame myself if she dies.'

'Please don't be ridiculous! She is a very sick lady, Sarah. She was dying anyway.'

'But the shock of discovering what Agnes had done brought on a relapse. I feel awful about that . . .' she broke off as a doctor in a long white coat came towards them from the depths of the shadowed corridor. She went to meet him. 'How is Miss Asbury?'

'I am afraid she is dying,' the doctor told her. 'The time is very short now, I am afraid, but it will probably be a few days.'

Sarah caught a sobbing breath. 'I am so sorry . . .'

The doctor smiled at her. 'You shouldn't be. I think she is more than willing to die, Miss Beaufort. She has asked to see you – if you wouldn't mind?'

'Yes, of course.'

'My nurse will show you,' the doctor said, and directed Sarah towards a nurse in a long dark skirt covered by a white apron. She beckoned to her and Sarah walked down the corridor feeling close to tears. It was depressingly dark in this hospital and she felt overwhelmed with sorrow. That was foolish because she didn't know Shirley Anne Asbury, but she wished that she might have done. Shirley Anne was fragile and ill, but her smile still had the power to charm.

They stopped outside the last door along the hall. The nurse put a finger to her lips and Sarah followed her into the small room. The lights were shaded with dark blue covers. Shirley had her eyes closed, but she opened them as Sarah approached and smiled at her.

'Thank you for coming,' she said, and held out her hand. 'I think I can trust you, Miss Beaufort?'

'Yes, of course you can,' Sarah told her, feeling the sting of tears. 'Is there something you wish me to do for you?'

'Two things,' Shirley said in a whispery voice. 'Please ask James if he will arrange for me to be buried close to our daughter – and ask him if he will see that Agnes has a good lawyer.'

'You want to help her?' Sarah felt surprised.

'She has been very loyal for many years. If I were not dying I might have hated her for robbing me of my child – but I do not wish to die with hatred in my heart.'

'I understand. I promise you that I shall tell Sir James what you have told me as soon as I see him.'

'Good, I can die easily now,' Shirley said. 'I believe you have been keeping a vigil for me here, my dear. You should go home to your family now.'

'Yes. Yes, I shall. Goodbye.' Sarah bent down and kissed her cheek, before turning away. The tears were slipping down her cheeks as she left the room and walked back towards where she had left Larch. He saw her coming and hastened to meet her, drawing her into his arms. Sarah stood with her head against his shoulder as the tears continued to slide over her cheeks. 'Please take me home, Larch,' she whispered. 'I want to go home . . .'

Sarah slept late into the day. They hadn't arrived back until the early hours of the morning, and she dimly remembered Larch carrying her inside and helping her upstairs, leaving her to the ministrations of Millie once he had got her to her room.

Would he forgive her for going off without him? She hadn't pointed out that he was the one who had shut her out first, even though it was true. He had been behaving oddly since the day he found Ronnie unconscious in the woods.

She yawned and threw the covers back, remembering that she had promised to pass on Shirley's message. Pulling on a warm dressing gown, she went down the stairs and picked up the telephone. She found Sir James's number quite easily in Amelia's book. He answered almost at once, as though he had been waiting for news.

'Miss Beaufort,' he said in a hoarse voice. 'Thank you for ringing. I don't deserve it after the way I behaved to you – but I believe Shirley gave you a message for me?'

'Yes, she did. She wanted two things – to be buried with her daughter, and a lawyer for Agnes.'

'That damned woman! I hope they hang her!'

'No one could blame you for thinking that way. But Shirley didn't want to die with hatred in her heart. She told me that Agnes had been good to her most of the time and that she wanted to help her.'

'I'll see what I can do when they catch her. I suppose I can't refuse if it was what Shirley wanted, though for myself . . .' He drew a deep sighing breath. 'As for burying her near to Morna, I can arrange that today. Shirley died last night. Mr Marshall rang me earlier this morning . . .'

'Oh . . . I am so sorry,' Sarah said. 'The doctor said a few days. I thought you might have had a chance to see her one last time.'

'No, that wasn't granted to me,' he said, his voice breaking with emotion. 'I'm not as forgiving as she was, Miss Beaufort. I can't help thinking that if that damned woman hadn't taken our child Shirley might still be alive. If it were not for her, my daughter would be alive now. I never really knew her . . .'

'Yes, I can understand your bitterness. I am so sorry – about your nephew too.'

'He was a good for nothing,' Sir James said harshly, 'but he was all we had. There's nothing much left now . . . damn him!'

The call was terminated abruptly. It was obvious that Sir James felt both bitter and angry over the way life had treated him and the people he loved. Sarah was moved to pity, though not to tears. She had wept for Shirley, but she couldn't cry for Sir James.

'Sarah dearest,' Amelia's voice was concerned. 'Should you be up? Larch said that you ought to stay in bed all day.'

'I was upset last night, but I am better now,' Sarah said, as she turned and saw Amelia standing at the door of the parlour. 'I think I shall have a bath if you don't mind, but I don't feel like staying in bed all day.'

'Just as you wish, my love. I'll ask Millie to make you some lunch when you've had your bath – just something light.'

'I think I could eat a horse,' Sarah said and stretched. 'Don't worry, Gran. I'm feeling fine. Glad that is it all over – at least it is up to the police now. They have two murderers to catch . . .'

'Two? I thought it was all down to that woman?'

'All except Simon's murder,' Sarah said. 'I doubt if she had the strength to do that – or the inclination. I believe now that she killed Miss Bates and Morna out of jealousy, and her sister probably knew too much to be allowed to live – but there was no reason for her to murder Simon. The police must realize that, I think. I am sure they are looking for Jethro Scaffry as well as Agnes Browning.'

'Well, I shall be glad when they catch them,' Mrs Beaufort said with a shudder. 'Then we shall all sleep soundly in our beds again.'

'I don't think Jethro Scaffry will dare to come back this way for a while,' Sarah said and yawned. 'As for Agnes . . . why should she want to harm any of us? I feel a bit sorry for her, Gran. It must be hard for her at her age. I can't see what she can do. I wouldn't be surprised if she turns herself in quite soon.'

'She would be better off dead. It isn't a very pleasant prospect. She might be put away in a mental institution, but they may hang her.'

'Gran . . .' Sarah said and shivered, because it was such a horrible way to die, even for a woman who had killed three times. 'Poor woman, I almost wish I hadn't solved the case now . . .'

'Oh, don't feel pity for her, my love. She had no pity for her victims.'

'No, I suppose not,' Sarah said. 'I shall see you later, Gran.'

Jethro glanced over his shoulder as he reached the wood-cutter's hut. He had abandoned his caravan, because he knew that the police were looking for him. He'd almost been apprehended once in Norwich, but he had slipped through the net and made his way back here. They wouldn't expect him to come here so that made it one of the safest places he could find until he could manage to leave the country.

He had hoped that he might be able to get hold of Morna's money – the five hundred pounds she had deposited in a bank – but they wouldn't let him have it without proof that he was her heir. The girl behind the counter had told him that he needed a death certificate and a letter from a lawyer saying that he was the rightful claimant.

'Damn you, Morna!' he muttered as he shut the door of the hut behind him. 'Why a bank? If you'd kept the money he gave you I could have been away and safe by now.'

He would never get out through the normal channels. The police would be looking for him everywhere by now, and when they found that spade in the caravan, they would hunt him down. He cursed himself for taking it with him that night. He should have left it lying on the ground beside the devil who had killed Morna. At least Simon Beecham had got what he deserved. He smiled as he remembered how easy it had been. Yeah, Beecham had got his comeuppance this time. Left to the police, he would probably have got away with it . . .

Hearing something outside the hut, Jethro tensed, ready to put up a fight. He would fight to the last, because he knew he didn't stand a chance with them. He was a gypsy and that meant he was guilty as charged as far as the police were concerned.

Jethro shrank back against the far wall of the hut as the door was suddenly flung open. A man stood in the doorway for a moment, his bulk outlined against the sudden light.

'It's you,' Jethro said, his fright subsiding as he recognized the figure. 'I thought it was the police.'

'I've been waiting for you to come back,' the man said. 'I knew you would when I heard that you had been seen in Norwich – and that's why I came here today.'

Jethro trembled as he saw the double-barrelled shotgun. 'Don't – please, don't!' he begged, feeling the sting of hot urine as he wet his breeches. 'I didn't do it! I didn't kill him. I swear it wasn't me . . .'

'You always were a liar,' Sir James said. 'The police might

believe you but you can't fool me . . .' He pressed the trigger and the sound of the blast was the last thing that Jethro heard.

He certainly didn't hear the second shot a few seconds later.

'They found Sir James first,' Sir William told his son the following evening as they gathered in the drawing room before dinner. 'It was one of those protestors out walking the woods. He heard the shots . . .'

'You are *sure* it was Sir James who shot Jethro Scaffry and then himself? Not the other way around?'

'Yes, quite sure. I dare say it was revenge for what the fellow had done to his nephew.'

'Yes, I think that must have been his reason. I do not imagine Sir James had much left to live for. He had lost all the people he loved – and Ben told me he was ill himself.'

'Well, that seems to wrap it all up – apart from the woman.' Sir William gave a grunt of satisfaction. 'It can only be a matter of time before they get her too.'

'Yes, I am sure it won't be long. Ben said they'll have pictures in all the newspapers for tomorrow and there will be something on the newsreel at the cinemas in Norwich. She may have gone to London, but she cannot hope to hide for long. They'll find her.'

'Bound to,' his father agreed. 'Are you going out this evening?'

'I'm not sure . . .'

'I should have thought you would want to see how Sarah is. Damned fine girl, that! You would go a long way to find another with the spunk she has shown in all this business.'

'Yes, I know,' Larch said, looking rueful. 'I am not perfectly certain that she will want to see me. We had a bit of a spat . . .'

'Not afraid of saying sorry, are you?' Sir William lowered his thick brows. 'Thought you might be keen on the girl . . .'

'We are friends, Father. I do not think either of us is ready for marriage just yet.'

'Well, you know your own mind,' his father said. 'But your mother was hoping you might settle down with her.'

'I might one day, but not yet. I haven't got over what happened out there, Father. I thought I had, but the other day in the woods when I found Ronnie lying there, it triggered something in my memory . . .'

'Got the shakes, did you? Nothing to be ashamed of, Larch. You're not the only one to suffer from something of the sort. If you would like to see a doctor I could make some enquiries.'

'Thank you, but I would rather try to get it out of my system myself. But I do thank you for understanding.'

'Least a man can do for his son . . .' Sir William sounded gruff, unlike himself.

'Father . . .' Larch broke off as the telephone rang and his father went to answer it. Sir William held it out to him. 'For me?'

'That Miller woman. Wants to talk to you about her son.'

'Mrs Miller,' Larch said pleasantly into the mouthpiece, 'how may I help you?'

'I wanted you to know that Ronnie is out of danger, thanks to you, sir,' Mrs Miller said, but sounded upset. 'The hospital told me today that they think he needs special care. They are going to send him to a secure hospital for . . . people who aren't quite right. I don't know what to do, sir. My Ronnie won't like being shut up in a place like that. He may be quiet now, because he has been ill, but when he gets better . . .' she broke off on a sob. 'I don't know what to do, sir.'

'Leave this to me,' Larch said. 'I'll have a word with my father, and then I'll go to the hospital – discover exactly what their intentions are.'

'I knew you would help me,' Mrs Miller said, sniffing. 'I found myself a little job at a shop today – just a few hours a week. I thought everything was going right for once and now . . . my poor Ronnie. He doesn't deserve to be shut away like that, sir.'

'I agree with you,' Larch said. 'I've spoken to my father about him before this and I know there are places . . . not mental institutions where he would be completely shut away, but secure homes where he would be allowed a certain amount of freedom. He might even be able to work in the garden if he behaved himself.'

'Oh, Captain Meadows!' Mrs Miller said, and now there was relief in her voice. 'I knew you would help me. My Ronnie isn't a bad boy. It was that gypsy that got him into bad ways and now he's been punished.'

'Yes, he has,' Larch agreed. 'I cannot promise, Mrs Miller,

but I shall certainly do all I can to see that Ronnie is treated decently.'

'Thank you. Thank you so very much, sir.'

Larch hung up and turned to his father. 'You heard what I've promised – do you think we can swing it?'

'Don't see why not,' Sir William said. 'I never did think the lad was a murderer. I'll pull all the strings I can and you can talk to the doctors at the hospital. Between us, we should sort this bother out.'

'Thanks, Father.' Larch smiled and turned away.

'Where are you going?'

'I think I'll drive over and see how Sarah is. She may still be angry with me, but at least I can tell her that we are going to do our best for Ronnie.'

'Yes, I dare say she will like to hear that,' Sir William said. He frowned as he looked at his son. 'It might be a good idea to get your hair cut before you visit the hospital, Larch. Don't want them thinking you're a tramp, do we?'

'No, sir,' Larch said. 'I'll get it done in the morning.'

Sarah was sitting with her grandmother in the parlour when she heard the car drive up. She knew at once that it would be Larch, and took a deep breath to steady her nerves. Was he going to give her another lecture?

She heard Millie answer the door, but remained seated until Larch entered the sitting room, getting up at the last minute to stand in front of the fire.

'Mrs Beaufort,' Larch said, 'I hope you are well – and you, Sarah? Feeling better, I trust?'

Sarah turned to look at him. The nervous tension seeped out of her as she saw that he was looking uneasy himself.

'Yes, much better, thank you,' she replied with a smile. 'Ben came to see us earlier. He told us that Sir James killed Jethro Scaffry and then himself.'

'Terrible business,' Amelia said. 'What will his poor wife do now? I cannot imagine what he was thinking of!'

'I expect he wanted revenge – for his nephew and his daughter. He can't know for sure if Morna was his daughter, but knowing that she had been murdered before he had a chance to find out must have been bitter.'

'Yes,' Amelia agreed. 'I dare say it was revenge – but his

poor wife won't know what to do with herself in that great house.'

'She will probably sell it,' Sarah said. 'If the money is tight she would be better off with something smaller where she can afford to be looked after. It was Sir James's family who had owned it for centuries. If I were her I should be glad to see the back of it.'

'Yes, well, she may have to,' Amelia said. 'Please do sit down, Larch. Would you care for a drink?'

'I came to tell you that Ronnie is out of danger. Unfortunately, the hospital think he ought to be shut away for his own good—'

'Oh, that is unkind!' Sarah said. 'I mean, it isn't as if he has done anything wrong, is it?'

'Not as far as we know,' Larch agreed, 'but he almost died and they think he's too difficult for his mother to manage. I've told her I shall try to get him into a more relaxed situation. Father knows of a couple of places where they treat lads like Ronnie sympathetically. He might even be allowed to help out in the garden.'

'Oh, that is a good idea,' Sarah said. 'I am so pleased, Larch. It is very good of your father to take an interest in him.'

'Well, his mother rang me and I said we would do what we could,' Larch said. 'I was wondering if you would like to come out for a drink, Sarah?'

Sarah hesitated and then smiled. 'Yes, if you like. I'll just pop upstairs and put on something a little smarter – if you don't mind waiting?'

'No, of course not,' he said. 'I'll talk to Mrs Beaufort for a few minutes.'

Sarah went out and Larch took her place by the fire. Amelia patted the sofa beside her, inviting him to sit with her.

'That's better,' she said when he did so. 'Now, may I ask what your plans are for the future, Larch? Sarah told me that you were hoping to go abroad to paint?'

'Yes, I was thinking of somewhere hot and exotic,' he replied. 'I feel that I need more experience in my work before I can exhibit.'

'That sounds very reasonable to me,' Amelia said. 'I'm thinking of taking a little trip myself after Christmas – but I had thought of the French Riviera. I have friends there, you see.'

'Shall you take Sarah with you?'

'Unless she has found herself a job by then. I understand she is going up to town in a couple of days. She has been told about another audition and she hopes that she might get chosen this time.'

'I hope she does too. It's what she wants, isn't it?'

'For the time being, perhaps,' Amelia replied. 'I love her very much you know. I should like to see her well settled before I die.'

'Yes, of course,' Larch said. 'In a year or two . . .'

'Yes, that will do very well,' Amelia said. 'She's quite young and adventurous. It may be better if she is allowed to stretch her wings for a while. Her mother married too young – and that turned out unfortunately.'

'A year or so will make all the difference.' Larch understood what he was being told. He stood up as Sarah entered the room looking lovely in a heavy silk dress of dark blue with a matching jacket that skimmed her hips. 'You look lovely, Sarah. Shall we go?'

'Yes, of course. Goodnight, Gran,' Sarah said and held out her hand to Larch. 'Please do not wait up for us. We shall not be late, but there's no need to worry.'

'Oh, I never worry when you are out with Larch,' her grandmother said. 'Enjoy yourselves, my dears.'

Sarah followed Larch out to the car. It was quite cool and she shivered, hurrying inside the car as he held open the door. She glanced at him as he came round and got into the driving seat.

'What were you and Gran talking about so earnestly?'

'She asked me what I was planning to do with myself for Christmas. I told her that I was hoping to be somewhere hot and exotic. I have been invited to hold an exhibition of my work in London, and perhaps New York after that, but I have put it off till the spring. I intend to spend the winter working intensively. Hopefully, I shall have something worth showing in the spring.'

Sarah listened in silence. It wasn't quite what she had hoped to hear, but in a way it was what she had expected. She was pretty certain that she meant something special to Larch, but he wasn't ready to commit himself yet – and if she were truthful, neither was she.

It had been a lovely evening, Sarah thought as they left the Chestnuts. Larch seemed to be almost himself again, though he had seemed a bit distracted when he came back from taking a phone call. She had asked him why he had been summoned to the phone, but he'd said it was just a message from his father. Sarah had wondered why Sir William should telephone his son at the Chestnuts, but Larch wasn't very forthcoming on the subject. In fact he had turned it once more, talking about Amelia's intention to visit the Riviera the following year, and asking Sarah if she would accompany her grandmother.

'Well, I might, you never know,' Sarah said, looking thoughtful. 'Some of my friends went to Paris for the Olympics in the summer. I might have gone with them if I hadn't been in the show.'

'But you wanted to stay in the show?'

'Well, wouldn't you?' Sarah asked. 'It was my first chance to prove myself, and I thought I was doing pretty well – but I'm not having much luck getting another job.'

'You might be luckier next time. You're going up for the interview soon, aren't you?'

'Well, it's an audition, but yes, I am,' Sarah said. 'I'm not sure what I shall do if I don't get in. I can't stay with Gran for ever, even though she says it's all right.'

'Yes, I see,' Larch nodded 'You wouldn't think of going home?'

'No! Daddy would think he had won and I have no intention of giving in at this stage. I'll find something even if it means waiting at tables somewhere. I wouldn't be the first to resort to being a waitress by any means.'

'No, but it wouldn't be much fun for you, Sarah. I can't imagine what your father would say.'

Sarah pulled a face. 'I dare say it would be unrepeatable.' She glanced at her little silver cocktail watch, the dial studded with tiny diamonds. It had been a gift from her father the previous Christmas. 'I think we had better go, Larch. It's getting quite late and I don't want Gran to worry.'

'I was thinking that I might show you some of my paintings,'

Larch said, and looked at his own watch, an odd expression in his eyes.

'I should love that tomorrow, but I really want to go home now. I have things to do.'

'Yes, of course,' Larch said. He got up, smiling at her in his usual lazy way. 'I'll just check at the desk if there have been any more calls for me . . .'

Sarah thought it was a little odd that he should be expecting a telephone call. She stood in the foyer waiting for a moment, but Larch seemed to be talking earnestly with the girl at the desk and she wandered outside. It was quite light that evening because the moon was full, and the hotel had several lights around the forecourt. She shivered and considered going back inside, but then decided to walk across to the car. She had left a thick coat in the boot, but she wasn't sure whether Larch would have locked it or not.

The gravel crunched beneath her court shoes as she walked towards the car. It was odd that Larch was so concerned about a phone call, she thought as she reached his car and tried to open the small luggage boot at the rear. It was locked and she was thinking of returning to the hotel foyer when she saw Larch come out.

'Hurry up, Larch! It is freezing out here . . .'

Sarah wasn't sure what made her turn just at that moment. Perhaps it was the crunch of gravel under someone's feet or simply instinct. As she turned, she became aware of the woman and of the menace in her approach. She was alert and ready when Agnes suddenly lifted her arm and came at her with the knife.

'You killed her!' the demented woman screeched and tried to stab Sarah in the chest. 'It was your fault for coming and upsetting her . . .'

Sarah put out a hand to save herself, grabbing at Agnes's wrist and struggling with her as she attempted to plunge it into Sarah's flesh. For one eternal moment they struggled for possession of the knife, and then Larch was there. He had seen what was happening and moved fast. He grabbed hold of Agnes from behind, lifting her off her feet and dragging her away from Sarah. She was screaming and shouting at the top of her voice, especially when he twisted her arm behind her, forcing her to drop the weapon. And then there was the sound of shouting and running feet and Sarah saw several men rushing towards them. She recognized one of them as Ben Marshall, and another as the local constable.

'Are you all right?' Ben asked, and put his coat over her shoulders because she was shivering. 'I'm sorry we were a bit late getting here. We've been watching your home, but we got a call a few minutes ago to say that she might have been seen here.'

'You've been watching Amelia's house?' Sarah asked, feeling a little sick and shaky. 'Then you expected her to turn up here? I didn't think she would dare . . .'

Sarah saw that the two policemen with Ben had put handcuffs on the still-screaming Agnes. She was shouting and spitting her venom at Sarah, threatening revenge.

'I'll kill her . . . I'll kill the interfering bitch!'

Larch came over to her, his face an odd shade of parchment in the moonlight. 'What made you come out without me? I was only a moment. I was trying to check with Ben whether anything had happened at your house.'

'So you knew . . .' Sarah's gaze narrowed. 'It was that phone call, wasn't it? Why didn't you tell me? Oh, it's always the same! You think I'm stupid or something, don't you?'

'No, of course I don't. I wasn't sure there was anything to worry about. Ben said they thought they might have her under arrest by the time we left here – but no one expected her to come here.'

'She must have seen us leave the house,' Sarah said. 'She probably followed us here, waiting until we came out . . . she wanted to kill me, Larch . . .'

'It's all over,' he said. 'They've got her now, Sarah. She can't harm you any more.'

'No, of course not.' Sarah was shivering despite Ben's coat. 'I think I should like to go home now.'

'Yes, of course.' He opened the car door for her. Sarah took off Ben's jacket and handed it to him. 'Thank you, but I have a coat in the boot of the car.'

'I'll call to see you tomorrow,' Ben said. 'There's just one or two things I have to clear up.'

'And then you will go home at last,' Sarah said. 'I think your wife is a very patient lady, Mr Marshall.'

'Oh, I've promised to make it up to her. Take care of

yourself, Miss Beaufort. You've done a splendid job – but it is all over now.'

'Yes, thanks to you and the police,' Sarah said. She smiled as he closed the door for her, but she didn't look at Larch as he got into the driving seat. It had been a pleasant evening, but she was feeling let down . . . upset that he hadn't seen fit to tell her what was going on.

When Larch drew up outside the house, she jumped out of the car without waiting for him to open the door for her, ran to the house and disappeared inside. She hadn't said good-night or thanked him for a lovely evening, because she was angry and upset. Larch had treated her as if she were a silly child and it really was too bad of him!

Larch spent the morning furiously painting in his studio. He was aware that Sarah was angry with him, but he felt a bit miffed with her himself. It had scared him to death when he saw her wrestling with that madwoman. He had been frightened that it would be too late, that he wouldn't be able to stop it happening. Afterwards, he'd been so relieved that he hadn't realized how angry Sarah was at being kept in the dark. He hadn't understood that until she ran into the house without saying goodnight.

They'd had their quarrels over the years, but Sarah had never gone off like that without a word, and it was his own fault. He ought to have told her, because she wouldn't have ventured outside alone if she'd guessed that Agnes was somewhere around.

By two o'clock that afternoon he had worked his own frustration and anger off, and he put his brushes to soak before going upstairs to change into some decent clothes. He would have to apologize, because he didn't want to part from Sarah like this, and if she got that job in London he might not see her again for months.

He drove up to the house feeling thoughtful. He hadn't felt that the time was right to ask Sarah if she would consider an engagement. However, his feelings when he'd known that she might die at the hands of that woman had shocked him, and he knew that he cared for her more than he had wanted to admit just yet.

He got out of the car, raising his hand in salute to Andrews, who was doing a bit of digging at the far end of the garden. Amelia's cat was lying curled up in his discarded coat in the wheelbarrow. Larch thought that he ought to have a word with him later, thank him for his part in the affair the previous evening. He had spent several hours keeping a vigil out there in the darkness with the others, waiting for Agnes to show up – but she had been one step ahead of them. It made Larch feel a little sick to think about what might have happened if Sarah hadn't put up such a struggle.

Millie opened the door for him. She smiled and told him that Mrs Beaufort was in the parlour. Larch went through into the comfortable room, feeling a bit disappointed that there was no sign of Sarah.

Amelia glanced up from her newspaper. 'Ah, Larch my dear, please come in. Millie will bring us some tea – but if you have come to visit Sarah I am afraid you are too late . . .'

'Too late?' Fear clutched at his stomach, but in another moment he realized what she meant. 'Sarah has gone to London?'

'Yes, she went with Mr Marshall earlier. He offered to take her to the station, you see, and she accepted. She seemed a little out of sorts, though perhaps it isn't difficult to see why. She must be nervous about this new audition.' Amelia smiled. 'Ben told us that they have caught Agnes. It was all such a pity, don't you think?'

'A pity . . . yes, of course.' Larch realized that Sarah hadn't told her grandmother about the attack on her outside the hotel the previous night. She had wanted to spare her the details, and Larch would do the same for the moment. He hoped that the news wouldn't get to Amelia via one of her friends. 'She wasn't a very nice person, Mrs Beaufort – but I daresay she had suffered herself.'

'Oh, I wasn't talking about Agnes Browning,' Amelia said. 'I meant Shirley Anne Asbury and poor Sir James . . . and their daughter. Morna had a lovely smile, you know, and they say her caravan was as neat as a pin. And of course she was very young. So many deaths and all because of one jealous woman. No, I don't pity Agnes at all.'

'I'm glad,' Larch said, and sat down. 'Because I don't either. I think she planned her crimes with a deliberate coldness and she didn't flinch from carrying them out. They think now that she killed her own sister as well. I think Madeline Lewis-Brown was a rather unpleasant woman herself, but she probably trusted her sister.'

'Yes, she may have done, though in my experience it is not always wise.' Amelia laughed softly. 'But I wanted to ask you about Ronnie Miller, the poor lad. Is there any chance they will let him come home again?'

'I don't know,' Larch said honestly. 'I've been to the hospital and they are willing to release him into care. I told Sarah about it. He will be looked after and allowed quite a bit of freedom, but not allowed to wander all over the place as he used to here.'

'Poor Ronnie,' Amelia said again. 'I was talking to his mother at the shop earlier. She said he was getting too much for her to control lately – but it isn't a pleasant thing to think of him shut away for life when he hasn't done anything.'

'It would have been a miscarriage of justice if they had sent him to a mental institution,' Larch agreed, but I think we've done the best we can for him, Mrs Beaufort.'

'Yes, I am sure you have,' she said. 'I've told Mrs Miller that we will take her to see Ronnie one day. She said she would like that and it is the least we can do for him.'

'Yes,' Larch said, and frowned. 'I shall have to go and see him when he is settled in myself.'

Sixteen

S arah looked at Liz in delight as she came off stage that morning. She could hardly believe her luck, because they had given her a part in a musical show at the Haymarket – and it wasn't just as a chorus girl. She wasn't the star, of course, but she was going to sing two songs of her own.

'I'm in!' she said, and laughed for sheer pleasure. 'They told me to leave my details with you and report for rehearsals on Monday morning.'

'That's good news, Sarah,' the older woman said. 'It will give you a chance to be seen on the London stage – and who knows where you will go from there.'

'I was on the verge of giving up and going home to eat humble pie. But now I shan't have to – and even Daddy can't say this is a second-rate show!'

'No, he can't. By the way, there was someone here asking for you earlier. I told him you would be out in about twenty minutes.' Liz's eyes twinkled at her. 'Most girls wouldn't bother about singing on stage if they had a gentleman like that waiting to take them out.'

'Did he give you his name?' Sarah asked, but in her heart she already knew it would be Larch.

She saw him waiting at the back of the theatre as she came out. He was wearing a smart grey suit and carrying a trilby hat, and he had had his hair cut. He turned, an uncertain smile on his lips.

'Sarah . . . I hope you don't mind?'

'No, of course not. It's awfully decent of you to come, Larch – especially as I ran off that night and didn't even thank you.'

'That was my fault. I was trying to protect you. I didn't want you to be frightened or worried, but I shouldn't have kept you in the dark.'

'No, you shouldn't,' Sarah replied, but she was smiling at him. 'I was cross with you, but I'm not now – and I do understand why you kept it from me.'

'Do you?' Larch turned the hat in his fingers, holding it by the brim. 'I know you're not stupid or easily frightened, Sarah. You were very brave through all this business, and clever at thinking things through. I'm not sure Ben would ever have solved the case if you hadn't put him on the right track.'

'Oh, I don't know,' Sarah said, and tucked her arm through his. 'He was getting there his own way. And it's all over now, isn't it?'

'Yes, I am sure it is. Ben told me that Agnes may not stand trial, which means your statement is probably enough, and you won't need to give evidence in court. Agnes hasn't confessed to the other murders, but the police seem to think that they have all the evidence they need. She had Madeline's lapis lazuli beads in her suitcase – and a silver photograph frame, which may have been taken from Janet's house. The doctors think she may be clinically insane.'

'I think it may have pushed her over the edge when Shirley turned against her,' Sarah said. 'She told Agnes she didn't want to see her again – and that's why she rushed off the way she did. Shirley forgave her before she died, but Agnes couldn't have known that. I feel a bit sorry for her.'

'Well, don't. Not after what she tried to do to you. She doesn't deserve your pity, you must know that?'

'Yes, I suppose so,' Sarah admitted. She stopped walking and looked at him. 'Have you heard any more about Ronnie? Your father was going to try and have him transferred to a place where he might be able to work in the gardens.'

'Yes, that's right,' Larch said, feeling pleased because he could give her some good news. 'He managed to arrange it and the last thing I heard was that Ronnie had settled well and they were letting him look after the vegetable garden.'

'Oh, that's good. I am pleased for him. It was so kind of your father to arrange it.'

'Father was pleased. We none of us thought Ronnie had a hand in any of that rotten business.'

'I expect Mrs Miller will be able to visit him. That will be nice for her – and him.'

'Amelia said that she would take her,' Larch said. 'I'm

thinking of going down myself one day soon – but let's talk about you. Did you get the job you were after?'

'Yes, I did. Isn't it marvellous? I'm going to be appearing at the Haymarket with all sorts of exciting people.'

'Why don't I take you to lunch?' he asked. 'And then you can tell me all about it . . .'

'Yes, I shall,' Sarah agreed. 'And you can tell me if Sir William has had any luck about finding out who owns that bit of land.'

'Well, yes, he has,' Larch said. 'It seems that Janet's brother was right. It does appear as our land on some old deeds, which means that Father will stop those houses going up. He has agreed to another plot for housing, and the council have re-routed the road, away from the woods.'

'Oh, that is good news! I am so glad that something has turned out well after all those tragedies. At last we can forget about the murders – can't we?'

'Yes, of course,' Larch said. 'It's all quite finished and there is nothing more for you to worry about at all . . .'

'Ah yes, Captain Meadows,' the matron said, smiling at Larch as he introduced himself that afternoon. 'How good of you to come down especially to see Ronnie. He is a little difficult sometimes, but I am sure he will settle after a while. He does seem to enjoy working in the garden, and he takes such good care of his tools – spends hours sharpening that spade of his.'

'I think he enjoys garden work. Would it be all right if I had a word with him, Matron?'

'Yes, of course. You'll find him working in the back garden. Go through the French windows there and walk down to the end of the lawn. The vegetable garden is screened by a hedge and—' she broke off as she heard a scream and they both saw an elderly woman come rushing across the lawns to the back of the nursing home. 'Oh, that's Mrs Hendry. I'm afraid she does this sometimes. Please go along, Captain Meadows. I am sure you will find your way.'

Matron went off to calm her patient, who seemed hysterical. Larch could hear her babbling . . . something about a cat. He frowned, an icy tingle at the back of his neck, instinct warning him that something rather unpleasant might have happened.

As he went through the gate into the kitchen garden, he saw the remains of the mangled cat, its head almost completely severed from its body, and his stomach turned. He had seen something like that once in the woods at Beecham Thorny, and it was what had happened to Janet Bates's cat, too.

He glanced a little further into the garden. Ronnie was sitting on an upturned crate, his head bent as he sharpened his spade. He was lost in concentration, his face intent as he slowly moved the file along the edge of his spade, sharpening it over and over and over, as if it were some kind of a ritual. As Larch watched, he stood up and, holding his spade in front of him with two hands on the stem, he lifted it high in the air and then drove it down hard so that it cut something in half. Larch was relieved to see that it was only a large clump of earth. Ronnie frowned, shook his head and sat down again, beginning to work at the edge of his spade once more, as if it weren't sharp enough for him.

Larch walked towards him but he didn't glance up, just kept sharpening the spade with a slow, deliberate action that was somehow sinister. It was only as Larch stood over him that Ronnie looked up. His eyes had a startling brilliance, an odd chilling light that made Larch feel slightly queasy. He took a deep breath, holding his nerve.

'Hello, Ronnie,' he said pleasantly. 'I thought I would come to see how you are.'

Ronnie stared at him for a moment, and then nodded. 'You're the one that helped me,' he said. 'I reckon you're Mr Larch . . .'

'Yes, that's right, Ronnie. I wanted to know if there was anything I could do for you?'

Ronnie stared at him for a moment, his eyes narrowing. 'They wanted to put me away after what happened,' he said, 'but you wouldn't let them. I like you . . .' He screwed up his face as if trying to think. 'I'd like some of the good stuff like Jethro used to give me . . . we used to drink it together after she went away.' His gaze narrowed and his face creased in an ugly expression. 'I didn't like them putting her in the ground. She were pretty, soft and white, and nice to touch. Jethro told me who hurt her. He said what we ought to do to him and we did it . . .'

Larch felt the chill spread through his body. 'What did you

do, Ronnie?' he asked. 'Was it something bad . . . the thing Jethro told you to do?'

Ronnie looked up at him; his eyes had suddenly become vacant again, as innocent as a newborn babe. 'I dunno what yer mean,' he muttered. 'I ain't done nuthin' . . . nuthin' at all . . .' He gave a little giggle and looked down at his spade, beginning the monotonous action with the file all over again. The edge of the blade was as bright as a new pin, and so sharp that it would cut through anything . . . perhaps even a man's neck.

Larch felt the sickness rise in his throat. Ronnie couldn't have done what he was thinking . . . he couldn't! They had all been so sure he was innocent of any crime, except perhaps for the cats . . .

Larch walked away. He couldn't get that peculiar look in Ronnie's eyes out of his head, the strange brilliance that had been there when he first looked up from sharpening his spade. In that moment he had seemed to have the eyes of a murderer, cold, calculating and disturbingly knowing. Larch was as certain as he could be without proof that Ronnie had murdered Simon, murdered him in cold blood as revenge for Morna's death – or had at least been there when the murder was committed. Larch wasn't sure who had committed the last violent act of decapitation, though instinct told him it had to have been Ronnie – but there was no way that he could prove it. Sir James had silenced the only person who might have known the truth.

Ronnie was never going to be tried for murder, but Larch was pretty sure that he had killed the cat that afternoon. He thought that maybe he ought to have a word with Matron before he left . . .

ρ